FABLED BEAST CHRONICLES

Maze Running and Other Magical Missions

LARI DON

Kelpies is an imprint of Floris Books

First published in 2012 by Floris Books
This new edition published in 2014

The publisher acknowledges subsidy from Creative Scotland towards the publication of this volume

Cover font designed by Juan Casco
www.juancasco.net

This book is also available as an eBook

British Library CIP Data available
ISBN 978-178250-140-4
Printed in Great Britain
by DS Smith Print Solutions, Glasgow

and
Other Magical Missions

ALSO BY LARI DON

ROCKING HORSE WAR

FABLED BEAST CHRONICLES

First Aid for Fairies and Other Fabled Beasts

Wolf Notes and Other Musical Mishaps

Storm Singing and Other Tangled Tasks

Maze Running and Other Magical Missions

FOR OLDER READERS

To Colin, Mirren and Gowan

Thanks for joining me on all those freezing winter walks to search for magic in the ice, wind and rain. I couldn't have written any of these books without *you*

Chapter 1

Clip clop clip...

Silence.

Helen couldn't hear anything. No hoofbeats. No whispers. No breathing.

Was Yann alright?

Silence.

She looked up at the fairy perched on a twig, at the phoenix on the tallest tree beyond the hedges, at the dragon circling in the sky. But they couldn't tell her anything, because they couldn't see past the smoke in the middle of the maze.

Where was Yann? Was he safe? Surely he couldn't have been captured without a fight? Without a lot of noise?

There was nothing but silence.

Helen glanced down. The maze floor was hard-packed

earth, edged with grit and old leaves. Yann wasn't great at sneaking, with those huge hooves. Perhaps she should have gone to the heart of the maze herself. She could move more quietly than Yann, though not as fast. And she certainly couldn't knock down as many fauns.

But if she couldn't hear him, where was he?

Helen and her friends hadn't had long to plan the rescue, because the baby's big sister had been too scared to ask anyone for help until the sun was nearly up.

In their hasty discussion on the dragon's back, the friends had decided that the winged fabled beasts should stay above the maze, to guide those inside. Rona had stayed outside too. The selkie was getting better at tackling sea monsters with her sealskin on, but was less confident in her human form, so she was guarding the exit.

Only Helen and Yann had entered the Traquair maze.

It was a traditional garden maze: tall hedges, right angles, long tunnels of new spring leaves and lots of confusing junctions. But their friends overhead had shown Helen and Yann the quickest way through the maze, and warned them about the fauns hidden round corners.

As they'd approached the middle, they'd heard the Master's rough voice start the ceremony. Then, over the goaty stink of the Master's followers, they'd smelt smouldering leaves and burning hair, and seen dark smoke coil through the hedges.

As the Master went silent after the first booming

verse, Yann had whispered to Helen, "That smoke will cover me. I'll grab the baby, you wait here ready to make a swift exit with her."

Helen had watched Yann move off into the smoke and she had waited.

She was still waiting, in the silence. Now she realised that although the smoke would shield Yann as he crept up to rescue the Master's victim, it also meant none of Yann's friends could see him, so none of them could help if he was in trouble.

Helen was crouched down, leaning into the hedge, listening. Hoping for a clip clop. Or a scrape. Or a yell for help. Anything that would prove Yann was alive.

But all she heard was the Master's rasping voice start the next verse in the song of sacrifice.

She glanced up. Lavender was just above her head, looking panicky. Catesby was shifting nervously in the tree. Sapphire was circling lower.

Suddenly Helen heard: *clip clop clip CRASH!*

Then a throaty growl, several splintering thuds, fast hoofbeats and a deep voice yelling, "Stop him!"

Helen stood up.

Yann galloped round the corner, a skinny silvery shape held to his chest. "Your turn now, human girl. Take her and get out. I'll hold them off..."

He shoved the pale baby into her arms, grinned at her, then swung round, pulling his bow and arrows off his back.

Helen clutched the long legs and light body, and tried not to let the baby's sharp spiral horn jab her shoulder as she ran through the maze.

The scorched smell from the baby's burnt mane was

choking her, but she tried not to cough so she could hear Lavender's instructions. "Turn left. Follow the tunnel. Keep running. You're nearly at a junction. Turn right, right again. You're nearly there!"

And Helen could see the back gate. A cheat's way out if you were playing a game; an essential get-away if you were being chased.

Rona yanked the gate open. Helen ran through. Rona slammed it and locked it. Then the selkie said softly, "Is she ok?"

Helen looked down. The fabled beast in her arms was singed and shivering. But the baby unicorn was still alive, which was all that mattered.

That, and getting all of her friends safely away from the maze.

So where was Yann?

Rona examined the base of the unicorn's slim horn. "We got here just in time. They hadn't started sawing it off. A unicorn this young couldn't have survived the shock of losing her horn."

Helen was relieved she wouldn't need the first aid kit on her back to heal any sacrificial wounds. She hugged the baby and smiled. She'd never been this close to a unicorn before; they were really shy, even of other fabled beasts. The panicked unicorn filly who had staggered into their midst this morning hadn't been able to look any of them in the eye, even when she was begging for their help.

But the baby in Helen's arms looked up at her with big golden eyes. Then Helen saw a blur of purple silk and feathers hover in front of her. "Stop gazing at the pretty pony," said Lavender, "we have to get away."

Catesby reinforced the point with a flick of his new copper feathers.

"We can't go without Yann," said Helen.

"We have to get the baby away first," insisted Rona, "because she's in the greatest danger. Yann will catch up with us."

Sapphire flapped above them, her blue wings blocking the dawn sky. But as Helen and the others stepped away from the maze into the rough ground where the dragon was going to land, Catesby squawked a warning.

Helen couldn't identify any words in the phoenix's croaking call. She couldn't understand Sapphire either. Even after more than a year, Helen couldn't understand any fabled beasts who didn't speak with a human voice. But it was clear from Catesby's jabbing beak that he was worried about the corner of the maze to her right.

Helen looked over and saw a herd of dirty white goats trotting round the sharp green corner.

Like the fauns the Master usually surrounded himself with, these goats were running on two legs, but unlike the fauns, they didn't have human torsos and heads. They were goat all the way up.

Helen didn't hang about to play spot the difference, she just assumed they weren't friendly and turned to run round the maze in the other direction.

But as she skidded round the corner and sprinted down a lawn bounded by the maze on one side and a straight line of trees on the other, she saw goat creatures coming from the ancient stone house at the front of the maze too.

Helen and her friends were caught in a pincer movement.

She yelled upwards, "Sapphire, there's no time for us to climb on your back before they reach us. We'll meet you on the other side of these trees."

Then Helen ran away from the maze, shouting behind her, "Yann! Get out of there! We're under attack! Meet us on the other side of the trees!"

Helen clutched the unicorn so tight that the baby squeaked and wriggled in protest. She ran with Rona at her side, Lavender and Catesby swooping above them.

But as they reached the trees Helen felt a tug on her shoulder. She spun round and the creature behind her jumped back to avoid the unicorn's horn.

Helen swung from side to side, pointing the horn at all the goaty creatures grabbing for her. She stepped further into the trees, aiming the horn like a spear at their chests.

The six beasts in a half-circle around her were overwhelmingly hairy and overwhelmingly smelly, not with the farmyard stink of fauns but a hotter sweeter smell of roasting rotted meat.

They looked like goats on two legs, with curved horns, yellow eyes, matted hair and hooves on their back legs. But their front legs ended in claws and their mouths were filled with fangs.

They moved towards Helen, barging each other out of the way to avoid the silver horn, their breath stinking and their fangs shining. Helen remembered what her mum always said, about why vets found goats so difficult to treat.

Goats will eat anything. Anything at all. Which probably included twelve-year-old girls and newborn unicorns.

She heard Sapphire roar in frustration above the trees, unable to help.

She heard Rona's terrified voice behind her. "Helen, get away. Run!"

Helen walked backwards, apologising softly to the unicorn for using her horn as a weapon to keep the clawed goats at a distance. But now they were close enough for her to see the flat black line in the middle of each eerie yellow eye.

Then she heard a bellow of anger and a familiar laugh, and she looked up.

Yann leapt high, ridiculously high, over the tall hedges and out of the maze.

His long chestnut horse's legs were stretched to their limits. His tangled red horse's tail was flying straight behind him, matched by the untidy chestnut hair on his boy's head. His pale bare shoulders and arms were twisted round to fire an arrow at his pursuers.

Yann laughed again as he landed with a controlled thud and, without missing a stride, galloped towards the trees.

Helen saw a wide grin on the centaur's face. He enjoyed this sort of thing far more than she did. He shouted, "Do you need help there, human girl? Or are you having fun with that herd of uruisks?"

The goats had turned to look at him, but now one of them whirled back and grabbed at Helen's throat. She lurched away, almost overbalancing as the unicorn wriggled again and the goat's claws got caught in her scarf.

"Oh no you don't!" Yann yelled. The goat bleated and fell away from Helen, ripping its claws out of her scarf to clutch at an arrow in its shoulder. The other goat creatures scattered, as Yann galloped up to her.

"Come on, Helen. This is a rescue, not a woodland walk. Let's get moving!"

"We were waiting for you," she said calmly.

"I'm here now, so let's go home."

They ran deeper into the tall grey trees. The goats didn't follow.

"What did you call them?" Helen asked, as they caught up with Rona and the others.

"Uruisks," replied Yann. "When that dim filly said the Master had goatmen with him, I thought she meant his usual wimpy fauns. If I'd known she meant those mountain goat monsters too, I would have brought heavier arrows."

Rona was waiting for them in the middle of the trees, the flower fairy on her shoulder and the phoenix hovering above.

Yann stopped beside her. "Well done, everyone. Now let's get this little one safely home." He smiled at the baby, then he glanced up at Catesby.

Helen saw the centaur's horse shoulders and human shoulders bunch with sudden tension. Yann whispered, "Catesby, Lavender, fly up and out of this wood. *Now!*"

Catesby squawked, but Yann repeated, "Now! Don't argue, my friend. Get Lavender out of here."

Then he whispered to Helen and Rona. "Look up slowly. We're caught in a trap."

Chapter 2

Helen looked up. There were rocks balancing above their heads in the trees around them.

Huge, rough-cut, dark grey lumps of stone, supported by the forks of branches or by networks of twigs.

Every tree in a wide circle held at least three rocks.

Rona edged closer to Yann.

Helen took a deep breath. “That's impossible. Those rocks must be really heavy, and these trees can't possibly take their weight. The branches are bending, but not breaking. What's holding the rocks up?”

“Magic,” said Yann. “Magic is holding them up.”

“So magic can let them fall,” whispered Rona. “On us!”

“Keep close to me,” instructed Yann, “and walk *slowly* through the trees towards Sapphire.”

Helen saw patches of bright blue through the grey trunks. Sapphire, waiting to take them home.

"Watch your feet," said Yann. "I don't know what will trigger it..."

"I will trigger it." The deep voice came from behind them, from the maze side of the wood.

Helen turned back, and saw a line of creatures at the edge of the trees. The fauns to the left, their smooth human shape above their hairy goat legs, standing still like sentries. The uruisks to the right, hairier, with longer horns, fidgeting from hoof to hoof.

And in the middle, the Master. Tall and broad, the massive burden of his bull's head carried on his man's shoulders. The Master of the Maze. The minotaur.

"I will happily trigger the trap, so stay exactly where you are."

Yann lifted his curved bow. "We will not give you back the baby. She will not die for your dark magic."

The minotaur laughed. "I'm not claiming her back, horse-boy. You got in and out of that toy maze, you got past my fauns and uruisks. You won the unicorn fair and square, so you can keep her, and she will be crushed with you in my stony snare if you don't do as I say."

Helen bent over the unicorn, wondering if her own body could shelter the baby from falling rocks.

Yann muttered, "Get under me. I'll shield you."

"I won't let you do that for me," said Helen.

"Why not? You're doing it for the baby. She'd be safer under my ribcage than under your narrow shoulders." Helen looked at Rona, who shrugged and ducked under Yann's chest. Helen stayed where she was.

The minotaur rasped again, his human voice

struggling past his bull's throat. Helen realised he was the only creature without a human head that she could understand. "You are getting a name for yourselves, young fabled beasts. Perhaps that's why the careless unicorn babysitter came to you for help. You have already completed many successful quests."

"We've defeated many enemies too," Yann called out. "Including you."

"Really, colt? Do you count that a victory? Last time we met face to face, I threw you to the ground. And your feathered friend had to burn up a life to free that human child from my grasp. You didn't defeat me, horse-boy. I'm still here and you've stepped right into my trap."

Yann shook his head. "You don't look like a victor though, do you? I'm back on my hooves, taller, heavier and harder to knock down this year. Catesby has hatched again and grown new adult feathers. We're both looking pretty good. How are you looking these days? Do you like your reflection in the mirror? Can you even *see* a mirror?"

The Master bellowed and stamped towards them, stopping just before the first tree booby-trapped with rocks. Now he was close enough for the sunlight seeping through the trees to light up his bull's head.

The sun gleamed on patches of lumpy pink skin between tufts of black hair on his forehead and ears. And it shone on his mismatched eyes: one bright and alive; the other pale and still, the eyelid drooping. Helen gasped. She'd never seen the burn scars left by phoenix fire before.

Yann called confidently, "The last time you tried to

beat us, you lost the Book you were chasing, and you lost half your hair and the sight of one eye to Catesby's flames. This time, did you hope the mild healing power of unicorn horn would cure your scars and blindness?" The centaur laughed. "Do you really think that if you look prettier, the fabled beast tribes will let you lead us? We will *never* accept you as ruler of our world, with one eye or two!"

"Don't insult me, horse-boy." The Master held up a small branch, with a pebble balanced in the top fork. He shook it and the rocks above them trembled. "If I drop this pebble, you will be crushed. But if you do as I say, I will free you from the circle before the rocks fall."

There was silence.

Not total silence. Helen could hear birds twittering, as if they hadn't noticed their trees had become a trap this morning.

And the trees were creaking, like a forest ruffled by a breeze. But Helen knew it was the sound of wood straining under weight, branches near breaking point.

Then the Master spoke again. "If you do as I say, you will be safe."

Rona whimpered, "What does he want? Why won't he tell us? Ask him, Yann."

Yann muttered back, "If we ask him what he wants, that's a step towards agreeing to it. Don't say anything. Don't move. Don't panic."

The noisy silence continued, for another hundred heartbeats.

The minotaur laughed. "Wise children. Wise with words and silence as well as weapons and clues.

Excellent. I want you skilled and talented, when you're on my side."

"We're not on your side!" shouted Helen.

The minotaur jerked the branch and the rocks shifted above their heads. After a terrifying moment, the rocks settled again.

"Oops," said Helen. "Sorry."

Yann shook his head at her. "Let him talk, Helen. While he's talking, we're still alive." Helen nodded and hugged the warm unicorn in her arms. The baby was breathing gently. Helen looked down. The baby was asleep.

The Master sighed. "I know you're curious, but I admire your good sense in not asking me. I want you to go on a quest for me, horse-boy. I want you and your followers to fetch me..."

"They're not my followers," interrupted Yann. "They're my friends. We don't quest for anyone else. We certainly won't quest for you."

"What happened to letting him talk?" Helen muttered.

Yann grinned down at her. "If you don't like how I negotiate, human girl, shelter under my chest."

The minotaur frowned. "You will follow my orders or you will die."

"Are you threatening a centaur with a bow in his hand?" Yann laughed. "Do you know what we call the target in archery? A bullseye. Would you like to find out how accurate I am? My arrows disabled four of your fauns and one of your uruisks when I was *galloping*, bullhead. Do you want to discover how accurate I am when I'm standing still, when I have time to aim? When I'm aiming at your only working eye?"

"Put the bow down." The branch twitched in the minotaur's fist. "Put the bow down and listen to my orders."

Yann raised the point of his arrow and drew his bowstring tight. "We will not agree to work for you. You know we won't. Stop posturing for your herd of goats. Let us go or I let this arrow fly."

"If you let it fly, colt, then I drop the rocks. You won't be able to shoot straight if you're turning to run away."

"I never run away. Whatever you throw at me, I will stand still and I will shoot straight." Then Yann whispered, "Helen, please shelter under me."

Helen didn't want to let Yann take risks for her. But she didn't have the right to make that decision for the unicorn, so she handed the baby to Rona. The baby snorted, then settled in the selkie's arms.

Helen looked up. There were seven rocks in the tree above them. Two were as big as the minotaur's head. The others were the size of her own head. She took one step closer to the tree trunk, hoping that would protect her.

Yann's voice was still low. "Do we agree that we can't do what he wants?"

"Of course," said Helen.

"Agreed," murmured Rona.

"Then take a deep breath, girls. We've had the words, now we'll get the sticks and stones."

The centaur called out with all the power of his two pairs of lungs, "We will never work for you, we will never call you Master. Put the branch down or I will shoot for that bullseye."

The minotaur smiled. He lifted his left hand and prodded the pebble. It wobbled. The trees creaked and

Helen heard a thud. But it wasn't the one solid thud of a rock falling, it was a drumbeat of thuds, getting louder behind her, like an orchestra made up only of percussion.

Could it be hooves? Dozens or hundreds of hooves?

Helen looked between the trees, past the dragon, and saw an approaching horde of horses. Some horned, some part-human, some with water dripping from their manes. An army, a cavalry of horses.

The minotaur snarled and threw the branch up in the air. The pebble fell out and dropped to the ground.

Then Helen heard everything at once:

the thudding of hooves;

the twang of Yann's bowstring;

the cracking of branches freed of an unbearable weight;

the crash of rocks all around her.

She crouched, her arms over her head.

She heard thuds and snaps and laughter and hoofbeats.

A falling rock grazed her elbow, numbing her left arm. Twigs pinged onto her hands and arms, scratching her.

There was a downpour of rocks and a lightning storm of breaking branches.

Another rock landed beside her, bouncing up and hitting her ribs. Suddenly there was a pause in the crashing, so she lifted her head. She saw a rock falling towards her, then a blur of chestnut legs as Yann reared up and kicked the rock away.

There was another chorus of pops and snaps as more branches cracked under the strain.

And Helen saw a long straight branch fly through

the air and hit Yann, in the smooth width of his horse's chest.

The branch didn't bend. It didn't bounce off. It drove right into his flesh, sharp and straight and true, like one of his own arrows.

Yann made no noise. He said nothing. He didn't scream or yell or whisper.

He just fell. His back legs crumpling, his front legs loose.

Helen hauled Rona out of the way, so Yann fell towards empty space, not towards the selkie and the unicorn.

His boy's body fell sideways as his horse body collapsed onto the ground. The long spear of wood jutted from his chest. A thin jet of blood splattered the leaves.

The rocks stopped falling.

The drumbeat behind them got louder.

Yann lay still and silent on the ground.

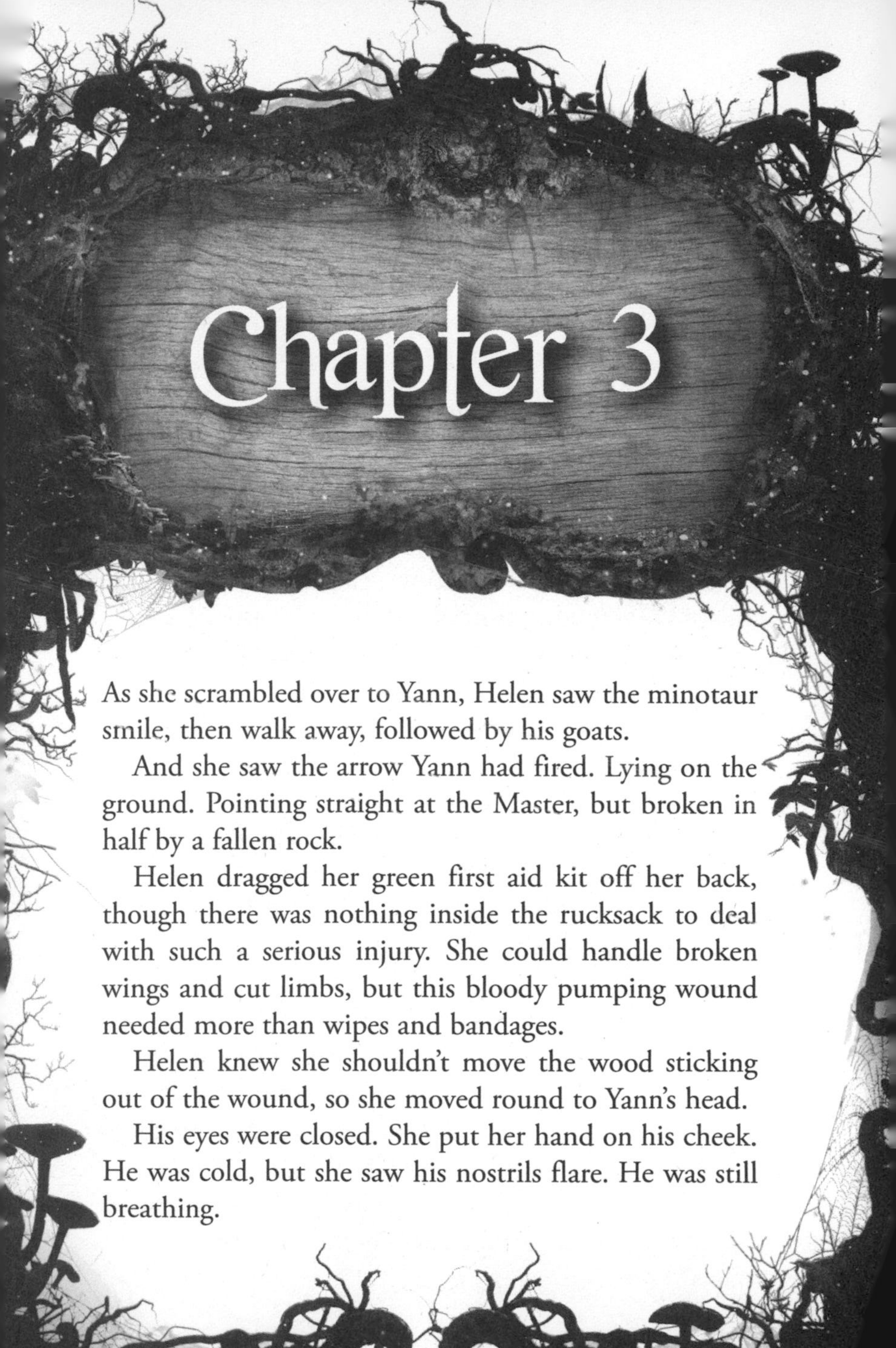

Chapter 3

As she scrambled over to Yann, Helen saw the minotaur smile, then walk away, followed by his goats.

And she saw the arrow Yann had fired. Lying on the ground. Pointing straight at the Master, but broken in half by a fallen rock.

Helen dragged her green first aid kit off her back, though there was nothing inside the rucksack to deal with such a serious injury. She could handle broken wings and cut limbs, but this bloody pumping wound needed more than wipes and bandages.

Helen knew she shouldn't move the wood sticking out of the wound, so she moved round to Yann's head.

His eyes were closed. She put her hand on his cheek. He was cold, but she saw his nostrils flare. He was still breathing.

The hoofbeats were now so loud, she could hardly hear Catesby screaming or Lavender and Rona yelling. But she caught enough words to know her friends were asking if Yann was alive and if she could heal him.

She looked at his white face, his limp arms and legs, the blood pooling under his body, the branch stuck deep into his chest, and she wondered whether anyone could heal him.

Then she was surrounded by a crashing which was almost as overwhelming as the rocks falling. The cavalry had arrived.

She ignored the long legs and heavy hooves around her, and concentrated on Yann.

She felt the pulse at his wrist. It was weak.

"Please be quiet!" she called out. "I need to hear his heart."

But everyone kept thumping and yelling and circling round.

"*Quiet!*" No one paid any attention.

Then Rona shouted, "Silence! Give the healer some space. Give her some respect."

The circling hooves moved back. The voices quietened.

Helen remembered that the best place to hear a horse's heart was from behind, so she crawled past Yann's hooves, then lowered her head to his ribcage, behind his left leg. She heard his heart ... beat ... slow ... and ... weak...

She sat up. She was kneeling in blood. Her knees were wet and warm with it.

She fumbled in her pocket for the only piece of equipment which could save Yann. Her phone. She dialled home.

"Hello! Who is that? Hello!"

"Nicola! It's me. Find Mum and give her the phone."

"Mummy said I am not to disturb her. Not less it's urgent, like a crocodile biting my leg. Call back later please. Thank you."

And her little sister hung up.

Helen dialled again. "Nicola! Don't hang up! There's a crocodile biting my leg *right now* and I need to speak to Mum. Please!"

"Okey dokey. Say hi to the crocodile."

Helen heard footsteps, a squeaky door, then Nicola's faint voice. "Mummy, Helen is being eaten by a crocodile and wants to talk to you."

Then she heard her mum's irritated voice. "Helen! I'm writing a lecture. What is it?"

Helen put the phone on speaker and laid it on the ground, so she could talk and use her hands at the same time. "Mum! Please help me. I have a ... a ... horse here with a branch driven into his chest and he's bleeding and unconscious and his skin is pale and cold and his pulse is very weak! What do I do?"

"Is there an adult there? Is the horse's owner there? And why aren't you getting ready for school?"

"*Mum!* Help me with the horse! School isn't as important as the horse!"

"Calm down. Staying calm will help the horse. Who else is there?"

Helen looked up for the first time.

She was surrounded by fabled beasts: by her own friends, including Sapphire, who'd pushed her long neck through the trees, now that she wouldn't spring the trap;

by a herd of centaurs, a dozen silver and gold unicorns and some wild-looking kelpies.

All of them staring at her.

"There's quite a crowd, Mum, but I'm the only one with a first aid kit."

"Is the wound still bleeding?"

Helen saw a steady stream of blood dripping down the branch onto the ground. "Yes. He's lost lots of blood and it's still bleeding."

"Where is the wound?"

"It's on the left side of his chest. I think it's pierced his heart! And his heartbeat is so slow and quiet, I can hardly hear it. What do I do? Do I take the branch out?"

"No. If it's penetrated his heart, even more blood will pump out when you remove it. You don't have the equipment to deal with that. We'll need intravenous fluids and... I'm coming now, Helen, just hold on. How slow is the heartbeat? Can you count it for me?"

Helen laid her head down again and heard one flicker of a pulse.

Then nothing. She waited.

Silence.

Nothing.

The birds had stopped calling. The trees were still. None of the fabled beasts were making a sound.

And she couldn't hear Yann's heart.

"His heart has stopped! Mum! What do I do?"

"You can't do anything on your own. I'm coming, in case there's anything I can do. It isn't easy to hear a horse's heart if it's weak. There may still be a very faint pulse. So cover him up, keep him warm, and tell me where you are."

"I'm at Tra—"

A huge hoof slammed down and crushed her phone.

Helen screamed in frustration.

She leapt up and faced Yann's father. "How dare you! I'm trying to help him! My mum can help him! She can bring equipment to save him. She's only a few minutes away, there's still time!"

Before the white centaur could answer, Helen flung herself back down and listened again for Yann's heart.

Nothing. She couldn't hear his heart beat in his horse chest.

She stretched up and put her fingers on his wrist. Through his thin human skin, she felt a slow throbbing beat. "A pulse! He still has a pulse!"

"Of course, you stupid human girl..." Yann's father grabbed her shoulder.

Helen pushed him away and heard Rona's soothing voice saying, "Petros, please, let her try. She has healed so many of us."

Helen wondered why Yann had a pulse when his injured heart had stopped beating. She scrambled round to put her ear on his human chest.

His boy's heart was still beating. Weak, but regular.

"He's alive! He has *two* hearts. And his boy's heart is still working! We can still save him."

She touched the branch, wondering if it was safe to pull it out of the horse heart now, to treat the wound.

But Petros hauled her away. "Leave my son alone! You've done enough damage. We will take him home to our healers, who will not be surprised to discover that he has two hearts. And *you* will stay away from him."

He dropped Helen to the ground behind the circle of

horses. She watched as four adult centaurs picked Yann up, the branch still sticking out of the wound, blood dripping more slowly off the end.

They laid him across his father's back, then all five centaurs moved off in formation, one bearing his weight, the others holding him steady.

As they galloped away, Helen watched her friend's blood streak red down his father's white flanks.

Chapter 4

Helen couldn't stand up.

Now that the danger of the rescue, the terror of the trap and the horror of Yann's injury were past, she could feel bruises on her elbow and ribs. The blood on her knees was cold and sticky. She shivered.

Rona sat down beside her. "Centaur healers are used to battle wounds..."

Then the baby unicorn woke up. She'd slept through threats, rockfalls and injuries, but when one of the adult unicorns whickered, she wriggled in Rona's arms.

A pale golden unicorn approached Helen and Rona on slim legs and pearly hooves. She called again and the baby replied. Rona opened her arms. The baby unicorn stood up, wobbling on her newborn legs, then staggered over to her mum. The baby reached her head up and the mother reached her head down, and they rubbed noses.

Helen burst into tears. Which was a bit embarrassing, because it was usually Rona who cried.

But Helen was scared that by trying to heal Yann herself she had delayed more useful treatment. Also, she was happy the unicorn was safe, she was sore in at least three places, her mum was going to ask impossible questions about that awful phone call, and she was nearly late for school.

Rona hugged her. "Yann is strong. He'll be fine." But she was sniffing too.

The mother unicorn raised her head and whinnied. Rona replied, "Thank you. I'll tell him when he wakes."

Then the unicorns left, their glittery outlines vanishing into the shadows of the trees. The kelpies turned and galloped on the trail of the Master. The remaining centaurs collected Yann's broken arrow and discarded bow, and followed Petros. Suddenly the friends were alone.

Helen looked at the blood on the ground, and her smashed phone. "Let's go after them. Let's see if there is anything we can do."

She stood up, but Rona gripped her wrist. "Don't be daft, Helen. Petros doesn't like you near Yann at the best of times. He's as big and strong as the Master, and he hates humans almost as much. It's not safe for you in the centaurs' grounds; that's why Yann never takes you there. Perhaps once Yann is recovering, you can visit. But not while his blood is still flowing and his father's blood is still hot. Anyway, you have to get to school."

"I can't go to school! I have to find out how Yann is."

Catesby chattered angrily above her head.

Lavender landed on Helen's shoulder. "Catesby's right. You have to act normally, or you'll give too much away. Go home, tell your mother something she can believe, then go to school. That might repair any damage you did to the secret existence of Scotland's fabled beasts when you called her."

"I'm sorry!" wailed Helen. "I thought she could help. Anyway, how can I act normally at school when Yann might be *dying?*"

"You've faced monsters, Helen Strang, you can do anything."

"This is worse than any monster..."

Catesby chattered again and Lavender translated. "Catesby will fly to the centaurs' moor, and if Yann gets worse, we will get a message to you."

So Helen climbed onto the dragon and they all flew, hidden high in the clouds, to Clovenshaws.

They landed behind the trees on the hill at the back of her house, and Helen hugged her friends goodbye. She didn't bother cleaning the blood from her hands or the tear-streaks from her face. They were part of her story anyway.

She ran down the hill, clambered over the wooden fence, jogged past the large animal surgery and crashed through the back door.

Her family were sitting at the table, eating breakfast.

"Helen!" her mum yelled. "Where were you? Why did you cut me off?"

Helen took a deep breath. "The horse jerked and smashed my phone with his hoof. No one else had any reception, so I couldn't call back. Sorry."

"And how is the horse?"

"He's ... he's fine. I overreacted. The wood only went in a centimetre or two. It must have hit a vein, because there was lots of blood, but once I remembered how to take a horse's pulse properly I realised his heart was beating fine. So we eased the stick out, cleaned and covered the wound, and the horse is being kept warm and calm to deal with the shock."

Helen's mum nodded, but she still looked worried.

Helen kept talking. "Sorry I panicked. Lavender loves her ponies and she was crying, which made me overreact. Sorry."

"That's a lot of blood though, Helen."

"It's not that much." She glanced down. Her legs were dark red from her knees to her ankles. It looked like she'd been wading in blood. "Ah. Some of that is mud, really. It's not so bad." Her mum didn't look convinced. And her dad and little sister were staring at her jeans.

Helen noticed her ripped scarf and hid it in her fleece. "I'd better get ready for school." She stepped away from the table, wondering if she had got away with that. She'd been getting away with lots of lies recently, because her parents believed that Helen had a new friend at high school with a passion for ponies, and that Helen went out early most mornings to help exercise them.

The pony story would collapse if her mum ever spoke to anyone at school, and discovered that the Lavender in Helen's maths set was far happier at a computer than out of doors and only had a goldfish. But Helen was hoping she would think of a way round that before parents' night.

Her mum stood up. "Not so fast, Helen. Is there a vet attending the pony? Should I go round?"

"No. Yes. No, you don't need to go round. Really, Mum, it was only a flesh wound, and you've shown me how to deal with those, and Lavender's granny has owned horses her entire life, so she knows what she's doing." Helen thought of her real friend Lavender's real granny, who was so tiny she could boss everyone around from inside a rhododendron flower. "It's fine. I panicked. I'm sorry. I'll pay for a new phone."

"And new jeans, I suspect," said her dad.

"These will wash out. I only use them for adventures anyway."

"For what?"

"Oh. For riding, going for walks, messing about in mud ... and blood," she muttered as she left the kitchen.

"You have fifteen minutes before the school bus goes!" her mum yelled after her.

Helen had a quick shower, wincing as the water hit her bruises, then got dressed without bothering to tie her tie. She pinned her dark curly hair back and grabbed her schoolbag.

Then, moving so fast she didn't have time to worry about Yann, she ran out of the house and down the lane to the main road through Clovenshaws, where she skidded to a halt on the grass verge. Two minutes early.

She had time to get her breath back before the bus drew up. Then she jumped on and sat beside her best human friend, Kirsty.

Helen knotted her tie and pulled out her French homework. "Can we revise this vocabulary, Kirsty? I didn't have time last night."

"Why not? I did it all before teatime."

"I was out on the hills, looking for new birds' nests."

Helen had invented several hobbies recently, including birdwatching and horseriding, to explain why she wanted to be outside in the evenings, early mornings and most weekends. She'd also become expert at doing her homework on the bus, at lunchtime and at the tea table. She was still getting good marks, because she was concentrating on getting it right first time, so her parents didn't have any excuse to keep her in.

"Birds' nests?" said Kirsty. "Really? That's a bit pathetic. Who is he, Helen?"

"Who is who?"

"Who is it you're seeing?"

Helen bit her lip. "What are you talking about?"

"Come on, Helen. I know this ponyriding thing is a lie too."

"What ponyriding thing?"

"Last week, when your mum gave us both a lift and you had to run back for your violin, she asked me whether I was exercising Lavender's ponies too. She said you were awfully keen, out pretty much every morning. And I covered for you, said you were always chatting about horses at school. But I know you and Lavender hardly ever talk and she's allergic to animal hair, so what are you doing? Is it a boy? Is it a mystery? Is it your music? What is it?"

Helen, who'd stopped breathing as she heard Kirsty destroy her carefully built castle of lies, grasped at that last suggestion. "Yes it is! It is my music. You know what my mum's like. If it's not got four legs and a fascinating wound, she thinks it's a waste of time. She disapproves of me spending more time on the violin than my other homework, so she's trying to cut me down to fifteen minutes practice a day. Just quarter of an hour! That's ridiculous. I'll never be a professional violinist at that rate. So I'm sneaking out to someone's barn and practising every morning. Please don't give me away. *Please!*"

Like most of Helen's lies, it wasn't far from the truth. Her mum didn't want Helen to focus just on her musical talent. She did insist on more maths and less music. And Helen did often take her fiddle with her when she met the fabled beasts, because Rona was a superb singer, and they sometimes composed and performed together.

But it was still a lie. A lie to her best friend. After the lies to her mum and dad.

The only people she didn't lie to were the people she was lying to protect: Rona, Lavender, Catesby, Sapphire and Yann.

Helen sighed. Yann. She hoped centaur healers could cure spears in the heart.

But Kirsty heard the sigh differently. "Oh, Helen! It must be so hard. To have a dream and not be able to follow it!" She sighed too. "I'm lucky, my mum drives me to Edinburgh three times a week to play football. She's so supportive. It must be hard when your mum is so strict..."

Helen smiled. Her mum wasn't strict. She had rules, like homework done, room tidy and limits on violin time. But so long as those rules were followed, she let Helen roam the countryside, and didn't ask too many questions when Helen came back. Unless she was drenched in blood.

"My mum's alright. So are you!" She hugged Kirsty, and they raced through a list of French animals until the bus stopped.

Helen had been at the high school for months now and was used to the timetable, the maze of corridors and the huge sixth years. Today, when her mind kept flitting back to the blood on the leaves and the moment Yann's heart stopped beating, she was grateful for the regular changes of subject.

The last period was music, her favourite. But she kept glancing at the windows, hoping, for once, that she wouldn't see a waving fairy on the windowsill. She didn't want to get a message from her friends today. She didn't want to hear that Yann had got worse, because the only way for him to get worse was for him to die.

But by the time she'd clambered on the bus, listened to Kirsty's chatter about what she'd burnt in Home Economics, then run home, she was desperate for news.

She dropped her bags in the hall and stomped upstairs.

She heard the door of the small animal surgery open. There was a muffled woof, then her mum's voice. "Homework?"

"It's Friday," Helen yelled. "I don't have homework for Saturday or Sunday. Give me a break!"

"Don't be smart with me, Helen. What homework do you have for Monday?"

Helen shouted back, as she reached her bedroom, "Not much. I have to plan out a story for English and do some maths." Then she shut her door. "Also, I have to find out if my grumpiest friend is still alive and I have to keep my other friends safe...

"Do you think I can do all that before Monday?" she asked the figures sitting on her bed: Rona on the duvet, Lavender on the pillow and Catesby on the headboard. "Do you think *we* can do all that?"

None of them spoke.

"Of course we can," Helen answered herself. "That's why even the Master of the Maze wants us to work for him."

Then she asked the question she'd been worrying about all day, but now didn't want to ask. "How is he?"

Rona stood up and put her arms round Helen. Helen felt the selkie's tears, damp on her shoulder.

Chapter 5

Helen pushed Rona away and stared at her pale face. "How is he?"

Rona shook her head, then slumped back down on the bed.

Helen couldn't ask again. She looked at Catesby, who squawked. Which, as usual, meant nothing to Helen.

So she looked at Lavender.

The fairy whispered, "He's alive, Helen. But only just. The centaurs stopped the bleeding. But his horse heart hasn't started beating again and he hasn't woken up. His human heart is too small to keep him alive. It's not strong enough to pump blood round a body the size of a horse. It's weakening already. If his horse heart doesn't restart, he only has a day or two left."

Helen said, "Right, let's go and help." She grabbed

clean jeans and a t-shirt, and gestured at Catesby to fly out of the window while she got changed. "Can Sapphire take us there?"

"No, Helen," said Rona. "You can't go to Cauldhame Moor."

"I know it's not *easy* to get there, but if you help me, I'm sure..."

"No, I don't mean you can't. I mean you mustn't. You must not go there, because the centaurs are still angry. They blame you for Yann going on that rescue mission, which is unfair, because we all know the hard thing is *stopping* Yann going on an adventure. But they think he'd have asked other centaurs to help when that unicorn came crying that she'd lost her sister, if we hadn't been willing to join him. They're blaming all of us, but mostly you, because you're human. So it's dangerous for you to go to the moor, and you can't get in anyway, can you?"

Helen shook her head. She'd never been to Yann's home. She'd stayed with Rona's family in Sutherland. She'd had sleepovers at Lavender's, though she always took her own tent because she couldn't fit into the flower fairy's bedroom. They'd all been to parties in Sapphire's cave. She'd even had a picnic below Catesby's nest. But she'd never visited Yann's home. Partly because she knew she wouldn't be welcome, but also because it was almost impossible for humans to get there.

There weren't walls or fences round Cauldhame Moor. Just what Yann had called an "unwelcome field" or a "general desire to turn around and go another way". Entire armies had changed their marching plans and at least two road-building schemes had taken a longer route, because human scouts or surveyors who tried to walk across the moor always found a better, easier, more attractive path. "It's the opposite of the grass being greener on the other side of the fence," Yann had joked. Helen could hear his voice in her memory.

She shrugged. "So what if his family shout at me? I can handle that."

"Angry centaurs don't just shout," said Rona. "They attack."

"But surely they know I only want to help."

"They don't want your help, Helen. They don't want *our* help. They won't even let the unicorns help. You know what centaurs are like."

"Stiff-necked, arrogant and rude," Helen said. "Just like Yann. I can cope with him, so I can cope with his family. I just want to see if I can help or if my mum can help. Please show me how to get in."

Catesby was back on the window sill, Rona was on the bed, Lavender was fluttering in the air. They were all shaking their heads.

Helen had lied to almost everyone she cared about today. She might as well lie to them all. She sighed. "I'll take your advice and stay away from the moor, but if I write a note offering help to Yann's mum, rather than his dad, will you *all* take it to her? Right now?"

Her friends nodded, so Helen scribbled a note. She gave it to Catesby, and watched as he and Lavender swooped out of the window.

Rona tried to smile at her. "Do you want me to stay here? We could work on our spring dance tunes."

Helen smiled back. "No. You'd better all go together, to keep each others' courage up against the nasty scary centaurs. I'll distract my mum while you go out the back."

She ran downstairs and opened the surgery door. Her mum was inside, with a sleeping spaniel on the black operating table, using tweezers to tug at something in its coat.

"What's wrong with the spaniel?" Helen asked.

"Thorns," her mum said. "She's not the brightest dog. She forgot how to reverse and kept running deeper into the bushes. Her owner is coming back soon and there are dozens to take out. Do you want to help?"

Helen washed her hands, then found the right size of tweezers.

There were thorns in the dog's nose. She gripped one and started to ease it out.

"So, Mum... I did panic this morning, but if I had been right, and that branch *had* pierced the horse's heart, what could I have done?"

"Not much, I'm afraid. If the branch had pierced the heart, it would bleed out internally and the horse would die."

"Is there any way a horse's heart can ever be restarted?"

"A vet could restart a heart with injections of atropine or adrenaline, or even with a few sharp blows with their knee. But that wouldn't work with a heart which was still bleeding."

"So with an injured heart, could you operate to repair it or transplant a new one?"

"No. Horses' hearts are too deep inside their chest cavity; vets can't open them up to operate. If a horse's heart stops for more than a few minutes, then the horse is dead."

"But, just say it *isn't* dead after a few minutes, what could you do?"

Helen's mum frowned. "That's impossible."

"I'm just asking," Helen said. "Just for ... em ... for the story I'm writing for English." But Helen realised there was no point in arguing about whether a horse could survive with no heartbeat, unless she was going to tell her mum that this horse had two hearts and one of them was in a boy's chest. She had to find out what else was possible.

"So what treatments *can* you give for problems with horses' hearts? Just so I can think of a realistic heart problem for my story."

Helen's mum smiled. She enjoyed answering this sort of question. "Well, if the horse's heart is beating irregularly, you can give a drug like quinidine, to get all four chambers beating in time again. But for a real kick-start for a horse with an uneven heartbeat, there are a few new techniques. You can use electric shock pads, or even put tiny electrodes in through the veins, to get the heart back to normal. That's called transvenous electrical cardioversion, which I can spell for you if you want.

"But you couldn't do that in the field, Helen, nor in my large animal surgery. You'd need to be at a specialist equine centre, like the one up at the university. You'd need an anaesthetist on the team..."

"Even if the horse is unconscious?" Helen asked.

"Yes. You don't want the patient feeling any pain. And you don't want the patient waking up in the middle of an operation either. Not with all those hooves. I even had to knock this wee thing out to remove the thorns without being bitten. So you need an anaesthetist as well as a surgeon, and all the right hygiene and recovery conditions. If you want to save a horse with a serious heart problem, in real life or a story, then you have to take it to a hospital.

"Anyway, that sort of heart problem doesn't usually occur in ponies; it's more likely to happen to racehorses. Horses with big hearts, very fit, under lots of stress."

Helen grinned. "A big heart, very fit and under stress. That sounds about right! Thanks, Mum."

"I'm just glad you're writing about real animals, not those imaginary ones you used to believe in. Now, how many thorns have you removed?"

"One. Sorry. I was thinking about the horse."

Her mum shook her head. "Go and write your story. I'll deal with Rosie here."

"Rosie?" Helen laughed. "Rosie and the thorns!"

Her mum smiled. "That could be the title for your story..."

Helen ran back upstairs. Her room was empty, so she pulled on hiking boots, and picked up her first aid kit and a warm fleece. It was nearly the end of March, but the weather was as cold as it had been in February.

She yelled to her mum, "I'm taking the bike out!"

Her mum replied, "I'm picking Nicola up from her play-date at six, so be home for tea at six thirty."

Helen cycled towards the hill where Yann had once pointed out his herd's lands from a distance, and told her that centuries ago a wise woman had gifted them a barrier to keep humans out. "You can't see the unwelcome field," he'd explained, "so people never know why they don't cross our moor."

"How do *you* get in?" Helen had asked.

"It doesn't stop us. It only works on our enemies."

Helen had said that not all humans were their enemies, but he'd just laughed and changed the subject.

When she got to the top of Bleakcairn Law, she saw the moor stretch out ahead of her. Already she could feel a desire to be somewhere else. She had lots of homework for Monday. Perhaps she should head home now...

Helen shook her head. She wasn't going home until she saw Yann. She leant the bike against a rock and headed downhill.

The desire to go back got stronger.

What if someone steals your bike? a familiar voice murmured in her head.

"There's no one else here," she said loudly.

What about practising that new violin melody?

"I know it already."

What about popping round to Kirsty's for a chat?

"She's playing football in East Kilbride this evening."

But it didn't matter how many answers Helen had, her head kept filling up with more reasons to go the other way. It was hard to keep her feet moving towards the moor.

It's muddy. Those boots will get manky.

"I can clean them."

It's dangerous. You could fall and hurt yourself.

"I have a first aid kit."

Soon she was at the bottom of the hill, right on the edge of the moor. But she couldn't walk forward any more. It took all her determination not to turn and run back.

It wasn't fear. People would remember being scared on the edge of a moor. You'd talk about running from something scary, but you wouldn't mention changing your mind about going for a walk and heading home for a cup of tea instead. You probably wouldn't even remember that.

Helen's desire to go home was so strong she was struggling simply to stand still. She was straining against thin air, pushing against her desire to leave and do something, anything, else.

Then she heard Yann's voice again, cheerful and confident in her memory. "It only works on our enemies."

She had to prove to the unwelcome field that she wasn't the enemy. So Helen started to talk, to herself, to the field, to the moor.

"I've healed a centaur's leg. I've ridden on a centaur's back."

She raised her right hand and pushed it forward. She felt something shove back, but then her right hand pushed further and slid through.

"I've answered riddles with a centaur. I've cheered a centaur in a race."

She raised her left hand and it met less resistance.

"I've made salad sandwiches for a centaur. I've cooled a centaur's poisoned hand."

She tried to step straight onto the moor with her right foot, but that met too many hidden worries about homework, family and friends. So she twisted and tried to move through sideways.

"A centaur kicked down my attacker in a cave.

A centaur held a beam steady for me to escape our enemies."

She pushed again, with her shoulder. *Go home!* her head shouted. *Wrong way, turn back! Go home now!*

But she kept talking calmly and pushing gently.

"I've held a sword to stand with a centaur against a pack of wolves. I've fought beside him. I'm a centaur's friend. He's my friend."

She stepped onto the moor.

Chapter 6

Helen wondered how she was going to find the centaurs in such a wide moor.

Then she heard the heavy beat of hooves, and realised the unwelcome field must be an alarm as well as a barrier. She didn't have to search for the centaurs; they would hunt for her.

She almost turned and ran back to her bike. But she tried to reassure herself. She wasn't their enemy, she was just there to see Yann and to tell the centaurs what her mum had said about treatment.

Twenty centaurs came into view over a low rise, galloping in a long line. Helen could see the glowing white of Petros in the middle, with pale grey centaurs to his left, shading darker grey through to black centaurs at the left wing; palominos to his right, shading through bays and chestnuts to darker brown at the right wing.

As they reached her, Helen stepped forward, away from the invisible barrier. She didn't want to be pushed back through before she had time to talk.

"Why are you here, human girl?" boomed Petros. "Haven't you done enough harm to my son?"

"I came to see Yann and to offer my help."

"We received your impertinent note. We require no help from you. Your presence here is an insult. Leave now, before we force you out."

"I also have information..."

Helen was interrupted by the centaur nearest to Petros. A young female centaur, a pale dappled grey, with plaited ash-blonde hair and a grey leather waistcoat. She called out, "Petros, you know the rules. Any humans who break through the unwelcome field must never be allowed back out. We can't let her leave. We must silence her. Permanently."

"Calm down, Epona. This human child has known our secret for over a year and has not given it away. We can safely let her leave. She has taken three steps onto our moor, so she can take three steps off again." He looked at Helen. "Do as I say, girl. Turn and leave. Or we will throw you out."

Helen looked at Petros, surprised to discover he wasn't the most anti-human centaur in the herd. She took another step forward.

Petros shook his head. "Misplaced courage will not impress us, child. Leave here now."

The grey centaur stamped her hooves. "This girl has been a risk for months. She's a risk to Yann, encouraging him to gallivant all over Scotland when he should be here guarding our lands. She's a risk to the whole tribe, knowing our secrets. Now that she is actually on our lands, and Yann can't defend her, we should get rid of her."

Helen could see that Petros was ignoring the girl centaur, so she ignored her too and spoke directly to him. "I want to offer my help and my mother's help to heal Yann. There are techniques which could..."

"Human techniques? You offer human healing to my son?" Petros laughed. "You think we're so primitive that we can't look after ourselves, that we need human help to heal our warriors?"

"Do you have a hospital," she asked, "with surgeons and anaesthetists, with drugs, electric shock paddles and tiny electrodes to kick-start hearts?"

"No."

"Then I think you do need help."

"We do not need human help."

Helen was finding it hard to stay calm. "You're just saying that because you don't want anyone to know about you. You're denying Yann life-saving treatment to protect your secret! That's so *selfish!*"

"Human girl, do you know my son so little? Do you think Yann would choose to be saved if the price of his life was our freedom?"

Helen bit her lip. She knew the answer to that. "But the price doesn't have to be your freedom. Humans can keep secrets. Yann trusts me. Don't you trust his judgement?"

"No, I don't. He is reckless and foolish, and risks far too much every time he meets you."

"Yann? Reckless? Taking risks?" Helen grinned. "Would you want him any other way?"

Yann's father almost smiled. Then he sighed. "I do not have time to debate with you. In memory of my son and his friendship with you, I will let you leave safely if you go now, but I will not let you take one more step onto our lands."

"In *memory* of your son!" Helen yelled. "Have you given up on him already? How dare you give up!"

Helen took three more steps onto the centaurs' precious moor.

Petros reared up, right above her. "I warned you! Are you as reckless as my son?"

"Not usually, but he's asleep, so someone has to be. Let me tell you what I've come to offer and then, if you still want me to, I will leave."

Petros snorted. "I begin to see why my son allows you to accompany him. Tell me what you offer."

"First let me check the symptoms and diagnosis. My friends say Yann's human heart is too small to keep him alive, so if his horse heart doesn't restart soon he will die. Is that right?"

His father nodded.

"My mother knows healers at the university in Edinburgh, who have equipment to kick-start horse's hearts. I give you my word they will do their best to save him and I will make sure they never tell anyone."

The dappled centaur muttered, "I know a way to ensure their silence..."

Helen said, "Lavender does memory spells. We could try that."

Petros shook his head. "The arrogance of humans, to imagine we do not have healers as experienced as yours. Our healers use cleansing herbs to prevent infection and mend wounds, and stimulating herbs and massage to restart hearts."

"Then why don't they restart Yann's heart?"

"Because my son's injury is not just physical. Your human healers would be as powerless as ours. The injury is not just to the flesh. It is a magical injury. It was inflicted by an object controlled by magic, and it resists ordinary healing."

"So heal it magically!" Helen shouted.

"*We are trying!* We have summoned the best magical healers in the land, and I should be at home waiting to greet them, not here arguing with you. You've given me your ignorant and insulting offer of help, now get out. And don't ever come back."

He folded his arms and stared at her.

She said softly, "But you don't think those magical healers can help, do you?"

He didn't answer.

"You're already mourning Yann and doing things in his *memory*, Petros. Why don't you think they can help?" Helen considered what she knew about the magic her friends used, or resisted using. "Or are you not sure about the kind of help they offer? Are they dark magic users, because the magic which injured him was dark?"

He shrugged. "The Three are neither dark nor light. They are something else entirely. But you are right: I don't want them or their magic to spend much time in my house."

"I don't use any magic," Helen said. "You don't need to be afraid of what I'll bring into your house. And even though I'm a small, weak, non-magical human, Yann isn't too proud to ask for my help. I know a little of your world and a little of mine, and that combination has worked so far. Please let me search for something, anything, which will undo the magic that's killing Yann."

Petros frowned. "What can you do?"

Helen had no idea, but she had to try. "Yann values my help, and you know the old legends say magical quests are more successful with a human involved. Rather than letting me leave safely to respect his memory, let me come through in respect for our friendship."

"Petros," hissed the young centaur, "she wants to find out our secrets. She may even have led Yann into that trap so she could get through our defences."

Helen laughed. "No one can lead Yann anywhere! He got himself into this, so why not use his methods to get him out? Let his friends try to solve this."

Petros scowled and looked at the low sun. "You are persistent. I have no more time to argue. I will let you see Yann, so you'll realise there is nothing you can do for him, then perhaps you will stop pestering us. But you will walk to my home. No human rides on my back."

"That's fine," Helen agreed. She didn't want to get any closer to him.

"We should blindfold her," said the dappled centaur.

"Why? To hide our secret grass and our confidential heather? Don't be daft, Epona. She is here as my guest, so stay out of her way if you can't be polite to her. Xanthos and Tolemy, escort this human to my house at her own pace." Petros looked straight at Helen. "I do this for my son. If you betray him, I will not stop Epona silencing you in her own way."

He galloped off, Epona still arguing at his side. Helen

followed, flanked by two bay centaurs, neither of whom were as tall as Petros, but both bigger than Yann.

After five minutes trudging, the centaur on her right spoke. "Is it true Yann lets you ride on his back?"

"Em. Yes. But only in emergencies," she said. Though nowadays, an emergency was any time Yann couldn't be bothered waiting for her to walk.

"That's disgusting," said the other centaur. "I hope he washes afterwards."

"Why do you all hate humans so much?" Helen asked.

"Why not? You cut down trees, and plant factories and shopping centres. You scar the land with roads and railways, and you poison rivers and seas."

Helen shrugged. "We don't all do that."

"What do you do to stop it then?"

"What do *you* do to stop it?" she snapped back. "Apart from hide behind that invisible barrier?"

After that, no one spoke as they walked across the moor.

Helen had always imagined Yann's home as a mix between a stable and a barracks, so she was surprised when they came over a ridge to see his father's house ahead of her.

It looked like a model out of an ancient history project. White stone, tall columns, flights of wide steps, and statues of centaurs and other fabled beasts round a fountain at the front.

Helen ran through the garden, up the stairs and into the villa. Then she followed the sound of subdued voices towards a bright warm room opening off the back corner of a large hall.

There was a gathering of fabled beasts beside the fireplace. Helen moved closer to see what they were all looking at.

It was Yann, on a low couch, with a dressing on his chest, and a face so white and still he could be another statue.

Gathered round the centaur were his friends. The friends Helen had hoped she might see: Rona, Lavender, Catesby and Sapphire, whose scaly head was poking through a window.

And others she hadn't expected:

Tangaroa, his black hair and blue tattoos gleaming;

Sylvie, crouched in her wolf form at Yann's head;

Lee, already holding his hand out to Helen.

Everyone was here. To say goodbye.

Chapter 7

Helen knelt down and took Yann's hand. "It's Helen! Can you hear me? Come back and join us!"

She heard Petros snort behind her. "We all talk to him. We all ask him to come back. If that's all you can offer..."

A faint knock echoed from the front of the villa.

"They've arrived!" Petros trotted away.

Helen squeezed Yann's hand, then looked at her friends. "Why are you all here?"

Lee smiled, his faery glamour almost blinding her. "News of the Master's reappearance travelled fast, and I heard our hoofed friend was injured, so I came to see what I could do."

Sylvie, who wouldn't change out of her wolf form just to speak to Helen, nodded in agreement.

Helen looked at the blue loon. "But Tangaroa, aren't you competing in the Sea Herald contest this weekend?"

He shrugged.

"You have to compete!" Rona said quickly. "You so nearly won last time!"

"I was beaten by a better competitor." Tangaroa grinned at the selkie, his white teeth bright in his blue tattooed face.

Rona whispered, "But I didn't win fairly."

Helen raised her eyebrows in warning at Rona. They'd never admitted to Tangaora that Rona had cheated, and he'd never guessed why she'd resigned after she won. Rona frowned at Helen, then said more clearly, "I didn't win fairly because of outside interference. You could have won last time, Tangaroa, so please go north and win this time!"

He shook his head. "I've missed the start now anyway. And Yann is more important than a title."

No one could argue with that. So they sat silently, staring at Yann.

Helen felt his pulse. It was slow and erratic. She put his wrist down. "I'm glad we're all together. But what can we *do*?"

"The injury was caused by a magical trap," said Lavender. "It has to be healed by magic. But strong magical healing has to be earned as well as found."

"Why is the magic so powerful?" Helen asked. "Was it doing more than just holding the boulders in place?"

"I'm not sure," said Lavender. "It was a strange trap. You, Rona and the unicorn came out almost unscathed, and Yann only has a couple of bruises from the rocks. If he hadn't reared up, the branch would just have scratched him."

"But he did rear up," Helen said, "and that branch stabbed him as effectively and accurately as a spear."

Lee, who was the Faery King's champion and experienced with more weapons than Helen was happy imagining, leant forward and examined the bandage over the site of the wound. "You're right. It was a perfect shot..." He looked at Helen. "Why was he rearing?"

"To kick a rock away from me. It was just chance he reared at that moment."

"No it wasn't," said Tangaroa. "If he saw a rock heading for you, of course he would kick it away. That's not chance. That's Yann."

"Then it was just chance the branch broke at the same time."

Lee frowned. "Was it?"

Helen shrugged. "We'll probably never know. But we can try to find out what the Master wanted us to do for him."

Lavender replied, "We may never find that out either. The kelpies lost the Master's trail in the Cheviots, so perhaps he's left Scotland for good."

They heard hoofbeats returning, so they stopped talking. Petros was walking towards them with a dark-brown female centaur and, between them, three human figures.

The three people were huddled together and wrapped up in red hooded cloaks, as if they were cold or hiding. As they got nearer, Helen saw glimpses of their faces. A very young woman, no older than the fifth or sixth years at Helen's school, a plump woman who was the right age to be the girl's mother, and a wrinkled woman old enough to be her great-great-grandmother.

The resemblance was very strong, as if they were all related. Or, Helen thought as she watched them glide towards Yann, as if they were all the same woman, at different ages.

Petros ordered, "Let the Three see my son."

Yann's friends stepped aside, to stand close together by the window, under Sapphire's blue head.

The three women knelt by Yann and laid their hands on him.

"He is badly hurt."

"He is dying."

"We feel the pain ... of the moment he fell."

"We feel the rip ... in his large heart."

"We feel the weakness ... of his small heart."

"Pain ... rip ... weakness." They repeated the words as if they enjoyed them.

"Shall we try ... to heal him? Or shall we sit with him ... and experience his death?"

Helen watched the three women closely. The girl would speak half a sentence, then the ancient woman would finish it. Or the plump woman would start saying something, and the girl would finish it. It wasn't a conversation; it was like one mind speaking, using different faces. Helen shivered.

"This one has ... lots of life and death in him ... lots of fire and pride and fight ... He will injure more ... kill more and spill more ... blood if we heal him ... He is worth saving."

The three women stood up, then turned to face Yann's father and the brown centaur beside him.

"The magic is deep ... but there are ways ... to heal him ... There are a few tokens ... of the healing force left ... in this old land ... If you can offer us ... a healing token ... then we can clear the magic ... from his heart ... so he can fight again."

Petros nodded. "I will find a token."

"No, centaur ... Your heart is filled ... with pride and arrogance ... You would save your son ... because you love him ... but also because he is your heir ... and you would be humiliated ... not to have an heir ... That is a selfish reason.

"The healing force ... will only reveal its tokens ... to those who approach ... with pure motives ... clean hands ... and innocent intent.

"You cannot save him, Petros ... You must search ... your own heart to discover ... if anyone can."

The Three laughed, giggling, chuckling and creaking in turn.

"We will return tomorrow ... at sunset on the spring equinox ... Spring brings new life ... so a healing at that moment ... will be most powerful ... If you offer us a healing token ... at sunset tomorrow ... we will save your son ... If there is no token ... he will die."

As they turned to leave the room, Petros asked desperately, "But what are the tokens?"

All three women spoke at once. For the first time three voices, soft and young, strong and healthy, old and cracking, spoke together.

"You must bring us:

"The scabbard of King Arthur's sword;

"A flower washed by seven waterfalls at dawn;

"The paired cliffs' hidden gems;

"Or water from the footprint of a king."

When they had left, red cloaks sliding silently over

the white stone, Petros put his head in his hands. "If I can't save my son, who can? Who can quest for these tokens for us, Mallow?"

The slim brown centaur by his side spoke for the first time. "Don't you see what is in front of you? Look at our son's friends, who have given up honours and braved dangers just to keep him company. His friends might quest for these tokens."

Petros looked at Helen and the group around her. "Perhaps we need your help after all."

Helen and her friends sat beside the fountain. They'd found Yann's silence distracting, and wanted privacy to discuss what they should do next.

Once they were settled in a rough circle, with Sapphire's body and tail curling all the way round them, Helen said, "So, those three creepy healers suggested four possible tokens. There are," she counted quickly, "eight of us. We could split into four teams and try to get all of them. Or we could stick together and go for the easiest or nearest or most powerful. We need to know where they all are first."

"Finding out where they are shouldn't be hard," said Lavender, from her perch on the silvery wolf's shoulder. "The Three *want* us to get a token, so they weren't setting riddles, they were giving directions. And we don't need to hide this quest from our families, so we can ask the elders about the paired cliffs, the seven waterfalls and the rest."

"Once we know where we're going, we should

split up," suggested Lee, adjusting the swords on his belt so they glittered in the glow from his cloak. "We don't need eight of us on one quest. We'd get in each other's way. We have just over 24 hours to find a token, so we should choose a couple of the likeliest and split up."

Sylvie nodded, and Tangaroa and Catesby murmured agreement.

"If we're splitting up," said Helen, "let's split into pairs and do all four."

Lavender flitted into the centre of the circle and shook her blonde bunches. "The last one is impossible, so we shouldn't waste time on it."

"Why?"

"Because there aren't any kings *in* Scotland these days to make a footprint."

"What about Lee's king? He might be a faery, but he's still a king."

Lee laughed. "He is more powerful than any human king, but he's not set foot in Scotland since your nasty little trick last summer, human bard."

"Don't any other fabled beasts and magical beings have kings?" Helen looked at Rona. "I know the selkies used to."

"Not any more," said Lavender. "Our political systems have changed, some even more than human ones. There are no kings here to leave footprints, and anyway," the flower fairy pointed to the clear sky, "it's not going to rain tonight, so even if we found a royal footprint, there wouldn't be any water in it."

Helen pointed to the fountain. "We could take our own water and pour it in."

Lavender shook her head. "We can't cheat the healing tokens. It has to be genuine rainwater for a genuine token. I don't think even water from one of my rain spells would work."

"What about the other three?" asked Helen. "Are any of them possible?"

"In a country with this many rivers and burns and mountains, I think we can find seven waterfalls," said Lavender.

"I'll go on that quest," said Rona. Everyone looked at her in surprise; the selkie didn't usually volunteer for anything risky. "If it's water," she said firmly, "then it's my job. Yann has saved me so many times, I have to do this for him."

Tangaroa nodded. "Waterfalls sound like my job too. I will go with our Storm Singer to wash a flower in seven waterfalls."

Catesby flapped his wings, then swooped up and dived down, his claws outstretched. He landed in front of Helen and tipped his head to the side in an obvious question.

"Am I meant to guess?" She frowned. "Was that diving down a cliff? You think your wings are a qualification for the high-up quest?"

He nodded and Lavender agreed. "The two feathered ones will search for gems at the paired cliffs."

Sylvie shimmered in the grey air, flickering in and out of sight. She was a crouching wolf, then a crouching girl, a wolf again, then a girl sitting calmly on the ground, dressed in grey top and trousers, with pale eyes, silvery blonde hair and sharp features. "You have the wings, but I can have hands, so I'll come with you to carry the gems." She smiled, showing long white teeth. "And to protect you from whatever may be guarding them."

Helen looked round the circle. That meant she was going on a quest with Sapphire and Lee. She trusted the dragon with her life, but she wasn't so sure about the faery. Like all forest faeries he was addicted to music, so his cleverness and tricks were a danger to Helen as well as to their enemies.

Lee grinned at her, which didn't help. His faery glamour, which made his rich green cloak glow softly in the dark and made his perfectly ordinary boy's features impossibly handsome, was just another danger.

He flicked his gold hair out of his blue eyes and held out his hand to her. "So Helen, healer and bard, shall we go questing together for King Arthur's scabbard?"

Helen blurted out, "I'm not taking my violin! And I'm only going with you if Sapphire comes too!" Then she sighed. "No, that won't work. We *all* need Sapphire. We can't do three quests at once, all over Scotland, with only one dragon..."

Sapphire grunted softly and looked up into the evening sky.

Helen looked up too and saw winged shapes spiralling towards them.

Lavender clapped her tiny hands. "Well done, Sapphire. If your classmates are happy to help us, this will be so much easier. If we all find a token tonight, we can save Yann three times over!"

Sylvie snorted. "Quests are never that easy, little

flower. Transport is useful, but finding the tokens will be more of a test than just getting there and back again."

The jet of water from the fountain stuttered as five dragons landed on the centaurs' lawn.

Chapter 8

The friends stood up to greet the dragons. Sapphire introduced them, with Rona translating for Helen. "The orange and yellow dragon is Bunsen," the selkie whispered. "The grey ones are Nimbus and Cumulus. The little white one is Jewel and the black one is Crag."

"Are they all Sapphire's classmates?" Helen whispered back. "They can't be the same age! Crag is four times the size of Jewel."

Rona nodded. "They all hatched in the same season and they're all studying dragonlore with the Great Dragon this year. They're classmates rather than friends, so it's amazing they've agreed to help out."

Lavender spoke formally, in language which reminded Helen of Yann at his most pompous. "Esteemed fire-breathers, we are honoured by your offer to transport us on our quests to save the centaur's heir. Before that, we would also be grateful if you could carry some of us to consult our elders."

Epona trotted up to greet the dragons too, then turned her back on Helen and spoke to Lavender. "Petros may trust you to collect these tokens, but I think there should be a centaur presence on the quest. Let me come with you."

"No thank you, Epona," said Lavender. "We have the right numbers for the three tokens we're seeking, and I'm sure Petros and Mallow want their herd with them just now."

"But I can't help Yann here." Epona sighed. "You're letting that horrible human girl help, why won't you let me help?"

Lavender said soothingly, "If collecting any of these tokens requires speed or hooves, I promise we'll call on you. Otherwise, let us get on with what Petros asked us to do, as Yann's friends."

"But I'm his friend too!" snapped the dappled centaur. Then she flicked her tail and galloped off.

Helen leant against Sapphire and whispered, "Will you still fly me to find the scabbard?" Her blue friend nodded. "Could you fly me home first?" Sapphire nodded again.

Helen said more loudly, "The rest of you don't have to hide these quests from your families, but I'd better go back to Clovenshaws to make excuses for being out tonight." She looked at Lee. "I'll meet you in the trees behind my house once it's dark. And I think I know where we can find the scabbard."

As Helen pulled herself up the edges of Sapphire's

scales, the faery walked over. He leant casually against the dragon's shoulder and arranged his cloak to show off its embroidered hem, before looking at Helen. "You already know where to find Arthur's scabbard?"

Helen settled herself between Sapphire's silver spikes. "I think so. Where would *you* expect to find it?"

"Despite his round tables and holy grails, Arthur was a warrior first. So he'll always have his sword by his hand. If we find him, we've found the sword and the scabbard. But then we'll have to steal it from his side."

"I agree," said Helen. "I don't want to steal from anyone, but saving Yann is more important than respecting other people's property. And it shouldn't be that hard, because I think Arthur is asleep. See what you can find out and I'll check out my idea at home. Meet you in the woods in two hours?"

Lee nodded. Then Sapphire flew off the centaurs' moor, grabbing Helen's bike in her claws as she swooped over Bleakcairn Law.

Five minutes later, Helen slid down Sapphire's shoulder in the clearing behind her house, patted her friend's blue snout and started to wheel the bike through the trees. It was nearly six thirty and she wanted to be home before her mum.

Sapphire grunted, so Helen turned back. Sapphire snuffed a cloud of smoke out of her nostrils and grunted again.

Catesby was better at miming than Sapphire, so Helen usually managed to work out what he was saying, but she had no idea what the dragon was telling her.

"Are you worried about Yann?" she asked.

Sapphire nodded, then shook her head.

"You *are* worried about Yann, but that's not what you want to tell me?"

Sapphire nodded, then waited.

"Do I have to guess?"

The dragon nodded again.

"You're worried about the quest?"

Another nod.

Helen grinned. "You're not scared, are you?"

Sapphire spat sparks at Helen's feet. Helen jumped back.

"So what is worrying you?"

Sapphire pointed a claw at Helen.

"Me? You're worried about *me*? You think I'm not up to it? But I'll try as hard as the rest of you to save Yann!"

Sapphire growled in frustration, then tossed her head back.

"Nope, not getting that."

Sapphire preened her face scales with a delicate claw, then tossed her head again.

"Oh! Is that Lee? Lee and his hair and that cloak! Are you worried about *Lee?*"

Sapphire nodded, then growled louder.

"Shh! You don't trust him?"

The dragon nodded.

"That's ok. I don't really trust him either. So we can both keep an eye on him, alright?"

Sapphire nodded, then flew off.

Helen scrambled down the hill, struggled to get the bike over the fence, and rushed in the back door just as her mum and little sister came through the front door.

She stood in the kitchen, listening to Nicola chattering about her friend Abby's new tree-house, and wondering why, out of all the friends she could go on a quest with, she'd ended up with the one friend she knew she shouldn't trust...

"*Helen!* Are you listening to me?" Her mum was staring at her and shaking her head.

"Em, yes?"

"Please take Nicola upstairs, wash that mud off her face, get those twigs out of her hair, then keep her out from under my feet while I make tea."

Helen picked her little sister up – the fastest way to get her anywhere near a sink – and carried her to the bathroom. Once she'd cleaned Nicola, she said, "Shall we read a book?"

They raced each other to the living room, where Nicola said, "The bottom book again!"

Helen laughed. "Not today! There's another book I want to find and it might have nice pictures too."

Helen looked on the shelves behind the couch for the books they'd taken from her gran's old house when she moved into a bungalow. Helen ran her finger along the spines. "*Ivanhoe, Old Curiosity Shop, Border Ballads, Odyssey...* Aha!" She pulled out a faded red copy of *King Arthur and Other Knights of the Round Table*.

"Nicola, do you want to look at this with me?" Her little sister clambered onto the couch and Helen opened the book. "Swords in stones, damsels in distress, Merlin the magician. Where's the scabbard?"

There wasn't an index and the chapter headings were all names of knights, like "Sir Lancelot's First Quest" and "Sir Gareth the Kitchen Knight", so Helen started at the beginning.

She sighed as she turned the pages. "This really isn't suitable for you, Nicola." Her sister looked at the pictures more closely. "What a lot of pointless violence. Men are described as good knights just because they could knock people off their horses, then slice off their heads. Nothing to do with honour or chivalry. I don't think I'd want to meet them."

She glanced out of the window at the darkening sky, then kept reading. "Here we are. The Lady of the Lake, the sword Excalibur. And a scabbard, woven with magic and worth ten times more than the sword, says Merlin, because while Arthur wears it he will not lose any blood. That must be why it's a powerful healing token. Here's a picture of a fancy leather scabbard with jewels round the top. I wonder if the artist just made that up?"

She kept flicking. "Round table, giants, dragons ... oh dear, Sapphire wouldn't like what they do to dragons. And listen to this. Arthur's evil sister Morgana La Fey stole the scabbard from him and threw it into a different lake. What if he doesn't have it any more? That would make it even harder to find!"

Nicola prodded Helen. "Are you going on a treasure hunt?"

Helen smiled and nodded.

"Can I come?"

"Not this time, wee one. Let's see what happens in the end." Helen flicked to the last chapter.

"Arthur's sleeping in a hollow hill, waiting for the call to fight again. He's surrounded by his knights and their horses. And this picture," she turned to the second last page of the book, "shows him on a stone bed, with the sword in the scabbard. So he did get it back before the end of the story. Great. Now I just have to steal it again."

"What are you going to steal?" asked Nicola.

"Not really steal. Just borrow, maybe. Anyway, King Arthur doesn't need it as much as my friend does. Arthur's only asleep. My friend is ... very ill, and I'll break any rules to help him get better."

"What about a get well card?" Nicola suggested.

"That might help. But this," Helen pointed to the scabbard in the book, "this might help more."

Nicola pulled the book closer and as Helen gently tugged it away, the back page fell out. "Oh no! We've ripped Gran's book!"

Then Helen realised it wasn't a page, it was a little booklet entitled *Legends of the Eildons*. She opened the brittle paper. There were four stories printed in tiny writing, and a beautifully drawn map. "This is the story I remember Gran telling me. There are three big hills in the Eildons, and one little hill which is meant to be magic. Listen Nicola, this story happened only a few miles from here."

Nicola bounced up and down. "Tell me a story!"

"A long time ago, a horse-trader called Canonbie Dick was crossing Bowden Moor, and he met an old man with a long white beard." Helen ran her hand down Nicola's chin and her little sister giggled. "The old man offered to buy the trader's two black horses. So Canonbie Dick sold the horses for a bag of gold. The next week, and the next, the same thing happened. The old man kept meeting the horse-trader to buy any black horses he had.

"Finally the horse-trader asked where he was taking the horses, and the old man said he was Thomas Rhymer or True Thomas, and he couldn't tell a lie. So he took Canonbie Dick and the horses across the moor to the wee hill on the side of the middle Eildon. It's called Lucken Howe – look, there it is on the map – and the hill *opened up...*"

Nicola's eyes widened and her mouth dropped open.

"The two horses and two men went into the hill. It was hollow inside, and there were lots of men asleep in a huge cave, with horses in stalls and a horn lying on a block of stone. True Thomas said they were King Arthur and his knights, then for some reason Canonbie Dick picked up the horn and blew it. The noise woke the knights up and annoyed Arthur, so the horse-trader was thrown right out of the hill and woke up on the moor. With no horses and no gold.

"Arthur is sleeping inside the Eildons. And the door is the Lucken Howe."

"Are you going there to look for treasure?" Nicola asked, snuggling onto her knee.

"Yes," said Helen, "but you mustn't tell anyone."

"I won't."

Helen smiled. It was nice to have someone she didn't have to lie to, because if her little sister did tell anyone that Helen was going to steal from a king, no one would believe her. Helen gave Nicola a hug, put the book in the bookcase, put the booklet in her back pocket, then went for tea.

Tea took less time to eat than it had to make, and

ten minutes later, Helen was in her room. She wasn't meeting Lee and Sapphire for another hour, so she used the time to practise her violin.

She played the three tunes she was learning for school, then the more complex pieces and scales she was working on with her violin teacher for her next exam. She was about to play something for herself, something as sad and scared as she felt about Yann, when her mum yelled from the bottom of the stairs, "Don't you have any *proper* homework to do, Helen?"

Helen sighed and lowered her bow. Her parents didn't realise her violin practice was more important than maths or English. Music was what she wanted to do with her whole life, so she had to pass as many exams as she could before she applied to music college. But her mum never let her practise as much as she wanted.

And she'd better not take the fiddle with her tonight on the quest. She often practised with Rona, but playing near Lee would be dangerous. If he heard her play, he might forget about the scabbard and instead try to force Helen to perform at one of the faeries' lifelong parties.

Helen put her fiddle back in its case, found her maths homework, and rattled through it as fast as she could.

Then she unzipped her rucksack to check the first aid kit was intact, and added a small torch. She put on her fleece and hiking boots, and went down to the kitchen. "Could you check my maths please, Mum?"

Once her mum was looking at her jotter, Helen said, "While you check that, I'll nip out to see if the birds

I'm doing a project on have laid eggs yet. I'll probably be back before bedtime. Is that ok?"

Her mum was nodding at the answers on the page, so Helen took that as a "yes" and walked out the back door.

She clambered over the fence and up the hill, to where Lee was leaning against Sapphire's high side.

The faery grinned and announced, "Arthur is asleep in the Eildons."

"I know and I even have a map." Helen waved the booklet at him. "We want the small hill on the west of the Eildons and we want to approach from Bowden Moor, because that's how the last person who saw Arthur got in."

She spoke to Sapphire. "It's not that far from here. We could walk or cycle..." She turned back to the faery. "Lee, can you ride a bike?"

He looked down at his perfectly polished red boots. "I'm sure I could if I tried."

Helen laughed. "Probably not cycle then. But we could walk, Sapphire, if you'd be more use to Yann flying someone to a token further away."

Sapphire rumbled and Lee translated, "Jewel is flying Sylvie and the feathered ones to some paired cliffs; Nimbus is flying Rona and your blue friend to seven waterfalls. So Sapphire is free to fly us. I think she wants to protect you from me." He smiled. "But I see you've left the house without your violin. I'm disappointed. What if you need to soothe some angry knights back to sleep with a lullaby?"

"If we need a lullaby, we can sing it. I'm going nowhere near you with a fiddle, Lee. It's too dangerous for both of us."

The faery climbed elegantly up the dragon's shoulder.

"Helen, if I wanted to impress my king and my people with your amazing music, I would just steal you as you are and find you a violin later." He reached down to pull her up.

Helen looked at his pale hand, then his shining smile, and she wondered how much she was prepared to risk to save Yann.

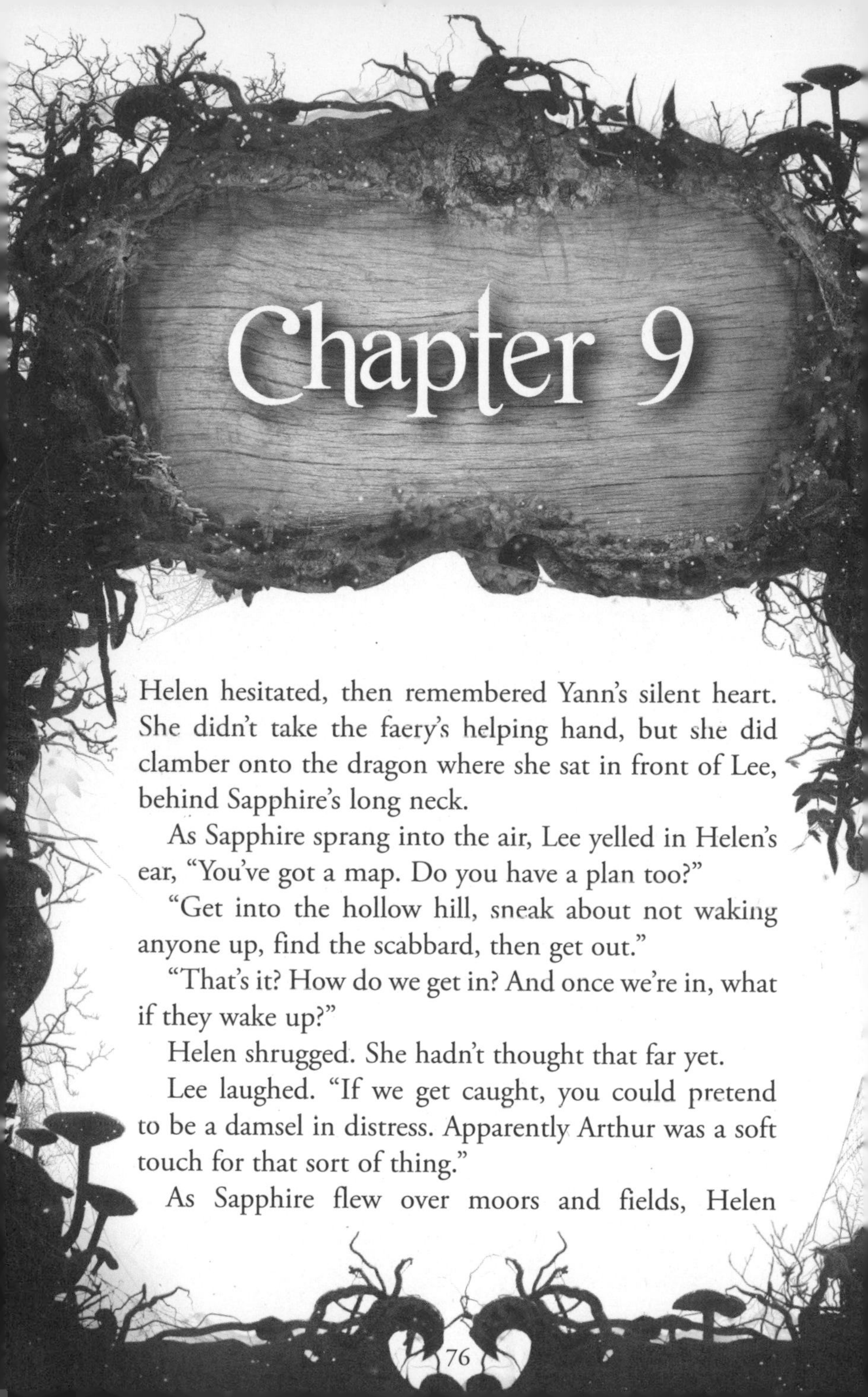

Chapter 9

Helen hesitated, then remembered Yann's silent heart. She didn't take the faery's helping hand, but she did clamber onto the dragon where she sat in front of Lee, behind Sapphire's long neck.

As Sapphire sprang into the air, Lee yelled in Helen's ear, "You've got a map. Do you have a plan too?"

"Get into the hollow hill, sneak about not waking anyone up, find the scabbard, then get out."

"That's it? How do we get in? And once we're in, what if they wake up?"

Helen shrugged. She hadn't thought that far yet.

Lee laughed. "If we get caught, you could pretend to be a damsel in distress. Apparently Arthur was a soft touch for that sort of thing."

As Sapphire flew over moors and fields, Helen

thought about the violent knights in her gran's book and about the trail of dead men, women and fabled beasts they'd left behind them. "I don't think a damsel in distress would be safe from their swords, especially if she was trying to steal from them."

"You're probably right. So let's not wake them up. And Sapphire should stay well away from the hill. A dragon would be in even more danger from those knights than thieves like us."

Helen had been thinking the same thing, but she was suspicious when Lee suggested it.

"Let's see when we get there," she muttered.

When they flew over the Eildons, it was obvious in the clear moonlight that there was nowhere for Sapphire to hide near the Lucken Howe. There was no tree cover, just fields of cows, sheep and ploughed earth on the lower slopes, and open moorland higher up.

Helen frowned. "There's a band of trees round that reservoir at the bottom of the hill. You'll have to hide there, Sapphire. You can't come any closer, where they could see you if they wake up, because they really didn't like dragons and they were very efficient at killing them."

Sapphire landed on the widest strip of grass between the reservoir and the trees. Helen leapt down and Lee jumped beside her, his green cloak glowing around him.

Helen walked round to Sapphire's head. "It will take less than an hour for us to climb up there, so if we aren't back in two hours, please come and look for us."

"We need a signal," said Lee. "To say we're safe and she can come up for us, or we're in danger and need a quick getaway. Or in case you suddenly get cold feet about heading underground with me, even without your violin."

Sapphire growled at him, but he said smoothly, "I'm not joking about it, dragon. I'm not joking about anything. Yann needs us to work together, and Helen is nervous. I'm trying to reassure her."

Helen sighed. "I'm not reassured, Lee. The more you talk about my violin, the more suspicious I get."

He held up his hands. "Sorry. If you can't trust me, stay here with Sapphire. My only goal tonight is to find the token for Yann. I can search for the scabbard by myself, if you'd be more comfortable with that."

Helen wasn't convinced. She knew Lee could easily twist words to hide his intentions. But she also knew he was Yann's friend.

So she shook her head. "You're an expert with faery weapons, Lee, but Arthur's sword is iron. You won't be able to touch it. Only a human can take the sword from the scabbard. We need to go together."

She turned to Sapphire, "I'll flash my torch three times from the summit if we need you. Otherwise, just hide here."

Sapphire rumbled and Lee laughed. "If she gets bored, she'll snack on the sheep in the nearest field."

"No, don't eat the sheep!" said Helen. "It's lambing season soon, so sheep are off the menu at the moment."

Sapphire blew a sulky smoke ring, then lay down on the grass. Helen patted her scaly foreleg and set off towards the hills.

As she walked along the side of the reservoir, on a root-ridged path between tall pine trees, she asked Lee, "Why *are* you doing this?"

"Yann saved my life. I must repay that debt."

"But did your life really need saving? The old legends call faeries immortal. Can you actually die?"

Lee put his hand on the hilt of his polished bronze sword. "Of course I can die. A sword in the heart will stop me breathing as fast as it will stop you. We're called immortal because of how long we can live, not because we can't die."

Helen glanced at his face. He didn't look much older than her, but perhaps he wasn't a boy at all. "How old are you?"

"I'm thirteen, the same age as Yann. We age the same way as humans for the first twenty or twenty-five years. Then when we reach our full adult height, weight and strength, we stop ageing, or we age so slowly it's hardly noticeable."

"But you're the king's champion, his senior warrior. How have you managed that so fast?"

"We have to use our first few years well," said Lee, "because once faeries stop changing physically, we find it hard to change our minds and our skills too. I need to reach the highest possible position while I'm still young, because whoever I am when I stop growing might be who I'll stay forever."

"You're already champion. What else can you possibly want to be?"

"My ambition is not as low as being the Queen's party planner, so your musical skills are not my priority." He smiled at her. "All faeries are addicted to music, so I'm tempted when I hear you play, but providing fiddlers for the faeries' feasts is not my career plan."

"What is?" asked Helen.

"Questing. Fighting. Not stealing fiddlers."

Helen looked at his open, handsome, sincere face, and laughed. "I have no idea if I believe you, but we have to go into that hollow hill together to save Yann, so I suppose I'd better trust you."

As they walked on, the path curved away from the water and towards a fence on their right. Lee stepped to the left, putting Helen between his body and the wire.

Helen shook her head. "You're not really cut out for quests in Scotland, Lee, there's far too much iron and steel here."

"I can manage. I'll just keep my distance." But the glow from his cloak was fading, so she switched her torch on.

They reached a small bridge made from wooden planks laid over a boggy burn. As Helen crossed it, she saw a layer of chicken wire stretched over the planks to prevent feet slipping on wet wood.

She looked back at Lee. He had stopped.

"It's very thin wire. Just run over it."

But he shook his head, his face getting paler, then took a few steps to his left and squelched through the mud and moss instead.

Helen walked off through the trees. Once Lee had caught up with her, she said, "I've been thinking. If Arthur wakes up, the damsel in distress thing won't work, so perhaps we should appeal to his honour."

"How?"

"We could ask him politely for the scabbard. As a favour or a lordly gift. Explain that this brave centaur was injured in an evil minotaur's trap while saving a baby unicorn. Would that appeal to Arthur's noble instincts?"

Lee shook his head. "Arthur and his knights only cared about humans. They hunted and killed fabled beasts. He wouldn't think that a centaur saving a unicorn from a minotaur was his concern."

Helen frowned. "So plan A: don't wake them up. Plan B: if they do wake up, describe Yann as a brave warrior who saved a baby, and don't mention all the hooves involved."

Lee laughed. "That sounds perfect!"

The path was curving further from the water, towards a stone wall and wooden stile, then up to the fields and hills. Lee stopped again. "The fence is still there, behind the wall. And that stile doesn't even go right over the wire."

The stile was built of two wooden steps with a high pole as a handhold, and it cleared the wall, but not the wire. There were three strands of barbed wire strung across the top step.

"That's not very safe," said Helen. "Little kids like Nicola would hurt themselves crossing that."

"So will I," whispered Lee. "I'll have to go back to Sapphire and find another way up."

"Lee, these hills are surrounded by fields. We have to cross a fence at some point." Helen climbed onto the stile and, with her thick hiking-boot sole, stomped down on the three strands of wire, pinning them to the wooden step. "Can you jump over that?"

"I can't. Getting close to iron is like running headfirst into a wall. I lose all strength. I can handle the pain, but not the weakness. I just can't do it."

"Yann could die if we don't find that scabbard, Lee. You don't have to touch the wire, you just have to jump over it. Show a bit of backbone, faery boy. Or I'll tackle Arthur on my own."

Lee bared his teeth and hissed in a breath. Helen couldn't tell if he was terrified, or angry, or both. "Don't try to shame me into this, human girl. I will do it for Yann, not to prove anything to you. Stand against the post to give me room and don't let go of that wire."

He took two steps back, then ran at the stile.

He landed with one foot on the bottom step, then leapt elegantly over the whole top step, clearing the wire by half a metre or more. But he stumbled when he landed, fell awkwardly and rolled onto the muddy ground.

Helen jumped down to join him, letting the wire spring back up. She saw his clothes fade from glowing velvet and embroidered silk to dull cotton and wool.

"Are you alright? Lee?" He was curled up and groaning. Helen put her hand on his back. His clothes started to shimmer and glow again. Helen sighed with relief. She didn't want any more friends unconscious and magically injured.

Lee sat up and ran muddy fingers through his blond hair, which looked as shiny as ever once he'd taken his hands away. He coughed. "Don't tell Yann about that."

Helen held out a hand to pull him up. "If we save Yann's life, I don't think admitting to a wee fall in the mud is going to worry you."

They trudged up the field towards the hills outlined against the smooth grey sky. Once Lee's breathing and colour had returned to normal, Helen asked, "Can't your people find a cure for that iron allergy?"

"You'd better hope not, Helen, because this weakness is the only thing stopping my people from using our magic and glamour to overrun your world."

As they squelched through ankle-deep mud, which shone almost as red as the faery's boots in Helen's torchlight, Lee said, "How are we going to open this door?"

"You're the magical being, so that's your job. I'll do fences, you do doors."

"But this isn't a faery door. It was closed by human magic, not faery glamour."

"Humans don't use magic."

"Some of you do," Lee insisted. "Merlin, Ceridwen, Taliesin, Morgana, Michael Scott, they all mastered magic. Arthur's human wizards closed this door, so perhaps human magic can open it."

"But how?"

"You should have brought your fiddle, my human bard. That's your strongest magic."

Helen shook her head. "Canonbie Dick got in, and he didn't play music."

They reached the top of the field. Helen opened a wooden gate in a stone wall, and strode onto the open hillside above.

The glow of Lee's cloak and her torchlight helped them find their footing on the slope, but Helen could only see the hill ahead because of the high yellow moon.

She hadn't needed the map, because the Lucken Howe was so obvious. On the smooth curved side of the Eildons, it was a jutting knoll with a rocky summit.

"Never mind how we open the door," muttered Helen. "How do we work out which bit it is? The Lucken Howe is bigger than I thought. We could search all night for a door. We could be searching for longer than Yann's weak heart has left."

Chapter 10

Helen stared up at the dark hill. "So where's the door?"

"I've no idea," said Lee. "But it has to be somewhere horses can get to and get through."

"Good thinking. Can I look without your glamour glow in my eyes?"

Helen switched her torch off, stepped ahead of Lee and let her eyes adjust to the moonlight. "There." She pointed to a slab of rock under the summit. "That outcrop is almost a small cliff. It's high enough and wide enough. It even looks like a door."

"It would be impossible to get horses up there. It's too steep."

"I think it's the most likely place." Helen started to scramble up the hill.

"You're having to use your hands to pull yourself up,"

Lee shouted as he followed her. "Horses can't do that. Canonbie Dick did *not* lead his horses up here."

"They could have come up in zigzags; that's what Yann would do." Helen put her hand on something rounded and slightly squishy. "Yuck! Watch out, Lee. Horses might not climb up here, but sheep use it as a toilet!" She wiped the heel of her hand on the heather and kept climbing.

She stopped just before the summit. There was a high jagged rock to her left, a jumble of fallen rocks in the middle and a wide wall of rock to her right.

Helen ran her hand over the wall. The rock seemed grey in the moonlight, but when she looked closely in torchlight it was deep red underneath papery grey lichen. There were no handles, no hinges, no buttons or levers. No way in.

Helen muttered, "Open sesame!" Nothing happened. "Do you know any magic words, Lee?"

"Lots. But none for opening human wizards' doors."

"Do you think there's a password?"

"Do we know enough about Arthur to guess?"

"I'll have a go." Helen spoke to the rock, in a slow serious voice: "Merlin. Excalibur. Pendragon. Guinevere. Lancelot? Possibly not ... Camelot. Avalon." But the rock stayed solid and rocky, and she'd run out of Arthur-lore already.

Helen sat at the base of the door-shaped rock and started whistling a bored sort of waiting tune. After a few bars, she leant back and prodded the rock.

Lee laughed. "What are you doing?"

"This is what happens in films. You give up and lean against something, then it opens and you get a big surprise. Lean against that bit there, like you've given up."

Lee smiled and leant against the rock, looking far more convincingly relaxed than Helen did.

The rocks didn't move.

"Maybe you're right," said Helen. "Maybe this isn't the door. Let's look at the rest of the hill."

She climbed round the jutting rock to the summit of the Lucken Howe, then stood on the highest boulder, just above the flat rock she'd failed to open. It wasn't easy to see the lower slopes in the moonlight, so she jumped off the summit and walked a few steps down a ridge which led towards the larger Eildons. Lee followed her.

"Maybe we should have brought that grumpy dappled friend of Yann's to test the best routes for hooves," Helen said. "But I think they could have led the horses round the foot of the hill, then up the gentler slope of this ridge, and round to the door-shaped rock face."

Lee nodded reluctantly. "But they could have got to anywhere on the hill from this ridge. Let's see if there are any other options."

Helen turned to her left, but Lee called, "Don't go widdershins; it can attract ill fortune. Walk sunwise." So they circled clockwise, following a sheep path which cut round the hill halfway up.

They didn't find any other big rocks or vertical faces. Just the sloping hillside, covered with grass, heather and moss, sheep and rabbit droppings, and a few small boulders.

"Nothing else looks like a door," Helen said when they'd walked all the way round.

"You're right," said Lee. "This is the best option."

So they stood either side of the wall of rock. Helen sighed. "Your faery magic is no use and I don't have any magic at all."

"Not when you're too much of a wimp to get your fiddle out in front of me."

"My music is not magic," she said firmly. "If we can't use magic, we'll have to use..."

"Force?" Lee rattled his weapons.

"Bronze against stone? No, let's use our brains. Let's think about the story. Canonbie Dick got in."

"You think we should come back with two black horses and a bearded man?"

"Take this seriously, Lee."

"I am taking it seriously. You're the one who's refusing to use your one true power..."

Helen interrupted. "But it wasn't Canonbie Dick who opened it. It was the man who brought him here: Thomas Rhymer. So it might be faery magic after all."

"Thomas wasn't a faery. He was just the Faery Queen's consort."

"Yes, and when she was finished with him, she gave him a really dodgy gift. He could only tell the truth. That was his true power. A faery power. I wonder if that will open this door. Some truth ... from a faery."

"Truth?" said Lee. "Truth like ... em ... I was really scared when I jumped over that wire?"

They looked at the rock wall. It didn't do anything.

Helen said, "Maybe that's not hard enough truth."

"I don't find it easy to admit being scared."

"But you're not telling me anything I don't know. I know you're scared of iron. Let's try more painful, dangerous truth."

Neither of them spoke for a long moment.

Then Helen said, "Lee, tell me this truth. Do you plan to take me from my home and my family to play music for you in the faeries' lands?"

Lee looked away. He looked at his clean boots. At Helen's muddy boots. At the rock, at his swords, then back at Helen.

He put his hand on the rock. "For Yann, I will speak the truth. Yes. Yes, I do plan to take you from your home to play music for my people. Your music is the most powerful that I've ever heard, that our King or Queen have ever heard. The faery who brings your talent to our lands will gain far more influence than a swift sword can ever bring. So yes, I do plan to steal you, take you to our lands and keep you there for hundreds of years, knowing that if you ever come back to your own world, you will crumble into dust."

The rock creaked.

Lee put his other hand on the rock and spoke clearly. "And I haven't taken you yet, Helen Strang, not because I think it would be wrong; not because I know you'd miss your parents, your sister and your friends. It's simply because if I stole you, then I could never come back to this Scotland, because I'd be afraid of the revenge your friends would take."

The rock rumbled.

"I want to steal you, because I'm selfish and ambitious; I haven't stolen you, because I'm a coward. That's the truth, and I'm not proud of it."

The rock slid open.

Helen stared at Lee. He didn't look at her; he stared into the black hole in the hillside.

Helen whispered, "I need to ask one more question. Does this door really lead to a hollow hill in this world? Or does it lead to your lands?"

"This is not a faery door, Helen. You will be safe in here." Then he smiled. A thin, tight smile. "Well, you'll be safe from me. Neither of us will be safe from your human knights."

He took a step in.

Helen hesitated. "Was that the truth?"

"You won't know unless you step inside." Lee walked into the hill.

Helen followed him.

Once she was inside, the rock door crashed shut. The slam echoed into the deep cold darkness. Lee and Helen looked at each other in the small pool of light they'd brought in with them. They didn't speak. Then Helen stepped in front of Lee, so her torch lit the way ahead and his cloak lit the tunnel behind them. And she walked forward.

Helen knew she should be pleased they'd found the key to open the door, to lead them to the healing token that could save Yann's life. But she was too shocked by Lee's answer, too upset because she knew she could never trust him again.

She had hoped he would answer "no" and the door would open, proving that he was telling the truth. But the truth he had told wasn't what she wanted to hear. Or was it?

In the soft echo of their footsteps, she heard her mum's voice: "Don't you have any proper homework to do?" and she wondered what answer she'd really been hoping Lee would give.

The stone tunnel was wide, with a cobbled floor, smooth walls and a high arched roof. The floor sloped downwards, deep into the ground, then it curved left, flattened out and headed for the larger Eildons.

When the noise of their footsteps changed to a broader echo, Lee drew his sword and moved in front of Helen.

They walked forward into a stable, stalls cut into the hill on either side. Each stall had a trough for water, hooks for hay and grooves in the floor worn by heavy hooves.

Helen stepped into the nearest stall. The trough was dry. Wisps of straw made dirty yellow lines on the floor. She picked one up and it crumbled in her fingers. Crumbled into dust, like a human returning from the faeries' parties.

She swallowed her sudden panic and continued down the long tunnel, checking every stall. But they were all cold, dusty and empty.

At the end of the stalls, the tunnel opened out into a dark chamber. Helen put her fingers over the torch beam so it didn't shine so brightly, and walked forward.

There was a smell, a warmth, a feeling of life, and Helen wondered if the horses from the stable were now in here.

She heard Lee whisper in her ear, "Pull back, now."

They both took a few paces back, and he stepped with her into the last stall. "Helen. We have to work together. We have to trust each other. Can you still do that?"

She nodded. "Yes. For Yann."

"Good. Turn off your light. We'll use my more subtle glow to find Arthur."

Helen switched off her torch and tried to think about the scabbard. "Let's walk straight towards the middle of the hollow hill. Arthur will be in the centre, won't he?"

"I'm not sure. He had a round table so none of his knights sat above or below anyone else. Perhaps they're all sleeping round the sides in a circle. Anyway, how will we know which one is Arthur?"

Helen shrugged. "He'll have the fanciest armour and fanciest clothing. You're the expert on overdressing, so I'm sure you'll recognise him."

Lee frowned and opened his mouth to respond, but Helen continued, "The simplest plan is to walk straight across, and if we don't find him, then when we get to the other side, we split up and come back here round opposite walls, searching as we go."

"No," said Lee firmly. "We do not split up. We stay together."

"Why? Are you planning to kidnap me on the way home?"

"No." He tried to smile. "No, I just need you to stamp down barbed wire on our way back. So we stay together. We can go straight across, and if we don't find him, we'll walk round the perimeter together. When we find him, you take the sword out, and I'll untie or cut the scabbard free."

Helen nodded. "Are you ready?"

"Always."

They moved out of the stable into the hollow hill.

It was impossible to tell how big the chamber was. The blackness was so absolute, outside the gentle glow of Lee's faery light, that the walls could be as close as an arm's length or as far as a stone's throw.

They walked slowly side by side. The light shone far enough ahead that they wouldn't bump into anything and nothing could approach them without being seen. But anyone awake would see them outlined in the darkness.

They kept moving forward.

The floor was paved with massive flagstones, worn smooth and clear of dust.

They moved deeper into the hill.

A dark shape appeared ahead of them.

Helen and Lee moved closer together. Lee swirled his cloak outwards, bouncing a curve of light off the shape.

It was a large block of stone, with a crumpled heap of fabric on top.

"Arthur's bed," Helen whispered.

She leant even closer to Lee. "Take one more step so I can see clearly, then stay out of the way while I remove the sword."

Lee squeezed her arm and whispered back, "Be careful, Helen. He's not a courtly king, he's a violent warrior."

They took one more step together, then Lee stopped and Helen went on alone.

The bed was cut from a chunk of red stone and covered by a cloak: not smooth golden silk like Arthur wore in pictures, but knobbly brown wool.

Helen stepped even nearer.

If Arthur was under there, he was huge. She couldn't tell which end was the head and which the feet. But the cloak was moving softly and regularly, as someone underneath breathed in and out. Arthur was asleep.

Helen grasped the edge of the cloak, lifted it a few

centimetres, then peered underneath to see if the sword was there.

But the cloak kept moving upwards.

The figure on the bed was sitting up.

Helen scrambled backwards.

Suddenly there was a blaze of light behind the bed, the cloak flew into the air and a tall figure leapt off the bed.

Helen crashed into Lee.

The figure in front of her shouted, "You are not Arthur!"

Helen replied, as calmly as she could, "You're not Arthur either!"

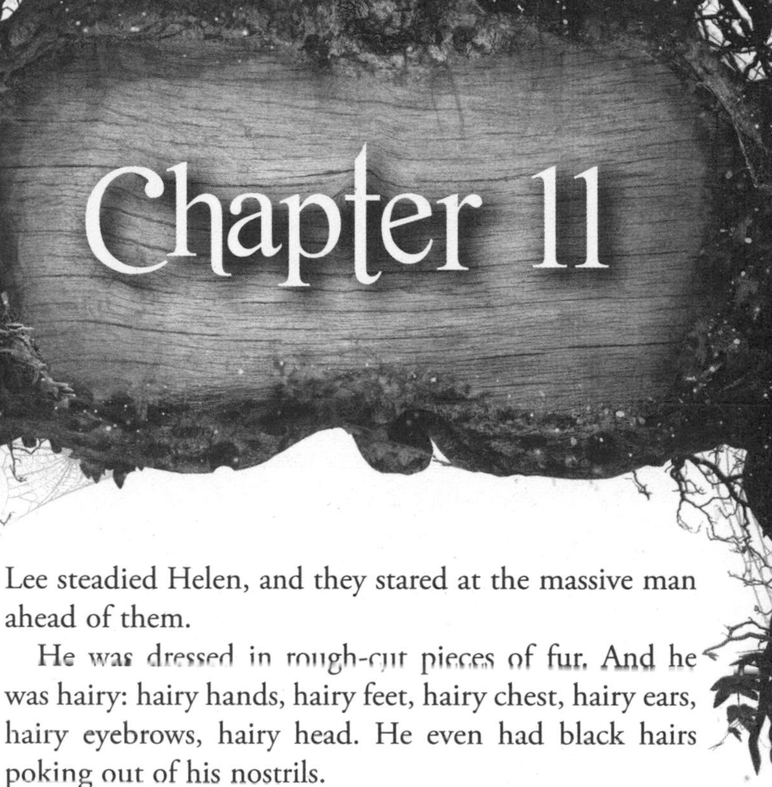

Chapter 11

Lee steadied Helen, and they stared at the massive man ahead of them.

He was dressed in rough-cut pieces of fur. And he was hairy: hairy hands, hairy feet, hairy chest, hairy ears, hairy eyebrows, hairy head. He even had black hairs poking out of his nostrils.

But his chin was bare.

The skin on his chin was pale and hairless, grazed and scabby. It had been badly shaved, and it looked cold and sore in the tangle of hair covering the rest of him.

"*You are not Arthur!*" he roared again. "Who are you?"

Helen answered carefully, "We're two companions on a quest. Who are you?"

"I am the giant Ysbaddaden. I wait here for revenge! We all wait here for revenge!"

The light behind him lurched closer. It was a line of lanterns, held in hairy hands, scaly hands, paws and claws.

The giant spoke again. "Arthur and his knights *shaved* me, to humiliate me! They used a razor stolen from my companion Twrch Trwyth."

A huge boar stepped into the light, with bristly shoulders as wide as a car and long yellow tusks jutting up out of its black jaws.

"When we heard that Arthur slept here," the giant rumbled, "we came, bringing others who hate the knights of the Round Table, to have our revenge."

"To kill them," said a voice from the darkness.

"To eat them," whispered another.

"But they're not here," continued Ysbaddaden. "So we'll wait until they return."

Helen looked at the shapes behind the lanterns. In the gloom, she saw a long low beast with a snake's head on a spotted cat's body, more tall hairy men and a wrinkled dragon's wing.

"But didn't Arthur and his knights kill everyone they fought?" she asked. "Aren't you lucky to be alive?"

"Lucky?" spluttered Ysbaddaden. "Was it lucky to be stolen from, to be left beardless and weaponless? Some of us they drove away: my friend the boar was chased into the sea. Some of us they made fun of." He touched his chin and shivered. "But many of us here are the mothers and sons of those they butchered in their pointless quests. We all wait here for revenge. Why are you here?"

"We're here to steal Arthur's scabbard, like he stole from your boar," said Helen. "Did they leave the scabbard behind?"

"They left nothing behind but dust and horse droppings."

"Then we should leave you in peace," said Lee in his most charming voice. "We wish you patience and good company while you wait; swift and satisfying revenge when your enemies return."

Lee took a smooth step back, pulling Helen with him.

"I'm hungry!" whined a voice.

There were screeches and growls from beasts Helen couldn't see and couldn't understand.

Lee whispered, "If we have to run, get ahead of me. Don't stop to help me. Don't wait for me."

They kept walking backwards through the hollow hill.

Helen spoke directly to Ysbaddaden, hoping he was in charge of the creatures behind him. "Where have Arthur and his men gone? When will they come back?"

"They've gone to water their horses, obviously. They will be back before morning. Did you see them on your way here?"

"Oh yes," said Lee, sincerely and convincingly. "We saw horses at the reservoir. They'll be back soon. We'll leave now, so we're not in your way when they arrive."

"How long have you waited?" asked Helen, as they moved further from the claws and fingers clutching the lights.

"One long night. It seems to have lasted centuries," moaned Ysbaddaden. "But they will be back soon, so get out quickly."

Helen and Lee walked faster.

But a voice rumbled, "No, Ysbaddaden. These children might warn the knights. And anyway, we are *hungry!*"

The line of lights broke, dark shapes rushed past the shaggy giant, and Lee shouted, "*Run!*"

Helen turned and sprinted through the cave towards the stables. She knew Lee was close behind; she could see the cloudy glow of his cloak on the stones at her feet. But she also knew Arthur's enemies were following; she could hear them clattering and cursing.

She reached the tunnel and ran straight into the darkness, fumbling for the on-button of her torch. She found it in time to stop herself running into a horsebox. So she kept going up the tunnel, hoping the footsteps behind her were Lee's.

Then she saw a flick of velvet at her side.

"It's just a shame," she panted, "that everything Arthur annoyed is so *big*."

"It's not a shame at all," said Lee. "Look back."

She swung round and her torch beam shone on a tangle of legs, arms and wings stuck at the entrance to the tunnel. They were too big to fit through together.

She slowed down.

"Keep running!" Lee urged. "They're not all stupid. Someone will sort them out."

Helen heard Ysbaddaden roaring, "Dragons and giants get to the *back!* Let the questing beast and the boar go *ahead!*"

Lee and Helen ran round the curve in the tunnel and up the slope. Helen's torchlight slapped against the rock door. It was still shut tight. How were they going to get out? She didn't want Lee to tell her more terrifying truths.

"How do we open it this time?"

"Your turn, human girl. You tell me the truth."

Helen tried to think of something hard to admit, something embarrassing or dangerous. "I lie to my mum about where I go at night!"

"Of course you do. We've all done that. Something else, something more."

Lee stood at her back, facing the darkness, and lifted his sword.

Helen could hear the claws and feet of Arthur's enemies racing up the tunnel. "I can't think!" She smacked her hand against the cold rock.

Lee called, "Come no closer, Ysbaddaden, my sword is sharper than any razor."

Helen shouted over the stamping from the tunnel behind her. "Lee! Ask me a question."

"With pleasure, Helen. Would you play your music for my people and my followers, if I asked you to?"

Helen knew the truth before he'd finished asking. But she didn't want to say it out loud.

She kicked the door. It didn't move. She would have to answer him.

Arthur's enemies had almost reached them. "Stay back, Ysbaddaden," warned Lee, "unless you want such a close shave that you lose your head as well as your whiskers."

Helen could hear the creatures shifting and slithering nearer. Perhaps only Ysbaddaden was afraid of Lee's blade.

"Quickly, Helen! Tell me the truth. Would you leave your world to play music for the faeries?"

As they stood, back to back, Lee facing Arthur's enemies and Helen facing the rock door, Helen told him the truth. "Yes. Yes, I would." The rock shifted under her fingers. "Because the faeries value music more than anyone else does. And because music matters more to me than ... anything."

The rock creaked and rumbled.

Helen gasped. "That's so selfish of me! I can't put music before my friends and family. I don't want that to be true!" But she knew it must be true, because the rock opened.

Lee was standing his ground behind her, holding back the line of Ysbaddaden's angry companions. Helen could run out and leave him there. She could signal Sapphire and get away from him.

But Lee was here to help Yann, and he was standing between her and danger. Helen grabbed his cloak. "We stay together, remember?" and she pulled him out with her.

As she scrambled up to the summit, she looked down. Past Lee's glimmering cloak, she saw giants, boars and the snake-headed beast squeezing through the door.

Ysbaddaden was at the front, his white chin leading the way.

"Sapphire!" screamed Helen. She switched her torch off and on, three quick flashes, aiming the signal towards the moonlit water below. But she couldn't see Sapphire, and the mob was already climbing after them.

"Sapphire!" Helen shrieked again and ran off the summit the only way she could, down the ridge. Lee followed her, but only for a few steps. Helen glanced back. The faery was now facing the white-chinned giant, who pulled a huge wooden mallet from his fur waistcoat and stepped towards Lee. But suddenly Ysbaddaden vanished. His feet flew into the air, he dropped the mallet and slid down the hill.

Helen heard him moan, "Sheep droppings! Sheep droppings on my boots and on my chin! These children have humiliated me too!"

She was about to yell for Sapphire again, when her torch beam bounced off a blue shape flying fast through the night air. The dragon blasted an arrow of fire at the creatures swarming up the hill, then swooped towards Helen and Lee, claws outstretched.

They ducked and Helen yelled, "Not from above! Fly lower and we'll jump!"

She and Lee stood together on the ridge, watching as Sapphire swerved round a single tree on the slope, sent a bolt of flame at the snake-headed creature, then sprinted along the side of the ridge below them.

"Too fast!" called Helen.

Sapphire swerved again, then flew past slowly enough for Helen to jump off the Lucken Howe onto her broad back.

But Lee didn't jump. He turned at the last moment to protect Helen's leap from the bristling boar.

The faery stood on the ridge, facing an opponent with two curved tusks as long and sharp as his one sword. Sapphire flew past again, but Lee didn't jump. He just pulled another sword from his belt and threatened the boar with both, one in each hand. The boar hunched its shoulders and took a step forward.

"Come on, Lee!" yelled Helen.

"I can't take my eyes off this brute in case he charges, so I can't judge when to jump," he responded calmly.

"I'll count, you jump after three!" Helen instructed, as Sapphire turned in the air.

The boar started to run, heavy and hurtling, at the faery.

The dragon flew below the ridge.

Helen shouted, "One, two, three, jump!" and grabbed Lee as he leapt backwards.

As Sapphire swerved up, then hovered above the summit, Helen and Lee could see Arthur's enemies waving weapons, fists and tusks at them.

Then Ysbaddaden, wiping his filthy chin with his hairy knuckles, yelled, "We can't reach the children. Let's hunt for Arthur and his gang at the water."

So Ysbaddaden led the scaly and bristly creatures, stomping and sliding, down the side of the Lucken Howe.

Helen said, "Let's run back into the hill while they're away, and see if Arthur left any clues about where he went next."

Lee said, "But the biggest monsters couldn't fit through the door, so they're probably still in there."

"I'm prepared to risk it, Lee. We *have* to find the scabbard. Sapphire, please fly us back down."

But when the dragon angled towards the Lucken Howe, a crunching impact knocked her sideways. Helen and Lee clung to her spikes as Sapphire tumbled screaming out of the air. They slithered around on her back until she recovered control of her wings and flew upwards again.

Two huge flapping shapes followed them up. Sapphire was being attacked by two massive dragons.

"If those are the dragons from the cave," Helen yelled, "then the cave might be empty! Sapphire, can you let us off and keep these dragons at bay while we run back in?"

But every time Sapphire flew towards the Lucken Howe, the two bigger dragons bashed and battered her, to force her away from the hill.

Helen was about to yell, "Why don't you use fire?" when she realised how daft that would sound. The other dragons would be fireproof, just like her friend. So the three dragons fought with their weight, speed and spiked armour.

The attackers used their heavy heads, wide wings, long claws and spiked tails to prevent Sapphire getting back to the hill. As they fought in the air, Helen wondered if these two huge beasts were ancient relatives of the dragons killed by Lancelot and Tristan.

Sapphire, lighter and slimmer, tried to fly round them, but the two dragons worked together, blocking every route, crashing into her from both sides. She kept trying, her body shaking and juddering, her grunts of pain drowning out Helen and Lee's shouts of shock each time they were nearly thrown off her back.

After half a dozen attacks, Helen screamed, "Sapphire, stop! There probably aren't any clues anyway. Fly away before they hurt you again."

But Sapphire roared and tried one more time. She stretched her neck out, drew her wings in and dived between the two enormous dragons. They both lashed out with their claws, and Sapphire screamed fire as her sides and tail were savagely clawed from left and right.

She dropped out of the air, falling toward the hills. One of the dragons flew under her and bashed his head against her stomach, stopping her fall, forcing her up, pushing her away.

Sapphire spread her wings, flapped jerkily and flew away from the Eildons.

The two dragons didn't follow. They stayed high in

the air above the Lucken Howe, circling like sharks, ready to attack if she approached again.

Helen called, "Sapphire, are you ok? Do you need to land?"

The dragon didn't answer. She just glided slowly towards the ground.

Helen sighed. They'd escaped from the giants and the dragons. But they hadn't found the scabbard.

Chapter 12

Sapphire almost fell into a hole, thumping down with a muffled moan.

Helen let go of the spikes, rolled over the dragon's wing and landed on her feet. They were in an old quarry: a bowl-shaped hole hacked out of the ground, with man-made cliffs all around and loose rocks underfoot.

Helen ran to Sapphire's head. "Thanks for coming to save us and for trying so hard to get us back in. Are you injured?"

Sapphire nodded slowly.

"Is it your belly, from those head-butts?"

The dragon shook her head gingerly.

"Your sides and your tail, from those claws?"

Sapphire nodded and moaned again.

"Let me look."

Helen walked along the bulk of her friend, shining the torch on her scales.

Lee walked with her, saying, "Where did those dragons come from? Were they the wrinkly dragons from the cave, or were they already waiting outside?"

Helen shrugged, looking at the shallow scrapes on her scaly friend's left side.

Lee kept talking. "They were quite fast for dragons who'd been mouldering in a cave for centuries, weren't they, Sapphire?"

Sapphire growled.

Helen said quietly, "You're not helping, Lee. Hold the torch." She stepped over the dragon's tail to look at her right side, which was also grazed.

But when she returned to Sapphire's tail, she found the really painful damage: three scrapes on the left side and two deep rips on the right side, four spikes up from the tip.

The scales were sliced open, a triangular flap of dragonskin was hanging loose, dark blood was welling out and the muscle underneath was glistening through.

Helen swung the rucksack off her back, cleaned her hands, then used swabs to wipe the largest wound.

"Lee, can you get the exotic animals textbook out of my rucksack?"

She wiped the smaller wounds, then took the book and flicked to the reptile section. She found pictures of snakeskin repaired with a complex mattress stitch, read a couple of paragraphs, then looked at pictures of dying lizards.

She walked back to her friend's head. "I'm sorry, Sapphire, but the right side of your tail is ripped open and a big flap of skin is hanging off."

Sapphire grunted. Lee translated, "She's never been cut before. One of the few things that can cut dragon hide is dragon claw. But she's confident you can heal her."

Helen sighed. "I can't sew the flap back on. I couldn't force a needle through the layers of folded skin your scales are made from, and anyway your skin has started to curl up, so the edges won't stay together. I'm also worried that the wound might get infected. Who knows what dirt and germs those old dragons had on their claws? And infection in a lizard's tail can travel up the spinal cord, until it paralyses, then kills."

Sapphire's head sank to the ground.

"But if I act fast, I can take away the pain and the danger of infection. If you trust me."

Sapphire looked at Helen, her silver eyes narrowed with questions.

"If dragons evolved from lizards, Sapphire, then you might have one very useful ability. Lizards can lose the end of their tails when their tail is grabbed by a predator, and their tails can grow back. If you're descended from the same reptiles as iguanas and geckos, then I can amputate the end of your tail and do you no lasting damage at all."

Sapphire roared and turned her head away. Helen didn't need anyone to translate. "Really, my friend, it is the safest thing to do. You won't get an infection and it will grow back. But I have to do it now, before the skin rips further and the damage gets worse."

Lee muttered in her ear. "Helen, if you cut off her tail, and it's bleeding and painful, how will she fly back to the moor? She can't stay here, near farms and roads, once it's daylight."

Helen answered loudly, "If I'm right, Sapphire's tail will be designed to snap between the vertebrae, and the nerves and blood vessels will shut off immediately. If I'm right, the tail will hurt *less* and bleed *less* once the end has been removed."

"If you aren't right?" Lee and Sapphire asked at the same time.

"If I'm wrong, the tail probably won't come off at all. We have to try, because you're already in too much pain to fly straight. So, Sapphire, will you stay still while I take a tiny bit of your tail off, just the very tip?"

Sapphire growled.

"Trust me, Sapphire. I know what I'm doing."

The dragon stared silently at Helen, then nodded once.

As Helen walked back to the tail, Lee whispered, "*Do* you know what you're doing?"

"I know what I'm trying to do, I just don't know if it will work on a lizard this big."

Helen picked up the end of the tail to see how much it weighed, then looked round. "I'm just moving your tail to the left, Sapphire." Helen staggered over to a nearby boulder. Sapphire shifted her back legs to follow her tail.

Helen laid the tail over the rock, like the plank of a seesaw.

"Lee, hold it steady."

"But that's not just the tip!" he objected.

"*Shhh!*" Helen hissed, then called out, "Sapphire, you're the bravest dragon in the world and I know you can do this. Just stay still."

Helen jerked the tail down.

It hardly moved. Sapphire had flinched in the other direction as Helen put pressure on the tail, and the dragon's tail muscles were much stronger than Helen's arm muscles.

"I've seen this done with an iguana. I *know* it's possible. I just need a little more force."

She tried again. The tail didn't snap, though there was now a pool of blood on the ground.

Lee grimaced. "Do you want me to do it? I could put more weight and strength into it."

"No. If it takes more strength than I have, then it's ripping her tail off, not allowing it to break naturally."

She called along the dragon's length. "Sapphire, you need to help me. Can you relax on the count of five?" There was a pained grunt from the front of the dragon.

"One, two, three..." *Jerk!*

And Helen was holding the end of the tail. Unattached. Snapped off. And wriggling in her hands.

She dropped it on the ground, then shone her torch on the tail's new end.

She looked with interest at the white curve of bone, and the confusion of flesh and scales around it. There was no blood oozing out of the new wound. The claw rip had bled, but the tail-snapping wound had closed up instantly.

"Sapphire, how are you?"

Sapphire rumbled.

Lee said with a smile, "She says it's stopped hurting. Now the tip just feels numb. She'll let you try again. But don't cheat this time, she says, don't jerk until you reach five."

Helen laughed croakily. "Sapphire, we did it. It's already off."

Helen and Lee had to leap out of the way, as the dragon whipped round in a circle, trying to see her own tail.

"No!" yelled Helen. "Don't get dirt in the wound! You don't want to get an infection."

Sapphire roared and Lee shouted over her. "She's saying that's not just the tip! That's about half of her tail! She doesn't believe that will ever grow back."

"I had to break that much off, because the damage went up that far. Now stay still!"

Sapphire lay down, with angry orange fire in her nostrils; Lee took the twitching tail-tip away to bury it; Helen cleaned the end of the tail and placed gauze over it.

"There. It will grow back, long and blue and spiky. Before midsummer, I'm sure you'll have a perfect tail again." Then Helen sighed. "There's no real rush to get back to Cauldhame Moor, because we don't have anything to show for our quest. So you don't have to fly me and Lee back if you can't carry us, Sapphire."

In answer, the dragon flapped her wings vigorously, and raised her snout to the sky.

As Helen repacked her rucksack, Lee crouched down beside her, wiping his hands on a swab. He spoke softly, "I'm sorry, Helen. I'm sorry we both said such scary things to open that door, and we haven't even saved Yann by doing it."

"The truth isn't always a good thing, is it?" Helen didn't look at him. She closed the book and slid it into her rucksack. "I'm sure you did tell the truth, Lee, and I have a horrible feeling I did too. But if you're really my friend, please don't test it out by asking me. Please."

He stood up and his cloak swirled round him. "I

won't ask you to bring your music to us this spring equinox. Right now, I'm here to help Yann. But I make no promises for after that."

"Then I promise you," Helen stood up too, "that I will try my hardest to find reasons to stay here. I'll find people who value my music here."

Lee smiled. "No one values music more than we do."

Helen frowned. He was probably right. But she would fight to stay in her own world, even if what she was fighting was her own desire to play for the most appreciative audience.

Once Helen and Lee were on Sapphire's back, the dragon struggled to rise into the air, then lurched from side to side, working out how to balance with a shorter tail.

When they were flying, slightly squint, away from the Eildons, with no sign of other dragons in the sky or giants on the ground, Helen called to Lee, "Should we warn someone about all those angry creatures loose around Melrose?"

Lee yelled, as Sapphire grumbled her way above the clouds, "They'll be safely back in the hill before anyone wakes up. They're too stupid to come up with another plan to attack Arthur. They'll hide in that cave for centuries."

"So where can we search for the scabbard now? I don't know any other local Arthur legends."

Lee replied, "He's linked with lots of different hills, mostly in England and Wales. He probably left here after he was woken by that horse-trader. The Eildons weren't secure after that. Perhaps anywhere there is a legend of him sleeping is somewhere he has already left.

If Arthur doesn't stay anywhere once he's been seen, we can't track him using stories. I hate to admit failure, Helen, but I don't think we can find Arthur and his scabbard fast enough to save Yann."

Helen shivered. "So we'd better hope someone else's quest is more successful than ours."

Chapter 13

Frass leant against the crumbling wall, watching his Master try to control the brawling uruisks.

"It's a risk, Master," he called out. "It's been a risk all along, but now so many of the centaur's friends are involved, they might discover that his injury was the real goal of the unicorn kidnap. Also, I'm not sure it's wise to trust the Three."

"Nonsense, you faint-hearted faun," the Master bellowed as he strode barefoot across the black and white floor. "My plan is unfolding perfectly. I trust the Three to heal my phoenix scars, because they know that once I have my new power and can force the fabled beast tribes to bow down to me, I will cause many more injuries for them to enjoy. And to heal me, they need one of these tokens."

Frass grunted. "But you could send me to get a token for you. I would do anything for the Master of the Maze. It is my inherited duty, my family honour, to serve the Master of the Maze, whoever that is."

"Yes, Frass, thank you for reminding me that you serve my title rather than me."

"Whatever my reasons for serving you, Master, I have served you well. You could send me to collect a healing token. You could even send those uncouth mountain goats, who serve you out of greed, rather than honour."

The minotaur scowled, rubbing at the scar between his horns. "The uruisks will serve me whether I have the backing of the Maze or not. But you are a civil servant and you would bow just as low in front of my brother or nephews, if they were Master of the Maze. However, I couldn't have used any of you to get the token. The healing tokens only give themselves to those with pure motives."

"I serve you purely," said Frass. "If you order me to do something, it doesn't matter how dark your motive, my motive in obeying is pure. Because you are my Master." Frass bowed, the stubby goat horns on his human forehead almost brushing the tiled floor.

The Master laughed. "The 'I was only following orders' defence is discredited these days, Frass. And if I sent you to get a token, you'd tarnish it with your stinking touch."

Frass turned away, pretending to examine the upside-down painting on the dusty wall beside him, hoping the minotaur couldn't see the expression on his face.

But the Master was still explaining his brilliant plan. "You may think it's too complex, but I believe manipulating these talented, lucky and innocent youngsters, so that they collect the tokens to save their friend, is the best way to get the healing power for myself."

"And do you plan to let them heal the centaur first?" Frass asked, quietly.

"The Three say the colt is a potential instrument of chaos, so they'd like him healed. But I don't want anyone with his strength and courage opposing me. I'd rather get rid of him while he's still young. So we let his naïve friends collect one of the tokens, we let them take it home, then we seize it before they can heal the horse-boy.

"And when I am healed, I will see clearly out of both eyes again and I will also see more than anyone has seen before."

Frass bowed again, then frowned as the Master walked off towards the wild goats. The minotaur was already roaring encouragement at them, as one uruisk broke off another's horn with an overhead kick.

Frass scratched his hairy left leg with his right hoof. He wasn't sure this particular Master of the Maze was still following the labyrinth's gradual global strategy. Perhaps it was time to send a message to the Maze.

Catesby watched the dragons leave: Crag, Cumulus and Bunsen returning to the Great Dragon after helping Lavender gather information for their quests; Nimbus carrying Rona and Tangaroa to the seven falls; Sapphire flying Lee to Helen's house. Only the white dragon was left.

Lavender tapped Catesby on the wing. "I've given everyone else their instructions and I think I know where the paired cliffs are, so we'd better..."

Sylvie interrupted, "I don't trust that shiny faery and his stupid smiles. Perhaps I should have gone with Helen."

Catesby shook his feathery head and said, "You may not trust Lee, but Yann does and I do. He's visited us many times this past year, and in return for archery tutoring, he's taught Yann swordplay and duelling. Once Lee stops trying to look cool, he's fine. He's less of a prat when there aren't girls about too."

Sylvie said, "He's going on a quest with Helen and Sapphire. They're both girls."

"He is Yann's friend," Catesby insisted. "He's here to save Yann, just like the rest of us. Come on, furball and petal person, we have a long way to fly."

Sylvie growled, then flickered from her wolf form into a girl. "Don't call me furball, cinders."

"Sorry, furless girl!"

Sylvie grabbed at him, but he flapped out of reach, chattering with laughter. She growled again, then they followed Lavender round to the gleaming head of the white dragon. Catesby put on a serious face and all of them bowed their heads.

Lavender said, "Noble Jewel, we wish to search for the gem at the Sutors of Cromarty, so we should fly to the Cromarty Firth, then find the best place to land near the cliffs. Do you agree?"

Jewel nodded, then peered at them down her pale nose. "I thought I was taking the wolf," she chirped, in the highest, most musical dragon voice Catesby had ever heard. "Where did the wolf go?"

"I was the wolf," said Sylvie, "but I changed."

The dragon looked confused.

"So I can hold onto your spikes," Sylvie explained, "with my hands."

Jewel still looked confused. Sylvie held up her hands.

"Oh!" The dragon's pink eyes got wider. "You were the wolf, now you're a girl! Clever! Those hands will make it easier to stay on my back!"

Sylvie sighed. "So they will. I hadn't thought of that." She walked round the dragon, shaking her head and muttering, "We've not got a very bright spark here."

Catesby shrugged. "So long as she can fly." Then he noticed the line of centaurs watching anxiously from the bottom of the steps. He swooped over and hovered in front of Yann's mother.

"Don't worry, Mallow. There are three quests, going in three directions. We'll return soon with three healing tokens. You just keep his heart beating while we're away, and Yann will be fine."

Mallow reached up and stroked the phoenix's head. "I hope you don't put yourselves at risk for my son, Catesby. I hope you are all sensible and careful."

Catesby ducked away. "We'll do as much for Yann as he would do for us."

She frowned. "That's what I'm afraid of. Please come back safe, Catesby."

He nodded to her, bowed in the air to Petros and flew back to his friends, who were already on the back of the dragon. Lavender nestled in Sylvie's hair and Catesby perched on the wolf-girl's shoulder. Sylvie used her useful human hands to grasp Jewel's pearly spikes as the dragon leapt into the air.

It wasn't comfortable for the phoenix to be a passenger. He'd prefer to fly at his own speed and height. But his plumage, newly grown since he burnt up then re-hatched, still wasn't strong enough to race a dragon in flight. So he tried to concentrate on the task ahead. He was doing this for Yann, for his best friend. And for the centaur herd, who had always made him welcome.

It felt strange to set off on an adventure without Yann. They might insult each other as often as possible, but Catesby always trusted the centaur's strength, good sense and courage. Maybe he'd be useless on a quest without Yann to guide and goad him.

He wasn't on his own, though. Lavender was so small a fast breeze could blow her off course, but she had more wisdom and magical knowledge than any of his other friends. And Sylvie was rude and selfish, but she was also single-minded, brave and ruthless.

Catesby gulped a breath of fast air and tried to think positively, listing his friends' powers and skills, remembering their victories. How could they fail to save Yann?

But as they sped up the high spine of Scotland, he remembered the bright colour of his best friend's blood.

He couldn't imagine life without Yann. They had to find the token. However, Catesby had no idea what they were actually looking for. After speaking to the oldest centaur and listening to information Rona brought back from the Fife coast, Lavender had simply decided where they were heading.

Catesby leant closer to Lavender's head and Sylvie's ear. "So what are we doing, nectar-nibbler?"

"Don't call me that," whispered the flower fairy, "or

I'll tell everyone about that feather mite infestation you had last month."

"Shhh!" But it was too late. Sylvie was already sniggering and pretending to scratch.

Castesby sighed. "Very well, Lavender Flowerdew, most wise fairy, what are we doing and where are we going?"

Lavender raised her tiny voice to reach both of them in the rushing wind. "The paired cliffs are most likely the North and South Sutors of Cromarty, headlands facing each other across the Cromarty Firth. Giant shoemakers or sutors used them as workbenches in ancient times. They threw pieces of leather and tools across the firth to each other."

Sylvie said, "What about the gems the Three asked for?"

Lavender smiled. "The Fife selkies told Rona a legend about an ancient gem in the cliff face of the North Sutor. The gem is visible only from a distance, with moonlight shining on it. It looks like a great treasure, and many humans and fabled beasts have tried to remove it, to sell it or tap its ancient power. But it either vanishes or is invisible close up, because anyone who climbs the cliff finds nothing but bare rock."

"How will we find it then?" said Sylvie.

"Catesby can hover far enough away to see it in the moonlight and guide me towards it."

"And what do I do?" asked Sylvie. "Am I just along for the ride?"

"You're our bodyguard and sentry. Many magical objects have guards. Wings are the most useful things for this quest, but your teeth might also be necessary."

"Your hands are useful now too," pointed out Catesby, as the dragon swerved round a mountain top and Sylvie grasped the spikes tighter.

It was a long journey to Cromarty, so Catesby dozed, knowing that his roosting reflex would keep him secure on Sylvie's shoulder.

He woke up when the dragon slowed down. First he was aware of water below them. But it wasn't the wide sea, it was a long firth, a stretch of sea reaching inland. The water was dotted with human-built towers, speckled with lights. The dragon flew high above them, heading for the mouth of the firth, which was narrowed by two rocky headlands. On Lavender's shouted instructions, the dragon turned left towards the northern headland and landed on the top of a grassy slope leading down to the cliff.

Catesby stretched his wings and flapped off Sylvie's shoulder. "Thanks. You're a good perch."

The wolf-girl stretched. "I'm not a branch, you know. Your claws are sharp and you're heavier when you're asleep."

"Sorry. I forget you're more delicate when you're a girl!"

Sylvie growled and slid off the dragon. Lavender fluttered out from her hair and looked up at the night sky.

The moon was high and bright, with only the occasional cloud blocking its light. "Excellent," said Lavender. "If those clouds don't get any thicker and the gem shines in the moonlight, we'll get a good view of it."

Sylvie twitched her head sideways to draw her friends away from Jewel, then muttered, "Are we taking this daft dragon with us to the cliff or leaving her here?"

Lavender frowned. "The offer from the dragons was for transport only. I don't think we can involve Jewel in the actual quest. Anyway, even small dragons are very heavy, so she might make the cliff edge crumble. Shall we leave her here?"

The other two nodded, so Lavender flew round to the dragon's head to thank her for the journey and request that she wait for them on the hill. Jewel shrugged and laid her head on her clawed forelegs.

Sylvie flickered into her wolf form and sprinted downhill.

Catesby followed, at a slower speed so Lavender wasn't left behind. They flew down the hill, swooped over a line of huge concrete curves, which the phoenix thought were gun emplacements from an old human war, then flapped over a low fence. They found the panting wolf, tongue hanging out and eyes bright, on the very edge of the cliff.

They all looked down into the darkness.

Chapter 14

"We won't see any gems from up here," sighed Lavender. "Catesby and I had better fly out to sea."

"I'll have to stay on dry land," Sylvie growled. "I'll stand guard here, to make sure nothing approaches the cliff."

So the phoenix and the fairy flew off the cliff and over the firth.

"Is it windier out here?" Lavender asked nervously.

"This breeze isn't strong enough to blow you away," Catesby reassured her.

"I hope this is far enough," Lavender said, as they reached the middle of the firth. They banked round in the air, then hovered and stared at the North Sutor.

The moonlight was bright enough for them to see the pale wolf on the cliff edge. But they couldn't see anything glitter on the rock below her.

Lavender sighed. "Maybe we came to the wrong cliffs."

A cloud slid over the moon and the world went black. Lavender shrieked and dived under Catesby's wings. Then the cloud slid off and the moon shone out again.

"There!" the phoenix called. "I saw it, a silver-white gleam in that first flash of moonlight. I saw it!" Then he shook his head. "But it's gone again."

Lavender peered out from under his wing. "You saw it? In the first moonbeam?"

"Yes, it was halfway down the cliff, just to the west of Sylvie."

"So the clouds are our friends rather than our enemies," said Lavender. "I'll fly to the cliff; you guide me when the next cloud passes."

"No, Lavender, I think you should guide me in."

"Why?"

"I'm not calling you *small*, my friend," the phoenix said gently, "but the gem would have to be lighter than the sequins on Lee's party waistcoat for you to carry it. And you're not really big enough for me to see you from a distance, so how can I guide you?"

"You'll see me if I carry a lightball, and if I can't get the gem out, I'll mark its place. Please. I don't want to be out here alone in this unpredictable wind above the waves."

The phoenix nodded. "Aim for halfway between Sylvie and the sea, and I'll guide you from there."

Lavender flew towards the cliff, lighting the end of her wand. Catesby saw the fluffy edge of a cloud start to eat away at the moon and called, "Ready!" as the night went black.

He waited. The cloud drifted slowly across the moon. Then suddenly the moon glowed again and he saw a cold glitter on the cliff, below Lavender's warm lightball.

He marked the place in his mind before it vanished, then squawked as loudly as he could, "Down ten yards. West a bit. You must be close now. Can you see it, can you feel it?"

He glanced up again. There were no clouds approaching the moon. "Lavender, did you find it?"

He heard a faint voice. "No, just bare rock."

"Stay there. I'll get you closer next time."

He bobbed up and down on the air, searching for currents which would support his weight without pulling him out of position.

The moon vanished again. Catesby held his breath.

The moonbeam reappeared, and he saw how close Lavender was to the gem. "Down just a few inches! You're at it! You must be able to touch it!"

Catesby heard a squeal and saw Lavender's light tumble off the cliff, falling towards the sea. He shot through the air, but before he reached her, the fairy slowed her fall and fluttered upwards.

That squeal had sounded like Rona when she saw a spider. Catesby was fond of spiders; they tasted like oatcakes. But it can't have been a spider which made Lavender squeal. She lived among flowers and bushes; creepy-crawlies didn't shock her.

The phoenix and the fairy met in the air, a safe distance from the rocky outcrops of the Sutor.

"Did you find it?" Catesby asked urgently.

"I didn't see it, not even in the first moonlight. But I did feel it. I think it's a buckle, the sort of thing Lee would wear. A metal square, with tiny sharp gems round the edge. Perhaps the sutors dropped it when they were making a fancy shoe."

"Why did you squeal?"

"Because the buckle is guarded."

"By spiders?"

"Not by spiders! By ... I don't know. I'm not sure what they are."

Catesby flew up the cliff until his eye was attracted by movement in the moonlight. He saw skinny shapes with long tails and short legs, writhing round a bare piece of rock.

More of the creatures were appearing out of crevices all over the cliff, scuttling towards that one spot, opening their tiny sharp-toothed mouths, flicking their forked tongues at him.

Lavender hovered behind him. "That's what I screamed at. What are they?"

"Lizards."

"I don't think so. There's something odd about them."

Catesby flew closer. "They are lizards. Tails, claws, scuttling. Definitely lizards." Then he looked again. Each lizard had a different skin colour and pattern. But they weren't scaly, they were smooth. They were covered in...

"Leather!" said Lavender. "They're made of shoe leather. Yuck!" She darted straight up to the clifftop.

Catesby followed and found her cuddled between Sylvie's ears. The fairy was explaining what they'd seen. "... and they're made of leather. They must be the cut-offs from the sutors' shoemaking. Ancient leather, come to life and guarding the buckle. They aren't real lizards. They're something dark and magical, something resentful of being cast off."

Catesby shrugged. "They're still little and lizardy."

Sylvie said, "Shut up a minute, mite-scratcher, and let Lavender recover."

"I'm fine. I knew it might be guarded, but I don't like things which scuttle and they all ran at me..."

"But you're safe up here," Sylvie said, "and now we've found the gem. So, can your magic get rid of the lizards?"

"I'm the worst in my class at combat magic, because my hands get shaky and I sometimes drop my wand. But I can try."

"Don't be daft," said Catesby. "I have a beak and claws. And I'm not bothered by scuttling; I sometimes eat scuttling things. I don't really want to eat lizards made of smelly old shoe leather, but I could give them a peck. They were circling round a bare bit of cliff. That must be where the buckle is. So I don't even need you to guide me, Lavender." He puffed out his chest feathers. "I will get the gem for Yann."

Catesby swooped down to the shifting knot of polished leather: grey, black, brown and blue, with beady eyes and flicking tongues. The lizards were writhing in a tangled ring round a small patch of rock. The buckle must be in the middle. Even though he couldn't see the gem, if he could get his claws to that section of cliff, he could grab it.

Catesby wasn't quite as happy about facing hundreds of toothed and clawed lizards as he'd claimed, but he wasn't scared either. Most of them weren't any longer than his primary feathers. Even the biggest black ones weren't as long as his wingspan. They had teeth, but he had a beak; they had claws, but he had talons.

So he dived towards the bare rock.

Before Catesby reached it, dozens of the lizards leapt off the cliff and threw themselves at him, like leather cut-offs chucked off a bench. They landed on his wings, his neck, his head.

Catesby jerked back from the cliff before more could spring onto him.

He felt the lizards all over him. Clinging and quivering, scraping and biting. He couldn't shake them off. He somersaulted, but they clung on. They wound round him, bending his feathers, making him too heavy for his wings, making him clumsy in the air.

He could hear Lavender squealing his name and Sylvie howling, "What's happening?"

Catesby was struggling to stay in the air.

He felt a lizard bite the back of his neck. He had to get rid of them before they injured him, or before their weight overcame his wings and he tumbled into the sea.

So Catesby did the only thing he could think of.

He started to burn.

The phoenix let the fire inside his heart spread through his body. He heard sizzling. He smelt burning leather. Some of the weight on his back and wings dropped off.

It was working! But he felt himself grow hotter, and the world began to turn orange and red in his eyes. The moon faded and the cliff slid away.

He felt lighter as more lizards let go. There were almost none of them left. But how much of him was left?

Catesby had been practising using his fire without

burning up completely, but it required lots of control. He felt a lizard's teeth digging into the back of his neck and he desperately wanted to burn it off, to cook it, to melt it. He wanted to become fire.

But if he became fire, he wouldn't be able to save Yann. He'd be trapped in an egg again.

He had to draw the fire back into his heart. He had to cool down.

The lizard nipped him again. He felt another flash of flame.

Lavender screamed, "No!"

The phoenix tumbled and spiralled in the air, trailing smoke behind him, twisting so fast that the lizard fell. Then he willed the fire back inside, and let the night air cool him.

Then Catesby just flew. He let his wings stretch, his feathers bounce back into shape and his eyes adjust to the moonlight.

He glanced down and saw dozens of lizards in the black water, paddling back to the base of the headland. Then he hovered a safe distance from the hundreds of dry lizards. They leant out from the cliff, waving their front legs at him, holding on by their back legs, like ants waving their antennae. But not as easy to eat.

He sighed, flew back up to Sylvie and Lavender, and perched on the cliff edge.

"Catesby, you were on fire!" whispered Lavender. "I thought you were leaving us again!"

"I'm fine. I'm learning to control it. But I can't barbecue all those nasty nipping lizards without burning myself up. So I can't get the buckle either."

"My turn then," said Sylvie. "I'll climb down and get it."

Catesby shook his head. "Perhaps you could scramble down there as a girl, but I doubt you could hold on while they attacked you."

Lavender said firmly, "It's not safe for any of us while the lizards are surrounding the buckle, so I'll have to move them to a different bit of the cliff."

"How will you do that?" Sylvie asked.

"The buckle is invisible close up, so the lizards are guarding something they can't see. If I can create the image of the buckle somewhere else and convince them we're trying to steal the image, maybe they'll move away from the real buckle, then Catesby can swoop in and grab it."

"But I won't be able to find the invisible buckle if the lizards move," said Catesby. "The circle of lizards is our marker."

"Then I'll have to find my courage and hover out at sea, so I can direct Sylvie to the false buckle and you to the true buckle. We'll have to use a code, so the lizards don't realise what we're doing. Sylvie, please fetch a stick, so you can fish for the false buckle without going too far down the cliff, and I'll practise my spell."

Catesby preened himself as Sylvie trotted off and Lavender drew on the ground with her toe.

She flicked her wand at the scratched sketch and Catesby watched a buckle appear at her feet. A chunky square of silvery metal and starry diamonds. The fairy held her wand steady for at least a minute, juddering with the strain, then the buckle shattered and faded away. She sat down, exhausted.

Sylvie trotted up with a branch in her mouth and, for the second time, they all looked down into the dark.

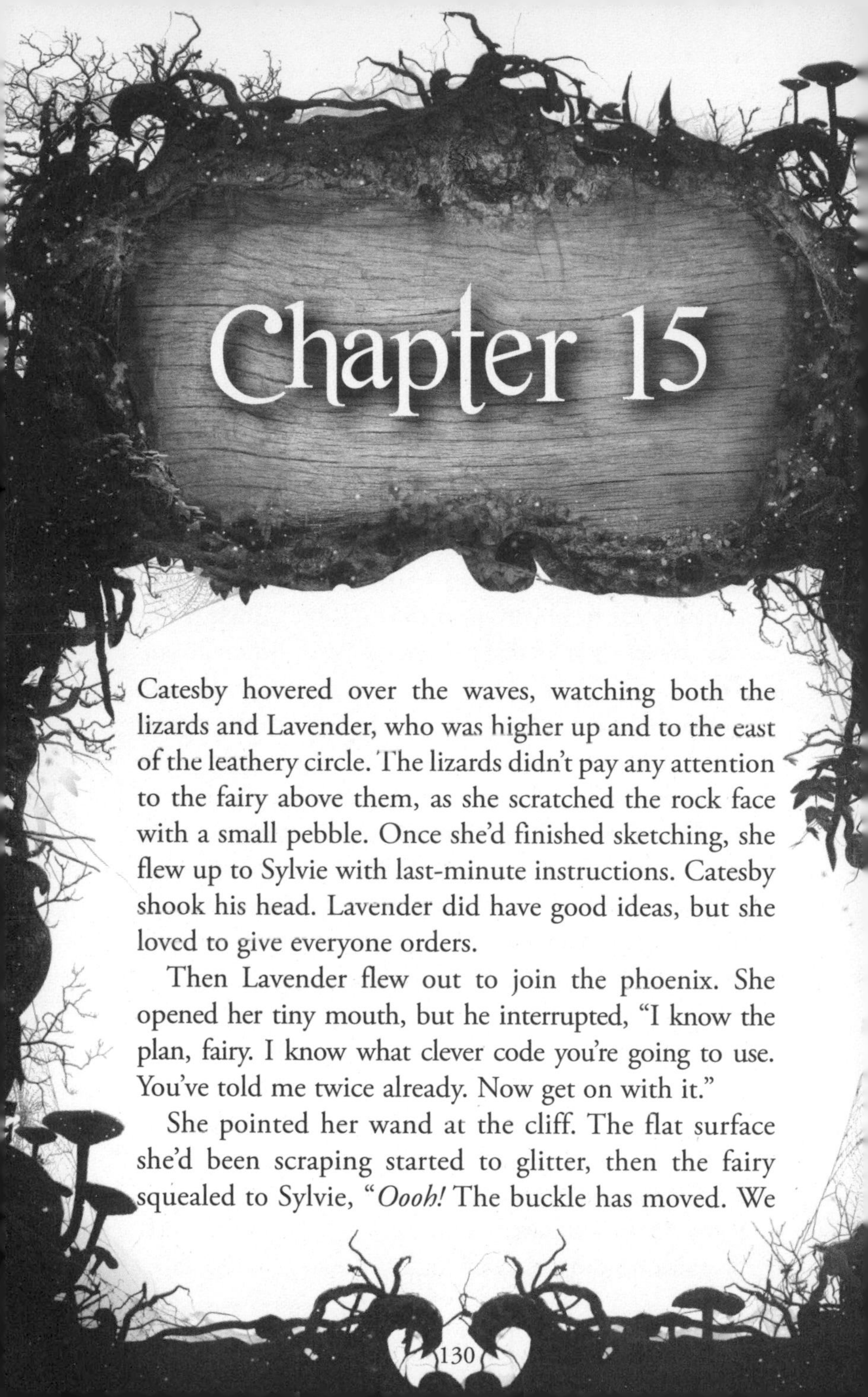

Chapter 15

Catesby hovered over the waves, watching both the lizards and Lavender, who was higher up and to the east of the leathery circle. The lizards didn't pay any attention to the fairy above them, as she scratched the rock face with a small pebble. Once she'd finished sketching, she flew up to Sylvie with last-minute instructions. Catesby shook his head. Lavender did have good ideas, but she loved to give everyone orders.

Then Lavender flew out to join the phoenix. She opened her tiny mouth, but he interrupted, "I know the plan, fairy. I know what clever code you're going to use. You've told me twice already. Now get on with it."

She pointed her wand at the cliff. The flat surface she'd been scraping started to glitter, then the fairy squealed to Sylvie, "*Oooh!* The buckle has moved. We scared it and it moved, but I can see it! It's beautiful!"

Catesby flew to the west side of the headland, hoping the lizards' attention was on the fairy's over-acting.

"*Oooh!*" she squealed again, "We could grab it now! Before those nasty little leather lizards work out what's going on! Can you reach it, Sylvie? It's just below you! Climb down for it! Oooh, it's so *shiny!*"

Catesby could see Sylvie scrambling down, using her human hands and feet to cling to the cliff face, holding the stick in her mouth.

The lizards were in turmoil. As Lavender called out exaggerated descriptions of the buckle's beauty and Sylvie inched down the cliff, the lizards kept creeping away from the real invisible buckle then scuttling back.

Lavender yelled, "Hurry, Sylvie. If you get it *now* we can rip it out of the cliff and take it away from Cromarty *forever*."

The lizards' circle broke. They all dashed up the cliff towards the false buckle and the scrambling wolf-girl.

Catesby dived towards the cliff. He hoped he'd fixed the circle's location in his mind, but when he scraped around with his claws, he found nothing but bare rock.

There was a cloud heading for the moon, so he backed away from the cliff, not wanting the lizards to notice his interest.

Lavender yelled, "The little leather rejects are nearly there. You'll have to rush, Sylvie, if we want to take the buckle away and leave this cliff dull and dark forever..."

The cloud covered the moon and the night turned black.

Catesby hovered, waiting.

Lavender was suddenly quiet and he heard the scrape of claws on rock high above him.

Then the moon lit the night again.

Lavender yelled, "Up a bit, Sylvie!"

So Catesby flew down, touching the cliff with one claw as he descended.

"Over to the east."

So Catesby went west.

"Down an inch!"

So he went up an inch.

"You're there!"

And he was. He could feel a cold metal corner.

He tugged. It didn't move.

Lavender shouted, "Sylvie, can you reach it? Now is *exactly* the right time to reach it!" She was trying to keep the lizards' attention on the false buckle and the wolf-girl.

Sylvie joined in the loud conversation. "I'll use my stick! Look! I'm using my stick!"

Catesby tugged harder.

Lavender yelled, "They're turning back, Catesby! They're scuttling at you!"

Sylvie yelled, "Stay away from him!" and he heard her lashing out with the stick above him. He also heard the claws getting closer.

He thought of the lizards' teeth and their weight on his wings. But he stayed by the cliff, tugging and pulling.

Suddenly the buckle jerked loose and he fell back into the air with the cold metal grasped between his talons. He flapped away from the cliff, much further than any lizard could jump, then looked down.

Away from the rock, the buckle glittered and gleamed. But Catesby didn't have time to examine it, because

Sylvie was still on the cliff and the lizards were swarming back towards her.

He flew up to Lavender, who was shouting even louder, but this time it wasn't over-acting. "Catesby has the token, so get out of there *now*, Sylvie!"

Sylvie had dropped the stick and was scrambling up the cliff with leather lizards hanging off her trouser hems.

The fairy and the phoenix flew nearer the cliff, Lavender yelling, "What can we do to help, Sylvie?"

Sylvie climbed onto an outcrop, crouched down and flickered into a wolf. The lizards clinging to her human clothes fell off. She snapped her jaws at the nearest lizards, then howled, "Go back to the dragon with that buckle. Don't risk the token to help me. I'll follow when I can!"

They both flew up to the clifftop, where Catesby hesitated. "I know she has strong jaws and long fangs, but she can't take on hundreds of lizards while perching on a little bit of rock. We can't leave her there."

Lavender fluttered above him. "We have to! If we lose the buckle in a fight, we could lose Yann. The token is our priority."

He shook his head. "We can't leave Sylvie to be eaten by lizards, or fall off a cliff, in order to save Yann. We can't abandon one friend to save another."

The phoenix flew back off the cliff, buckle tight in one talon. The buckle felt strange in his foot, not as solid as before, but he ignored that as he dived towards Sylvie.

And Lavender dived with him.

Sylvie was balancing on the rock, snapping at lizards,

biting them off her shoulders and paws, knocking them into the sea.

"I'm fine," she panted. "They aren't getting through my thick fur! Really, I'm fine..."

One of them bit her nose. "Ow! Really, I'll be fine. Get that buckle away from here!"

"*No!*" they both said.

Then Catesby yelled, "Here's the buckle!" The lizards turned, all their leather heads pointing at him like arrows.

He flew closer. "If you want it, come and get it." He held it out, stretching his talons towards them. The diamonds on the buckle flashed like stars in the moonlight.

The phoenix flew even closer.

Every single lizard, on the cliff face and on the wolf's fur, stared at the buckle.

Catesby swung his foot, so the buckle moved from side to side.

They all swung their heads.

He moved one wingbeat closer.

And they all jumped.

Every single lizard leapt off the cliff, off the wolf, all leaping for the phoenix.

But this time he was ready, and the moment the lizards were in the air Catesby flicked his wings and flew backwards, so the lizards all missed him and fell in a tangle towards the sea.

All except one big black lizard, which jumped furthest and grasped Catesby's leg, nipping the thin skin over his bone.

Lavender flew right up to the black lizard and jabbed it with her wand, muttering under her breath.

Catesby felt a terrible weight as the lizard suddenly got much heavier. He struggled to keep his position in the air, then the lizard let go and fell into the sea with a splash.

"Weight spell," explained Lavender. "Don't worry, it'll wash off. He'll float to the surface in seconds."

"I wasn't worrying about the lizard! But thanks."

They watched Sylvie climb to the top of the cliff as a girl. Then she flickered back to a wolf, and sprinted away.

By the time Catesby and Lavender arrived at the top of the slope, Sylvie was speaking with careful politeness to the dragon, suggesting that they take two minutes to get their breath back, then leave.

Jewel stretched her wings. Sylvie ducked, then trotted over to Catesby and Lavender.

"Thanks for coming back!" she said, flickering into a girl and hugging them both.

"Just as well those leather lizards don't have very big brains," said Lavender, "or they wouldn't have fallen for that false buckle."

"Or for your terrible over-acting! *Ooooh!*" Catesby laughed. "But well done, honeybunch, that was an excellent plan." He waved the buckle in the air. "We have the gems! We've saved Yann!"

"Don't speak too soon," warned Sylvie. "We still have to get it back to the Borders."

"No problem," he cawed. "We have a dragon taxi service."

Then he looked down at the buckle. It wasn't glittering and gleaming as brightly now. He looked closer. It was going dark around the edges, almost black at the corners. "The metal is changing! It's corroding! We'd better get it home as fast as we can."

Lavender peered at the buckle. "It's corroding so fast you can see the tarnish move across the metal! We may not have time to get it home. Give me a minute to think." She flew off in a distracted zigzag.

Sylvie put out her pale hand and Catesby gave her the buckle. They both looked at it.

It was silvery metal, with a line of bright white diamonds all around the square. But the edges were black and, if he looked carefully at one corner, Catesby could see the darkness blooming and creeping across the buckle. At that speed the whole buckle might turn black and disintegrate before they even got back to Cauldhame Moor, let alone before the Three arrived at sunset tomorrow.

Had they found the token which could save Yann, only to watch it die even faster than their friend?

Lavender fluttered back. "It's our heat! We're corroding it by holding it and breathing on it. The buckle has been held cold and still in solid rock for thousands of years. Now that it's in our hands or claws, it's warming up and time is catching up with it."

Sylvie placed the buckle on a stone and the moving black stopped. But it didn't retreat.

"So how do we get it home?" demanded Catesby.

Suddenly the dragon spoke above their heads. "I could carry it," said Jewel. "I am a reptile and my claws are as cold as the stone that bauble is used to, so I won't corrode it as fast as you warm-blooded mammals and birds."

Lavender bobbed in the air. "Thank you, noble

dragon. If you carry the token to Cauldhame Moor, the elders may have the skills to preserve it. Thank you so much."

The dragon picked the buckle up delicately between two pearly claws, then the friends climbed her white scales and settled on her back. Catesby was aware of little bites and scratches all over, and he could see a nasty bite on the end of Sylvie's nose. But he crowed, "We got it! We got it, we got it, we got it..."

"We're not home yet," said Lavender. "Don't count your dragons before they hatch."

"This dragon is proving pretty useful," whispered Sylvie, as Jewel took off. "And not as daft as she seemed."

Once Jewel was flying south at cruising speed, they murmured to each other about the cliff, the lizards, the great age of the buckle and how wonderful it would be to see Yann up on his hooves again.

Then they heard the unnatural mechanical buzz of a human engine. The dragon below them jerked in shock.

"An aeroplane!" screamed Jewel. "A plane! At night! I'm not very good with..."

The plane's roar got louder and the dragon dropped out of the sky.

Sylvie screamed, Lavender shrieked and Catesby just concentrated on holding on as the dragon fell towards the mountains and lochs below.

The plane passed far above them and Catesby yelled, "It's gone, Jewel, calm down!"

If the dragon didn't regain control, Catesby and Lavender could let go and stay in the air, but Sylvie couldn't survive a fall to earth.

"Use your wingtips, Jewel! Angle upwards!" Catesby

screamed. "Slow your descent! Get a grip on the air!"

The dragon frantically flapped her wings, sculling against the air rushing past them.

They were falling towards a long thin loch between two lines of jagged mountains. In the moonlight they could see their reflections getting larger as the dragon twisted and fell.

Finally, she got control, and swooped back up again.

But something kept falling. Something fell out of her claws and kept falling towards the loch.

Catesby launched off Sylvie's shoulder and dived down, trying to catch the buckle before it landed in the loch.

But he heard it splash. He watched as the buckle fizzed and fell apart. And he saw the diamonds sparkle as they sank into the loch.

Jewel was flat out on the ground when Catesby flew to the loch shore. She was moaning, "I'm sorry! I don't like planes and I panicked! I'm so sorry!"

Lavender called to Catesby, "Did you mark the place where it fell?"

"No point," said Catesby. "It's gone."

Sylvie said, "No it isn't. Someone will be able to search underwater. Rona, Tangaroa ... If their quest doesn't succeed, they can dive for it."

"No. It's *gone*. When it hit the water, the buckle disintegrated and those tiny diamonds sank into the water. They aren't much bigger than grains of sand. It would be impossible to find them all, and there's no buckle left to set them in. It's gone.

"We've failed. We've failed Yann."

Chapter 16

Tangaroa and Rona stood together as they listened to Lavender's final hurried instructions. "The healing power will be transferred to the flower by the washing action of seven waterfalls in new clean sunlight, so be careful not to get the water dirty as the flower goes down."

Rona's cheeks were pale as she nodded, but Tangaroa wasn't worried about the selkie's apparent nervousness. She often *looked* nervous, but it must be her way of dealing with tension, because he knew she was a fearsome fighter and powerful athlete, as well as a fast thinker.

Tangaroa knew Rona's abilities far too well, because she'd beaten him in the Sea Herald contest last year: overtaking him in a race, then answering a riddle, fighting a giant eel and escaping a killer whale much faster than he had answered his riddle and fought his monsters.

As they walked towards Nimbus, the dragon who would take them to the waterfalls, Rona was knotting her smooth dark hair round her fingers. Tangaroa grinned. He wasn't fooled. If he tried to match her skills and courage on this quest, she would probably embarrass him all over again.

He gestured for her to climb the dragon first. Then he followed her, and sat right behind her, wrapping his tattooed arms round the waistband of her sea-coloured dress. She murmured, "If you sit further back, you can grab the next set of dragon spikes. You don't have to use me to hold you on."

He sighed and slid round another set of spikes. "I just thought it would be useful to be closer together, so we could discuss our strategy."

"We'll have hours on the ground before the sun rises," she called back as the dragon leapt into the air. "We don't have to talk on the way."

Tangaroa shrugged and sat silent during the journey. He'd never been on a dragon before and he was fascinated by the landscape below: towns glowing underneath them, roads traced by cars' lights, rivers lit up by the moon.

Tangaroa was an expert navigator by sea, but the potential for finding his way around the land using flight and light fascinated him. He could tell by the stars that they were flying northwest. But he wasn't absolutely sure where they were headed.

Lavender had consulted many elders and they'd all suggested different waterfalls. There was so much rain in Scotland, so many burns falling down so many mountainsides, that there were hundreds of possible locations.

Tangaroa, as a coast-based blue loon who knew every island and cave round the Hebrides but knew very little about mountains and glens, had almost nodded off during the long argument about which seven waterfalls to choose.

All he knew was that they were heading for Glen something, to a burn called Allt something else. Lavender and the dragon Crag had chosen these particular seven waterfalls because the foliage in the glen meant there should already be flowers growing upstream from the falls, and the angle of the glen meant the team would have a good view of the sunrise.

Remembering the long discussion made him yawn. But he couldn't fall asleep or he might fall off the dragon. So he gazed at the dark land passing below to keep himself awake.

Finally Nimbus descended into a long glen, calling over his shoulder, "Where do you want me to land?"

Tangaroa yelled, "Apparently it's a burn coming down the highest mountain on the north side."

Rona added, "It's called Allt Ban, because the waterfalls make it look white from a distance, so it will probably be the burn we see clearest in the moonlight. Please fly up the glen slowly and we'll look out for it."

The dragon flew westwards along the glen, as Rona and Tangaroa looked carefully at the mountains on their right.

They both called out at the same time, "*There!*" when they saw a ribbon of silver against a black mountain. As the dragon landed on the heather, Rona turned round to smile at Tangaroa. He grinned back. She didn't look so nervous now.

They slid down the dragon's bumpy side, stretched their stiff arms and legs, then Tangaroa said, "First we need to find the seven waterfalls."

"There are two here," said Rona, stepping close to the steep side of the burn, "and I hear more further up. We might be at the right place already."

She crouched down, unwrapped her sealskin cloak and took out two fist-sized shell lamps.

"Don't light those!" Tangaora said.

"Why not? I don't want to sit around in the dark."

"You're not *scared* of the dark, are you?"

Rona shrugged. "I'm used to unlit water in my seal form, but in my human form, I get hairs rising on my arms in the dark. I'm not very brave as a girl."

"You're brave enough for me in either form, Sea Herald. Please let me see the location in moonlight, before your lamplight ruins my night-vision."

He stepped away from the dragon's bulk, stood on a rock at the side of the burn and looked round.

The glen ran almost directly east to west, which was why it had been chosen. They would see the sun rise earlier here than in most Scottish glens, because there weren't any high peaks to the east, just a line of distant rounded hills.

They were on the lower slopes of a mountain on the north side of the glen. Tangaroa glanced up at the peaks, then shifted his focus nearer, examining the darker than black blur of a line of trees to the west and a shadowy jumble of large rocks to the east.

He jumped back down, and walked towards the dragon and the selkie. "It's not a very secure location. There are too many places for enemies to hide."

"What enemies are you expecting, Tangaroa?" Rona glanced behind her.

He laughed. "I'm not, but we have to be prepared." He turned to the dragon. "Hey, Nimbus. Do you mind helping with a quick recce, then taking turns with us keeping watch? And while we're getting the token, could you perch on that rock there as our sentry?"

Rona whispered, "Lavender said the dragons offered to transport us, not to actually help us get the token."

Tangaroa grinned at the dragon. "We're all on the same side, aren't we? You'd get bored waiting to be a taxi. You'll muck in and help, won't you?"

The dragon looked at him. Stone-coloured scales, stony hard eyes.

The blue loon wondered if he'd pushed too hard, been too familiar. He wasn't good at diplomacy.

Then the dragon grinned. "Of course, small blue swimmer. I am glad to help."

"Great. Thanks," said Tangaroa. "First we should make sure we aren't being watched. Rona, you're the most experienced at quests, so could you go upstream, see if anyone is about, count the waterfalls, check for likely plants and also for any obstructions? Dead sheep or whatever they have up here."

Rona muttered, "If I find a dead sheep, I'm not touching it. One of you can move it."

Nimbus laughed. "If you find a dead sheep, I'll happily move it for you. Into my stomach!"

Tangaroa smiled. "So, Rona will go upstream. I'll go

to that band of trees. If you don't mind, Nimbus, you could check those rocks. And we can all scan the heather as we go."

Rona asked, "Can I light my lamp now, and does anyone else want one?"

Nimbus said, "I don't need one," and blew a fountain of flame into the night air.

Tangaroa sighed. "Thanks, everyone. Now my night-vision has been blasted away, I'll take a lamp. What is it? Seal oil?"

Rona shuddered as she lit the lamps. "Of course not. It's fish oil. I wouldn't use seal oil!"

"No. Sorry. But seal oil burns better. Smells better too." He sniffed as he took a lamp and jumped over the burn.

The blue loon walked towards the trees, wondering if the selkie was being such a wet blanket because she was worried about Yann. Tangaroa was worried about Yann too, but he also thought this was an opportunity for adventure in a new and scary environment. Rona just seemed to be seeing the scary and not enjoying the new.

Tangaroa was also a little nervous so far from the sea. He was less experienced than Rona at inland quests, even though he was totally human, because his all-over tribal tattoos made him too eye-catching out of the water.

After a five-minute walk, his lamplight glinted on metal. A high fence, as if someone was trying to stop the tall trees running away. The blue loon smiled. He didn't know a lot about trees but he did know they only walked in stories.

He tugged at the fence and it wobbled. It was too

flimsy to hold back a walking tree or anything else hefty. He moved along the fence to a post, climbed up and jumped over onto the strip of grass before the trees.

As he stepped forward, he was glad of Rona's lamp. He wouldn't have been able to see without it, because no moonlight reached under the trees. The blue loon pulled his fishing spear from its holder on his back. Its three barbed prongs should deter most forest animals from attacking.

If he was exploring a kelp forest, a sea cave or an underwater wreck, he would know from the local sounds and smells, from the movement of the water, whether there were any threats.

But in this narrow forest, these small creaks and green scents might be normal, or warning of an attack. He couldn't tell. This was Sylvie's environment, not his. They'd picked the wrong quests. She was probably on a clifftop right now, smelling the sea, and he was here, smelling pine bark.

He kicked his foot into a shadow. Nothing there. He couldn't search every shadow under every tree. Tangaroa turned to go. If anyone was watching them, at least they knew he was armed.

He swung back for one last look, in case something was creeping up behind him. As the lamplight shifted, he saw a shape sway over his right shoulder.

Not at tree height, but lower, the height of a tall man or a bear.

Tangaroa whirled round, aimed his spear, and lifted the lamp higher.

It was a small hillock, and the movement was tall purple flowers on the top, nodding in the moving air.

Foxgloves. Purple and beautiful, but their essence could save life or take it.

He'd only learnt basic land-based herb lore, but he didn't think this plant should be in such heavy bloom at this time of year. The flowers were open all the way up to the top of the stem. Was it left over from last year? Was it a trap? Was it a gift?

He reached out with his gutting knife, and cut the top four blooms off the tallest stem. He would give them to Rona to cheer her up. Perhaps they would bring luck and life to their quest.

With the knife in its sheath, the spear on his back and the flower in his hand, Tangaroa walked out of the trees, and tried to pretend that his deep breath wasn't a sigh of relief; it was just him enjoying the cool still night air.

Once he was over the fence, he scanned the heather as he returned to the falls, but didn't see anything threatening.

Nimbus was back already, crouched on the widest rock by the burn, and Rona appeared from downstream, in a circle of warm fishy light, just as Tangaroa sat down.

"I counted seven waterfalls," she said. "We're at the third here. There are two above us and four below. I dropped a twig in and it travelled safely down all seven falls. Do we want to camp by the top fall?"

Tangaroa looked around. "No, I think that rock is best for Nimbus, and we can be comfy here on the heather. What else did you see?"

"There's a sheltered dip a few dozen steps up from the first fall. It's got as many flowers as Lavender promised, almost like it's been planted. There are a couple of birch trees, some alpine flowers already in bloom and a few of last year's heather blossoms. There are no obstructions between it and the falls. What did you both find?"

"The rocks are secure," said Nimbus.

Tangaroa nodded. "Nothing in the trees either, except this." He handed her the foxglove. "I saw it and thought of you."

Rona frowned. "What? In the wrong place, at the wrong time, and potentially poisonous?"

"Em. No. I didn't mean that. I just thought you were worried about Yann and it might cheer you up."

The selkie smiled. "That was a kind thought. I am worried about Yann. But nothing will cheer me up until I'm back at sea. There's no salt in the air here." She sighed. "I was daft to volunteer for this quest. I can't swim as a seal in this shallow water. We're both out of our element."

"I thought that too in the trees. But we're not really out of our element, Rona. We have legs and arms, and we shouldn't limit ourselves to the sea. This is our Scotland too. Let's enjoy it."

He leant back and looked at the stars framed by the mountains. He could learn to find it beautiful. He could just fall asleep here...

But it wasn't safe for all of them to sleep at the same time. He sat up abruptly. "Nimbus, you've done more work than the rest of us tonight. Are you tired?"

The dragon yawned.

"So do you want to sleep first?"

"I need to rest before I fly you back," the dragon answered, "but I want to sit for a while and relax my wings. Why don't I take first watch?"

The blue loon nodded. "If Nimbus takes the first

watch, Rona could take the second watch and I'll take the final watch, so I can wake you both up in time for sunrise. We'll need to check the perimeter again before dawn, then be up at the top waterfall before the sun is up. Let's split the watches equally." Tangaroa pointed at the sky. "Nimbus, do you see the star at the bottom of that line of three? When that star touches the peak of that mountain, wake Rona up. And Rona, when the star at the top of the line hits the horizon, wake me up for the last watch. Alright?"

They both stared at him.

"Don't you tell time by the stars?" he asked.

Rona shook her head. "I tell time by the tides, which is no use here."

Nimbus shook his head too. "I tell time by how hungry I am. You two little ones go to sleep. I'll guard the waterfalls until the blue loon's star hits the edge of the earth."

Tangaroa and Rona settled down and tried to sleep, with the strange feel of dry heather under their heads.

Chapter 17

Frass sidled up to the Master. The faun was no longer sure of the Master's invincibility, but he was still afraid of the Master's anger. It was never safe delivering bad news. "Master?"

The minotaur looked up from the bone puzzle he was polishing. His right eye, hot and orange, stared at Frass. His left eye, cold and drooping, stared into blind space.

"Master, our watchers have reported." Frass stepped back, nearer the walls of the maze, out of reach of the Master's fist. "The first two quests failed. The scabbard wasn't there, and Arthur's enemies chased the girl and the faery away before they could work out where he is now. Then the white dragon dropped the gems on the way south."

The Master's fist crushed the fragile ivory box, but he

didn't lash out at Frass. However, the faun wasn't safe yet, because that wasn't the really bad news.

The Master prompted him. "So, there are still two tokens left?"

Frass nodded. "Let's look on the bright side, sir, I agree. However, there's been another development. The ancient one, she who takes the long view, has become aware of your interest in the tokens."

The Master growled. "Is she mobilising her forces?"

"They are already in play, Master."

"Then you must defend my interests at the third quest, Frass. Given the nature of our opponents, take shields as well as blades. Take the uruisks too. They know the land up there. Don't return with more bad news, faun, because if I'm forced back to the labyrinth in disgrace, I'll drag you with me in several soggy little bits."

When Rona shook Tangaroa awake, he stretched and looked at the sky. She'd let him sleep longer than he'd suggested, but even so, it was still a long time until sunrise.

Rona whispered, "Should we go up now?"

"No, Lavender and the elders were quite clear. We need a flower which starts to travel down the seven waterfalls as the sun is actually rising. We don't have to be at the top waterfall until the sun is just below the horizon. You grab more sleep; I'll keep watch."

Tangaroa walked to the burn to wash his face in the stinging cold water, then looked around.

The dragon was asleep on the rock, curled up and looking like a rock himself.

Rona was lying on the heather, her sealskin cloak over her, but not wrapped so tight she would turn into a seal. Her eyelids were flickering, as if she was dreaming or thinking.

Tangaroa looked to the west at the line of trees. He couldn't see anything in the shadows at the edge. He looked to the east. There would be a better view of the rocks from Nimbus's perch, but Tangaroa didn't want to disturb him. The dragon needed his sleep so he could fly them back.

Tangaroa kept glancing around, at the rocks, the trees, the heathery slopes, at the other burns coming down other mountains and joining the narrow river at the bottom of the glen.

The next time he looked at his companions, Rona's eyes were open, staring at him.

She frowned, then stood up and moved to the burn side. They sat together, watching the white water crash to the bottom of the third waterfall.

"I can't sleep," she murmured. "I'm too worried about Yann."

"Do you want to talk?" Tangaroa asked gently.

She shrugged. "I've known Yann all my life. My mother and his father are senior elders, so we've met at solstice gatherings and fabled beast councils since we were tiny. Yann had the best ideas for games when we were small and for adventures when we got bigger. He always looked after me, Lavender and Catesby. I don't think we'd cope without him."

"You won't need to. He'll be fine. There are three

quest teams out and we're probably the unlucky ones."

Rona looked worried. "Why?"

Tangaroa laughed. "The others were doing their quests by moonlight. They're probably back already with the scabbard and the gems. We'll show up with some damp flower mid-morning, and they'll be having cups of tea and saying, where were you guys? We'll get no glory for turning up last with the third token."

She smiled. "I hope you're right. I'm not in this for the glory. I just want to help Yann."

"I know you're not big on glory. I still don't understand why you resigned as Sea Herald after winning last year."

The selkie looked down at her feet, then pushed her toes into the water. "Oh! Cold!" She jerked her feet back out. "I don't mind Arctic waters with my sealskin on, but that's freezing on my human feet!" Rona waggled her toes. "When do we wake the dragon?"

"In half an hour, so we can do one more recce, then wait for a flower."

"I've been wondering about that, Tangaroa. Are we hoping that a flower falls in at sunrise or can we drop one in ourselves?"

"Didn't we get advice on that from Lavender?"

Rona shook her head. "We were too busy working out where and when to worry about what."

"But Lavender told Helen we couldn't take our own water to a footprint, because that would be cheating." He saw Rona flinch, as if her toes had touched the water again. "So probably we can't put our own flower in. Probably we have to hope a flower falls in as the sun is rising."

Rona frowned. "But the flower becomes the token

when it's washed by seven falls and new sunlight. Perhaps it doesn't matter how it gets into the burn."

They looked at the diamond-sharp water running under their feet.

"The water is completely clear," Tangaroa said. "No twigs, no leaves. And there's no wind to knock any blossoms off into the water."

Rona looked at the glow on the eastern horizon. "How long is the sunrise?"

Tangaroa looked at the low hills to the east and considered his answer carefully. "It's the morning of the equinox, which is the shortest sunrise of the year. But we can count from when the sun's rim first appears in that U-shaped glen, until the bottom of the sun moves off that rounded summit. I reckon just over five minutes."

Rona said, "So let's watch at the top waterfall for four minutes, and if no flowers come past, drop one in ourselves."

Tangaroa thought about her suggestion. "So we hope it happens naturally, but if it doesn't, at the last minute, we cheat?"

"Stop saying cheating!" she snapped. "It's not cheating! It's just helping the magic."

He laughed, "Ok, you're the boss! So it's not cheating. Just as well, because Yann wouldn't want to be saved by cheats."

Rona didn't answer, so they sat in silence as the world slowly grew brighter around them.

Tangaroa wasn't sure if he had offended the selkie. Perhaps he should try to be nicer to her. "What shall we do to pass the time?" he asked. "Make up rhymes? Ask each other riddles?"

"No," Rona muttered, "I'm not that good at riddles."

"Yes you are, you're great at riddles."

She shook her head. "Helen and Lavender are the riddle-masters in our team."

"Nonsense, Rona. Don't give them all the credit. You must have solved the Sea Herald riddle faster than anyone to win by such a margin."

He smiled at her, still trying to cheer her up. Then he saw the shocked look on her face.

Rona stammered, "Oh, yes, that riddle."

There was a moment's silence while Tangaroa considered everything he knew about this selkie, her friends, and the contest he'd lost to her. Then he considered the conversation they'd just had, that look on her face and that shiver in her voice.

He stood up. "You did answer the riddle yourself, didn't you?"

She didn't speak.

"Rona Grey. You did answer that riddle yourself, didn't you?"

He stepped closer to her. "Rona? Tell me the truth."

Her head moved, in what might be a tiny shake.

"Did you cheat?"

She looked away.

He grabbed her shoulders and turned her round. She was trembling, but he just gripped harder. He tried to keep his voice down, so they didn't wake the dragon, but he couldn't keep the anger out of his words.

"Did you beat me by cheating? Did you win that contest and humiliate me in front of my tribe by *cheating*? Tell me the truth!"

She whispered very quietly, "Yes. I cheated. In the last

task. Only the last one. I got help from Helen and the others to answer the riddle and defeat the guardian in the cave. I wasn't even in the cave. Helen got the map, Yann knocked the eel down. I was sitting outside. I'm a coward, really."

He opened his hands and let her go.

"Yann helped you cheat? Yann cheated?"

Tangaroa turned and scrambled up the side of the burn. If he stayed near this lying cheating treacherous selkie he might hurt her. So he should get as far away from her as he could.

She called after him, "But Tangaroa, you know why we did it! You know what disaster we were trying to prevent!"

"I know exactly why you did it," he bellowed back. "You did it to win. You did it because I was the strongest contestant and the only way to beat me was to cheat. Anyway, I don't care *why* you did it. I just know what happened when you did. After you won and I lost, I thought I was useless. Not as clever or fast or brave as some little seal-girl.

"And you know what's almost funny? I let your tame centaur comfort me. I went inland to his moor, and became his friend, and let him tell me that I wasn't useless, that I could win next time. And then what did I do? I cared about him *so much* that when I did have a chance to win the title which should already be mine, I gave it all up, to help the very people who beat me by cheating last time.

"You humiliated me. You ruined my life. You *cheated!* And now you can get that damn token yourself!"

Chapter 18

Tangaroa scrambled up the slope by the west side of the burn.

When he got to the top waterfall, he could see all seven falls: seven drops high enough to force the water to leap in a white frenzy, separated by gentler slopes where the water ran clear and slow.

The selkie was crouching by the third fall, sobbing into her hands. Tangaroa shook his head. She wasn't a Sea Herald. She had never been a Sea Herald. Those tears proved what a nervous, useless, over-emotional, cowardly wimp she really was.

Nimbus was yawning and staring at the weeping selkie. Then the dragon glanced up the slope towards the blue loon, who turned and walked further up. He didn't want to explain.

Tangaroa wasn't sure what he should do now.

The selkie and the centaur had lied to him and cheated him, so no rules of honour compelled him to save Yann or comfort Rona.

He should leave the dragon and selkie here, walk to the coast, swim back to the Western Isles, congratulate whoever had won the Sea Herald contest and get on with what was left of his life.

But he had come here for a healing token and he still wanted to collect it. Then shove it under Yann's nose and say, "See what I did for you, when you did nothing for me."

Tangaroa was walking up a shallower slope now, towards the sheltered area Rona had described. The banks of the burn were peaty here, rather than rocky. He reached the stunted trees and scowled at a patch of low plants with tiny blossoms. He wouldn't be picking any more flowers for that selkie.

He sat down by the burn. He'd keep out of Rona's way, keep her out of the way of his anger, until the sun was up. Then he'd get the token all by himself and fly back to Cauldhame Moor in righteous triumph.

He sighed. One small success with a flower wasn't going to make him feel better.

He leant over the burn to get a drink. He dipped his hands in the water, and felt something scratch his wrist.

Biting back a yelp of pain, he pulled his hand out. His wrist was bleeding.

He looked down into the water and saw a line of gold. There was a net stretched across the width of the burn. A net woven from golden wire.

It was letting water through, but stopping everything else: leaves, a feather, gravel.

Someone had placed this net to trap any flowers floating down the burn. That's why the water had been so clear when he was chatting to Rona.

Tangaroa pulled at the net, but it didn't move. He ran his hands carefully along it and discovered it was anchored by two wooden posts, hidden deep in the peaty sides of the burn.

He tried to slice through the net with his gutting knife, but even his sharp blade couldn't cut the fine shining wire. So he used his blue tattooed hands to dig at the sides of the burn, sending clods of mud and grit into the water, until he freed the posts and dragged the net out.

He wrapped the wire round the posts, then leapt down the hillside to the third waterfall.

Rona looked up, wiping her eyes.

He threw the posts and wire on the ground by her toes. "Your recce last night was worse than useless, seal-girl! Look what I found, blocking the burn just below the flowers. A net! Trapping anything going downstream."

"I didn't miss that!" she protested. "I ran my hand through the water all the way down. I can't have missed that. It must have been put there overnight."

"Nonsense," he said. "That's impossible. One of us was on guard all night. Unless you dozed off on your watch?"

She started to protest again. He spoke over her. "Don't bother! I'm not going to believe anything you say anyway." He turned his back on her. "Nimbus, it's just you and me now. This selkie is no longer a trusted member of our team."

Rona barged back into his eyeline. "Are you still trying to get the token? I thought you'd stormed off home."

"Your geography is no better than your riddling or your reconnaissance! If I was going home to the Minch, I'd go downstream to the sea, not upstream to the summits. Foolish seal! And yes, I am going to collect the token, because I need that cheating centaur to wake up again so I can tell him exactly what I think of him and exactly what he can do with his friendship."

He stepped round her to talk to the dragon, but she pushed in front of him again. "Hold on, blue loon. Your tactics aren't any better today than they were last year. Stop and think. Whenever that net was set, it means someone is trying to prevent us collecting the token. That someone might still be here. Don't you think we should prepare to defend the token?"

She was right, but he was hardly going to say so.

"*You* are not doing anything, girl. You just sit there blowing your nose and wiping your eyes. But of course Nimbus and I will check for threats."

He looked at the sky. The stars in the east had faded in the pale glow of the sun under the horizon. They didn't have long. "Nimbus, can you please see if there are any surprises lurking in the rocks or the trees? I'll meet you at the top waterfall in two minutes."

As the dragon took off, Tangaroa noticed Rona fiddling with the posts and the wire.

"Leave that alone, selkie. It might be useful."

She ignored him, and pulled a wire at the top. The net started to unravel. "The net-maker used a knot I know, so I can undo the wire, wind it round a pebble to give it some bulk, twist a point at the end for a blade and use one post as a handle. Then we'll have another spear, which I can use while you use your trident. One of us should watch any flower going down and..."

Tangaroa interrupted. "Stop trying to boss me about. I'm not listening to you."

"Don't be daft. You said yourself I have more experience of quests than you do, even if I didn't always follow the rules. Do you want me to turn this lovely sharp wire and this nice straight stick into a weapon, or don't you?"

"Do that. But only that." The blue loon was completely wrong-footed. He had thought Rona was a champion, then discovered she was a cheat. Then he was sure she was a wimp, but now she was taking charge. He couldn't keep up.

He climbed to the west side of the top waterfall, and scanned the hillside. He couldn't see anything hiding in the heather and the only thing in the sky was the dragon hovering above the rocks, then swooping over to the forest.

Rona yelled up, "Tangaroa? Did you look for tracks where the net was laid?"

He hadn't, but he wasn't going to admit that. He didn't answer.

She yelled again, "You didn't, did you? Is there time to look now?"

He glanced at the horizon. "No. I need to be watching for a flower now."

Nimbus landed heavily behind him and said, "I didn't see anything unexpected at the rocks. The forest edge looked clear and the fence is still standing."

Rona appeared on the east bank of the burn, with a short golden spear in her left hand and blood running down her right wrist.

Tangaroa shook his head. "Couldn't you wait for our enemies to appear and injure you themselves? That's a new way of cheating: cheating them of their fight."

She held up her hands. There were cuts all over her fingers and palms. "The wire was sharp," she said simply and turned to face east.

He remembered the sudden pain of his single wire cut and almost apologised. But he couldn't get the words out.

Then the sun came up, one dazzling edge over the horizon. They all looked at the burn.

The water was clear. No more swirling earth from Tangaroa's digging. No flowers either.

"We wait," said Tangaroa. "We wait and see if the mountain gives us a flower."

The water ran clear and clean.

"I could go up to the trees and stamp around a bit. That might dislodge something," Nimbus said impatiently, after the first minute.

"No! That would be cheating!" Tangaroa and Rona spoke at the same time, in the same tone of voice. But they didn't look at each other.

Another minute passed silently, with the blue loon and the selkie staring at the water, and the dragon standing sentry, watching the brightening world around them.

The air was still and the water was clear. There were no knotted heather stalks flowing past, no white stars or blue trumpets.

The only flower Tangaroa could see was the purple foxglove pinned to the neck of Rona's dress.

The sun was almost halfway over the horizon. Tangaroa sighed and looked up at the dragon. "Anything we should know, sentry?"

"Nothing. All quiet. All still."

"That's the problem," said Rona. "Everything is still. That's why nothing is coming down the water. This mountain isn't going to give us anything."

"It gave us that foxglove," said Tangaroa.

"You probably stole it."

"No, it offered itself to me. It was blowing in a breeze that didn't exist outside the trees. It almost leapt out at me. It felt right to take it. It even felt right to give it to you, you cheat and liar."

"Do you want it back?" She pulled it off her dress and held it out to him, over the burn. "Do you want it? Or should I drop it in?"

They both stared at the clear water. At the purple flower. And at the sun, hot and bright over the eastern hills. Almost free of the horizon.

Tangaroa shook his head. "If we put it in ourselves, it's probably cheating. It might not have any healing magic."

"But there isn't another flower coming past. A non-existent token can't save Yann. A token we've given a helping hand *might* save him."

"No. I think it's wrong. I think we should wait and see what the mountain gives us."

He looked to the east, but he wasn't seeing the sun, he was seeing Yann, pale and silent. Tangaroa was angry with the centaur, but he was also scared that he might never see Yann again, might never wrestle or argue or train or laugh with him again.

He looked back at Rona, at the flower rolling between

her slim fingers. "Do you want to drop it in? Do you think it will work?"

She shrugged.

"Come on, selkie. You're the world expert on cheating. Do you think you could get away with it?"

"*Getting away with it* is not the point of cheating, Tangaroa."

"You didn't like getting caught out this morning though, did you?"

She turned away.

He looked east, then at the water upstream. "We have less than a minute and I don't see any flowers coming down the burn." He turned to Rona. "So, cheat expert, do you want to cheat again?"

She snapped at him, "Oh no. I'm not going to decide this. I'm not a trusted member of the team."

"You are more experienced at this sort of thing."

"Then it's time you got experience with difficult choices, Tangaroa. You decide."

"What?"

Rona spoke clearly. "You cut the flower, you gave the flower to me. So you decide. You decide if we should break the rules, if we should cheat, to save someone we both care about. If you want this flower in that water, Tangaroa, then *you* tell me to drop it in. You tell me to cheat."

He looked at the sun rising over the hills, at the water falling down the mountain.

Seven waterfalls. Would that be enough to wash this flower clean of a false start? Did it matter? It was the only chance Yann had.

"I get the point," he muttered. "Sometimes you have to do the wrong thing to do the right thing. I get it."

"Tell me."

"Drop it in, Rona."

She let the purple flower fall and it tumbled through the still air into the moving water.

Chapter 19

The flower vanished over the first fall.

"Your flower," said Tangaroa.

"Your decision," said Rona.

They jumped down the sides of the burn, Tangaroa on the west, Rona on the east, following the flower.

It was already at the bottom of the first fall, bouncing up and down under the white water, battered by the weight landing on it.

"Can a flower survive seven of these?" Rona whispered.

A shift in the water flow let the purple foxglove break free. It floated to the second fall, a longer wilder fall, and leapt over that.

Rona and Tangaroa scrambled down the sides, struggling to keep their balance, to hold their weapons, to keep the purple petals in view as the flower fell through the churning water.

This time the flower's momentum brought it safely out from under the fall. But the flower drifted into a pool to the west, which it circled twice, then the current pressed it against a rock.

Tangaroa and Rona stared at the flower, willing it to move. The blue loon glanced along the glen. The sun was free in the sky now. This flower was their only chance. But the water was pinning it to the rock.

He looked up at Rona. She raised her eyebrows.

The flower was stuck at his side of the burn. It was his decision. Again.

"The sun is up now. It has to be this flower." He bent down and eased the foxglove free with his finger. It leapt back into the current, circled the pool once, then escaped into the forward flowing burn.

They watched it bob gently along a calmer stretch to the third fall. Then they heard the dragon call, "Blue loon, selkie. Look to the west!"

As the flower tumbled over the third drop, Tangaroa and Rona saw the fence around the trees glitter in the morning light, then collapse slowly to the ground. And they saw a line of goats run forward.

Goat-legged men and goats on their hind legs. More than thirty goats, all with shields, many with swords, hammers or maces, all running towards them.

"The Master's minions," gasped Rona. "They must have set the net! They want to stop us collecting the token, to make sure Yann dies. We have to keep the flower safe!"

Tangaroa nodded. "You watch the flower, I'll watch

the goats. Maybe they won't reach the burn until the flower has reached the last fall."

Tangaroa stood steady, with the burn, the flower and the selkie behind him, and the fauns and uruisks running towards him. Nimbus flapped downstream, and settled in the heather between the blue loon and the goats.

"Thanks, friend," said Tangaroa. "But I think there are too many even for you."

Rona called, "The flower is past the fourth fall. I'm following it."

Tangaroa leapt down to stand opposite her and turned to watch the goats. They were shouting as they ran, but he couldn't hear what they were threatening.

He glanced back at the flower, moving through shallow water. Stopping, circling, starting again lazily. It wasn't moving nearly as fast down the burn as the goats were moving across the mountain.

Then he looked at Rona, watching the flower, her hand relaxed around her spear.

"Rona, we're being attacked! Why aren't you as scared and nervous and basically useless as you were earlier?"

She shrugged. "I was really worried about you finding out I'd cheated. It was the worst thing I could imagine, but now that you know, nothing else quite as terrible can happen."

"You were more scared of me than of those creatures running at us?"

"You're my friend. I care what you think. I don't care what they think."

"You care what I think?"

She nodded. "But, right now, I think you should watch the goats rather than me."

He checked on the goats again. The fauns and uruisks were getting closer, so their words were clearer:

"Don't trust..."

"We're here..."

"Guard..."

Rona said, "The flower is over the fifth fall," and leapt down again.

Tangaroa followed her. The flower was already floating free of the chaos at the bottom of the fall. "I think this flower is going to make it."

"Only if the goats don't stop it, blue loon. So let's see if your blades are as sharp as your tongue." She lifted her spear. "Are you ready?"

"Are you planning to fight them, Rona?"

"Of course. Aren't you?"

"But you usually let Yann and Helen fight for you, don't you?"

"They're not here. Ready?"

Tangaroa turned his spear round, so the three blades pointed down. "No. I don't think we can hurt them."

"What?"

"Remember what Lavender said: if we get the water dirty, it might damage the token's healing power. I think we have to keep the magic clean and pure. We can defend the flower, stop the goats grabbing it out of the water, but we can't dirty the water with blood, or mess the magic up more than we already have."

Rona frowned. "You want us to collect the token, while being attacked by the Master's minions, without drawing blood? That's not going to be easy."

They walked on opposite banks, following the foxglove as it headed for the sixth fall. The slope wasn't as steep here, so the falls were further apart, and the water wasn't moving as fast.

As the fauns and uruisks got closer, Nimbus crouched low, his wings out and his neck stretched aggressively. Tangaroa could hear the tallest faun, with a black bull's head painted on his shield, yelling clearly, "Don't trust..."

But his voice was drowned out by flapping wings and roaring fire.

Four dragons landed in a line beside Nimbus. The huge black bulk of Crag, the shining flame colours of Bunsen, Nimbus's grey brother Cumulus and the bright whiteness of Jewel.

The flapping hid the goats from view, and the roaring covered up their shouting and yelling.

Rona called, "The flower is over the sixth fall."

"Don't injure them!" Tangaroa yelled to the dragons, now sure that they could only heal Yann if they didn't cause injury themselves. "Keep them back, but don't draw blood!"

"Can I fry them instead?" boomed Crag.

"Please don't, friend. We can't risk it."

The goats reached the dragons, who built a fence of wings, spikes and scales. Tangaroa could see hooves kicking under wings and blades crashing into scales, but the goats couldn't damage the dragons or get past them.

"Where did the dragons come from?" he asked Rona.

"The rocks which Nimbus checked." She raised her voice. "You said you didn't see anything, you tricky dragon!"

"I said I didn't see anything unexpected," Nimbus called back, "but I did expect reinforcements. You didn't need to know about them, unless we were attacked."

The flower was nearly at the seventh fall.

The orange dragon yelled, "This hairy animal is hitting me with a big axe! It's not good for my complexion. Can I just singe him?"

Tangaroa shouted, "No, Bunsen, we must respect the magic of this place!"

Suddenly half a dozen uruisks broke through the line of dragons at the lower part of the slope, and three of them leapt the burn. The goats sprinted up both banks towards the seventh fall, as the flower floated gently downstream.

Tangaroa pointed the blunt end of his spear. "I'll hold them off; you get the flower out after the fall."

They both slid down the heather by the final waterfall, keeping pace with the flower as it spiralled down.

Uruisks ran towards them, waving hammers, maces and axes. Dragons flapped overhead, landing on both banks.

Tangaroa saw the flower bounce up from the fall. Clean and bright, purple and beautiful, just like when he had picked it last night. But now it was twirling in the middle of a wide pool, more than an arm's length from either bank. Neither of them could reach it.

The earth was shaking, pounded by hooves and clawed feet. Tangaroa saw a pebble drop into the burn and screamed, "*Get the flower out* before the water gets dirty!"

Rona stepped off the east bank, balanced on a small wet rock in the middle of the pool, leant down to scoop the flower out, then jumped to the west bank. Tangaroa grabbed her arm to steady her.

They were standing in the heart of a battle.

Goats were whacking at the dragons' thick scales with blades and shields. Goats were running at Tangaroa and Rona, then being knocked back by wings and tails.

A faun with a huge sword ducked under Bunsen's flailing yellow tail and sprinted towards them.

"We have the flower now," shouted Rona, "so we don't need to worry about blood in the water." She jabbed her spear out in front of Tangaroa. The faun nearly ran onto the golden point, but before he reached them, Bunsen's tail flipped him into the air and over the burn.

Tangaroa laughed. "You are a warrior, after all, Rona! But we can't enjoy this fight; we have to get the token out of here. How do we get through that chaos to a dragon?"

"You go. You're faster and stronger. Take the flower, climb onto the nearest dragon and go."

"What about you?"

"I'll cover your back, then follow on another dragon, but I want the token safe first. You'll get it onto dragonback faster than I will." She held the foxglove out to him. He reached for it, and they both held the stem of the flower.

But two massive black scaly forelegs shoved them apart. As they fell to either side, they both let go of the flower.

Tangaroa saw a white uruisk loom over them, hammer raised high, shield covering his chest. Then a jet of flame shot between the selkie and the blue loon. The fire hit the uruisk's shield, knocking him backwards. The hammer fell harmlessly to the ground.

The flower fell too. The flower was caught in the bright white light of the black dragon's flame. The foxglove blazed crimson, then pink, then burnt to ashes before it hit the ground.

The tallest faun sighed and the goats ran off.

The grey dragons chased after them, but Crag yelled, "No. Let them run like rats. The token is gone. There's no need to chase them."

The dragons circled round the selkie and the blue loon.

"I'm sorry I burnt the token," said Crag. "But that hammer was aimed at the selkie's skull. I am sorry."

Tangaroa stood up. "No one blames you. Thank you all for trying."

He helped Rona up. He could see new tears running down the old stains on her cheeks. "You're fine, Rona. We're all fine."

"We're fine, but Yann isn't. We failed him. We tried everything, we helped the magic, we didn't injure those goats, we maybe even cheated, but we failed anyway."

Chapter 20

Helen was woken by a thumping noise outside and she sat up, wondering if the shaved giant from the Eildons had followed her home. She looked out of the window and saw her dad chopping firewood.

She still felt wretched about failing Yann last night, but she was sure the other teams would have collected one or even two tokens. The sun was up, so Rona and Tangaroa must be on their way back. If she hurried, she might get to the moor before them, then she could find out who had succeeded, and sit with Yann until the Three returned this evening to heal him.

She heard her mum clattering downstairs and Nicola singing upstairs. How could she avoid getting sucked into a family weekend?

She hunted for her mobile, then remembered it had

been crushed by a centaur. She crept into her parents' room, lifted the phone by the bed and dialled Kirsty's mobile.

"Are you awake?"

"No. Go away."

"Come on, Kirsty, rise and shine."

"Go away! I don't have a match this morning. I want a lie in." Kirsty yawned.

"I need your help. I have to escape from the house again, and I've already used ponies and birds' nests, so I need to use a human being this time."

"And I'm the human being you want to use?"

"Could you phone back and ask Mum if I can go round to yours today, then intercept any calls and cover for me? Please!"

"Why?" Kirsty demanded.

"Because you're my best friend?"

"No. Why do you want to escape?"

"Oh, you know."

"No, I don't know, Helen. I hardly ever know these days. Is it violin practice?"

"No, it's not music. It's something else."

"What else?" Kirsty asked.

"I can't say."

"You want me to lie to your mum and you won't tell me why."

"Yes," said Helen. "Because I don't want to lie to you."

"I suppose that's honest."

"So will you, please?"

"OK, I'll call your mum and ask if you can come out to play. Just this once." Kirsty cut her off.

Helen crept back to her room. As she was pulling on

her jeans, she heard the phone ring. Her mum answered it downstairs.

Helen shoved her feet into her boots. It was getting harder for her two lives to grow side by side, without crashing into each other. Helen knew that eventually she'd have to choose who she really was.

But right now, it was simple. She had to concentrate on Yann. She picked up her first aid kit, but left her fiddle case on the floor. She'd be much safer if she left that at home.

Helen looked round at her friends, slumped in a ragged circle on the grass by the white fountain. Everyone looked terrible.

No one had managed a full night's sleep, or washed all the night's dirt off. Sapphire was gazing unhappily at her tail, which no longer wrapped round the whole circle, as if she'd expected it to grow back already. Helen and Lee hadn't mentioned their difficult conversations, but Rona had just told everyone what Tangaroa had discovered, so it wasn't surprising that the circle was less cosy this morning.

But that wasn't why they looked terrible.

They'd all hoped someone else had succeeded. Now they all knew no one had collected a healing token.

They'd endured the centaurs' sympathy, questions and contempt. Petros had refused to speak to them. Mallow had offered food, drink and comfort. Epona had offered to take over, claiming that she could do better than any of them. Finally the centaurs had left them in peace. Helen could see Yann's parents pacing up and down behind the columns on the terrace.

She sighed. "I can't believe we made such a mess of it."

"I can't believe we had such bad luck," said Lavender.

"There's no such thing as luck," snapped Sylvie. "We just all did something really stupid. Or several stupid things." She glared round at everyone.

Helen was trying to make sense of their failure. "So we lost one token because it wasn't there, we lost another because Catesby, Lavender and Sylvie had a very nervous dragon, and we lost the final one because Rona and Tangaroa were ambushed by the Master's minions."

She thought for a moment. "The scabbard must be somewhere else, but we can't search the hollow hill for clues while that giant, the boar and those dragons are there." Helen frowned and kept thinking out loud. "The buckle did exist, but a dragon dropped it. The flower was washed by the waterfalls, but another dragon burnt it."

She lowered her voice. "Do you see a theme here? I know Arthur's enemies attacked the Eildon team, the lizards attacked the Cromarty team, and the goats attacked the Allt Ban team, but the ones who actually destroyed the tokens..." her voice was almost a whisper, " ...were the dragons!"

Sapphire growled.

"Not you, my blue friend," Helen said. "You've lost more than any of us trying to save Yann. But where did those dragons above the Eildons come from? And why has your classmates' help cost us two chances to save Yann? Who sent them here?"

Sapphire rumbled angrily and Lavender translated.

"The Great Dragon sent them. When Sapphire explained why she would be missing dragonlore classes, the Great Dragon sent her pupils to help." Then Lavender spoke for herself. "Helen, those dragons helped us gather information and decide the best locations. They've been very helpful."

"*Very* helpful," repeated Helen. "Right up until they dissolved or burnt the tokens."

"Helen! We couldn't have managed without them!"

"The point I'm making, Lavender, is that we didn't manage *with* them. Have the dragons been helping us or hindering us?"

Sapphire rose to her clawed feet and roared. The centaurs on the terrace turned to look. Catesby sprang into the air, screaming and shrieking at the dragon.

Tangaroa turned to Helen. "He's angry that Sapphire's classmates seem to have betrayed his best friend, in case you're not catching the subtleties of their argument."

As Sapphire's answering roars got louder, Helen said, "Neither of them are being that subtle! But you have human ears like me, Tangaroa. How did you learn to understand them?"

The blue loon shrugged his tattooed shoulders. "I don't know. I've always been able to. All the blue men of the Minch can understand fabled beasts. You just have to listen."

"That's what Lavender says and I do listen, but I don't understand."

"All you're missing right now are some rude words and insults they'll both regret later..."

But the insults were broken off, as Catesby flew straight at the dragon's face. Sapphire lashed round with her tail, and if it hadn't been shorter than she expected, she would have knocked the phoenix out of the air. He swooped up and dived at her head. She stood on her hind legs grabbing at him with her front claws, her huge feet ripping the centaurs' neat lawn.

Helen didn't need words to understand this. She jumped up and raced over. Rona, Sylvie, Lee and Tangaroa joined her, and they all started shouting:

"Stop it!"

"Don't hurt each other!"

"Calm down!"

But the shouts didn't help anyone calm down.

Lavender hovered above their heads, and waved her wand in a circle.

And there was silence.

Helen felt her mouth moving and her throat straining as she yelled, "Calm down!" but no sound came out. The dragon's mouth was open but she was silent too. All of them were shouting, but no one was making any noise.

Lavender whispered, "That's better. Now, move away from each other. Catesby, perch on Rona's shoulder. Sapphire, sit on your big blue bottom. Now!"

The dragon and the phoenix did as they were told. Everyone else stopped trying to shout.

"I'm cancelling the silence spell and I don't want anyone shouting another word. We are friends and we will stay friends, because Yann needs us together. Do you agree to keep quiet?"

Everyone nodded.

Lavender flicked her wand. Helen murmured "oh" and heard her own voice, very quietly. She smiled and sat down beside the quivering dragon.

Lavender said, “Let’s think about this calmly.”

After thinking calmly for a moment and failing to come up with a better plan, Helen said, “If this Great Dragon, her pupils or any other dragons are sabotaging our quests, we need to speak to her.”

Sapphire’s roar was such a clear NO that Helen flinched.

“We have to! We can search for healing tokens in every hill and waterfall, every cliff and footprint in Scotland, but if we’re going to be undermined by dragons every time we succeed, we have no chance of saving Yann. Either the Great Dragon is on our side, or she isn’t, and I want to know which before I try again. So I’m going to speak to her. Who’s coming with me?”

Helen wondered if everyone else was still held in the silence spell, because no one answered.

“Now I really miss Yann,” she said. “He wouldn’t be scared.”

“Yes, he would,” whispered Rona.

“If he *was* scared, he wouldn’t let it stop him. Who’s coming with me?”

Lee nodded. “Of course I’ll go with you. But only if you understand what you’re doing.”

“So someone explain, please.”

Lavender said, “The Great Dragon is older than Scotland. She was here before stone brochs or iron tools. She is the oldest fabled beast on the island.”

“Why is she called the Great Dragon?” Helen asked. “What’s so great about her?”

Rona said, “She’s great like you have a Great-Aunt Elsie. She is the ancestor dragon. Every dragon in Scotland is her direct descendant, and so are most dragons in the British Isles, and a large number of dragons in Scandinavia and Russia. She is their great-great ... for many greats ... grandmother. So they call her the Great Dragon. She's old and sleeps for many months of the year, but she always teaches young dragons their dragonlore in the spring."

"Whose side is she on?" Helen asked.

Rona frowned. "What do you mean, whose side?"

"Humans, or baddies, or goodies, or what?"

Everyone around her laughed.

"You know what I mean."

"No, I don't think *you* know what you mean," said Sylvie. "There are no sides in the fabled beast world. There is ambitious evil like the Master and gentle goodness like the unicorns. There are those who prey on humans and those who stay out of their way. But there isn't a line with goodies on one side and baddies on the other. To be honest, Helen, if there was an uncrossable line, we'd be on one side and you'd be on the other.

"But the Great Dragon hovers above it all. She takes the long view. Though she's never approved of humans, so she's unlikely to talk to you."

"Who will she talk to?" Helen looked at Sapphire. "Will you speak to her?"

Sapphire moaned and twitched her injured tail.

"Are you afraid of her?"

Sapphire slumped on the ground.

"Who will she talk to?" demanded Helen.

"She only speaks to those who earn a place in her presence," Lavender said reluctantly.

"How do you earn that?"

"By answering riddles."

Helen shook her head. "Riddles. Again."

"If you get an answer right, you get to ask her a question. If you get an answer wrong, you get..." Lavender paused.

"I can guess. If you get the answer wrong, you get eaten."

"We don't have to see her," said Rona. "We can just keep looking for tokens."

Helen shook her head. "We can look for tokens, find them, fight off their guardians and hold them in our hands. Then we can see them destroyed by dragons. That's a waste of time and Yann doesn't have time. We need a token by sunset tonight. So I'm going to ask the Great Dragon why she's trying to kill Yann. Who's coming with me?"

They all stood up.

Even Sapphire, who had turned almost grey with fear.

And they flew to meet the Great Dragon.

Chapter 21

Flying to meet the Great Dragon wasn't simple.

Sapphire announced that non-dragons were not permitted to know the location of the Great Dragon's hall, so her passengers must be blindfolded for the entire flight there and back.

Mallow provided a ribbon for Lavender and silk scarves for everyone else. They blindfolded each other, then set off on Sapphire's back.

Helen had flown at night before, but even the darkest night isn't totally black: there's moonlight, or starlight, or light from the land below. But with a scarf tight over her eyes, she was completely blind, and with the unpredictable movement of the dragon under her and the fast air pummelling her, she felt very insecure.

The flight seemed to last for hours. Tangaroa, who

was sitting behind Helen, whispered, "I think she's flying in circles to confuse us."

Then Sapphire slowed and Helen felt the familiar jolt of the dragon landing.

She put her hands up to push the scarf away, but Sapphire roared and Sylvie, sitting in front of her, said, "Keep the blindfolds on."

Then there were more roars from all around them. Sapphire reared up, the friends on her back bumping into each other, held in place only by her spikes. Helen heard Sapphire roar in anger and felt a lurch as the dragon leapt forward. Lavender whispered in her ear, "Crag and the twins are here. Sapphire's not happy with them."

But Helen could hardly hear Lavender's explanation past a crescendo of roars. This was even less secure than flying blind: sitting on the back of an arguing dragon, not able to see what was going on, not even able to understand the argument.

Suddenly, there was a lighter, higher dragon roar. All the other roars stopped. Whoever this dragon was, the rest listened and obeyed.

"Jewel is taking us into the great hall," whispered Lavender.

Sapphire lurched into the air again, and Helen gripped her spikes tighter. But Sapphire didn't fly upwards, she went straight forward. The sound of her wingbeats bounced back loud and close.

"Are we in a tunnel?" Helen whispered.

Tangaroa replied, "A tunnel or a gorge."

When the echoes faded away, Sapphire landed, then growled. Helen felt Sylvie and Tangaroa slide away from her. Still blind, Helen followed, slipping down Sapphire's bumpy sides.

Jewel chirped again. Sapphire argued loudly, but Jewel must have prevailed, because soon Sapphire grumbled at her friends. "Sapphire has to leave," explained Lavender from Helen's shoulder. "She can't stay, in case she's tempted to help us with the riddles."

Sapphire roared one more comment, then Helen heard her flap off.

Lavender murmured, "She says she'll see us outside."

"Actually she says she *hopes* she'll see us outside," Sylvie muttered.

Jewel spoke again, in a formal singsong voice. Lavender translated more loudly now, as if she wanted Jewel to hear and approve her translations.

"Jewel, dux of the dragonlore class, will ask us one riddle now, and if it is answered correctly we may remove our blindfolds and see the great hall. If the second riddle is answered correctly, we may see the Great Dragon herself. If the third riddle is answered correctly, we may hear the Great Dragon and she will deign to hear us."

Lavender paused as Jewel continued with her instructions. Once the dragon stopped, Lavender whispered, "Oh dear," before speaking clearly again. "But the riddles are not for us all. The human is an intruder in our fabled world, so the human must answer the riddles herself and the human must pay the price if the answers are wrong. Do you understand?"

Lavender repeated, "Helen. Do you understand?"

"Yes," sighed Helen. "I understand."

Jewel asked the riddle, singing it like a bird. Lavender translated.

"The first riddle is:

You fight so hard against it,
Though fighting the wrong opponent will bring it closer.
You fear it every day,
Though once it arrives, you no longer care.
It can look good to the old, and impossible to the young.
It is the spice which gives flavour to life.
It is the full stop which gives meaning to the sentence.
It is...

Despite the blindfold, Helen could see the answer. The one thing they were all fighting, because Yann had fought the wrong opponent.

"It is..." she said into the darkness, "it is ... death."

The dragon she couldn't see grunted and Lavender said, "We can take off the blindfolds."

Helen tugged the scarf up onto her forehead.

First, she looked round, to check that all her friends were there. Lee, Catesby, Tangaroa, Sylvie, Rona and Lavender. All rubbing their eyes, or blinking.

Then she looked up. They were in a massive hall. The largest indoor space she'd ever been in. Bigger than the Chambers Street museum in Edinburgh or the Museum of Flight in East Lothian.

It wasn't a cave. The black walls were built of cut stones the size of cars or cottages. Ledges jutted out from the walls, like balconies with no railings, occupied by dragons of all colours. Their scaled heads were peering down, watching the group below. Between the ledges were arches wide enough for flying dragons. The highest arch was so distant that it looked like the entrance to a doocot; the highest ledge was so far away that the dragon on it looked like a jewelled beetle.

Helen couldn't see any stairs, no way to get higher than the floor without flying. That was probably why the dragons had nailed their treasure to the walls. Cups, swords, shields and crowns were glittering in the light of the flaming torches hanging around the hall. No thieving human could reach this treasure.

Jewel roared. Helen looked down from the dragons watching and the gold shining, and saw the white dragon staring at her.

Not wanting to show too much interest in the treasure, Helen glanced at the floor. The dragons were flying creatures and lived on the walls, so there was nothing on the stone floor but a layer of dust and a huge pile of grey rocks at the far end of the hall.

Now that her blindfold was off, Lavender hovered in front of Helen. "Jewel will ask the second riddle."

Sylvie muttered, "I don't see why we should pay any attention to a dragon who's scared of aeroplanes."

Jewel laughed and spat a ball of fire over the wolf-girl's head.

Lavender murmured, "Apparently that was a ruse and we fell for it, just like the buckle fell."

"I'm ready for the next riddle," Helen said hastily, to stop Sylvie making more unwise comments.

Lavender translated, as Jewel grunted. "The second riddle,

We hope it lies behind most of our words,
But it never lies.

It is as sharp as a sword between friends,
Yet friendship is meaningless without it.

Helen glanced at Lee. He raised an eyebrow at her. She smiled and said, "The truth."

Jewel nodded and called again. "Now we can see the Great Dragon," Lavender explained.

Helen wondered which of the magnificent dragons above her was the ancient ancestor dragon.

But the floor rumbled, as the rocky grey pile at the end of the great hall stood up and thumped towards them.

It was a massive dragon. Bigger than a house. Bigger than the hill Helen had climbed with Lee. A knobbly crusty ancient dragon, with bright red eyes.

The Great Dragon roared.

"The third riddle is for us to hear her," called Lavender.

The dragon shook her wide grey head and grunted.

"No, the third riddle is for *Helen* to hear her."

"I can hear her now," Helen muttered. "She's pretty loud."

"And so," Lavender went on, "Helen must answer this herself."

"We've already done that," Helen said clearly. "Lavender will translate and I'll answer."

The Great Dragon stomped closer and roared again.

"Oh!" Lavender sounded surprised. "We all have to go. We have to leave Helen here on her own."

At one huge rumbling roar from the Great Dragon, all the other dragons flapped off their ledges and glided out through the arches.

The dragon stepped right up to the fabled beasts and growled.

Lavender's voice wobbled as she said, "The Great Dragon wants us to leave now. She wishes to speak to the human girl alone."

"We can't leave," said Rona, "because Helen won't understand the Great Dragon on her own."

"We can't leave," said Lee, "because Helen won't be safe on her own."

The Great Dragon growled again.

Lee drew his sword. He stepped forward to stand between Helen and the Great Dragon. He was joined by Catesby flying above him, Tangaroa gripping his three-pronged spear, and Sylvie flickering into a wolf and crouching low.

The dragon rumbled.

Lavender flew to Helen and hid behind her head. "She's not happy. She wants us to leave you alone."

Lee said, "We will not leave her unprotected."

Another roar. Lavender whispered, "Then she says we will not get the answers we seek."

Helen pushed her way gently between Lee and Tangaroa. "Thanks for defending me. But she won't help us if you threaten her. The Great Dragon isn't our enemy. Please don't turn her into one. So thanks, but leave me."

The others stepped back, but Lee stepped forward to the huge dragon's head.

Then the faery seemed to change shape. Helen could only see his back, not his face, but she thought he was growing taller and that the glamour of his shiny boots and glowing cloak was changing to something darker, almost scaly.

He spoke in a voice she couldn't understand. He

screamed something harsh at the Great Dragon and the dragon roared back.

He spoke again, looming a metre taller than normal, his shoulders hunched but also higher, his back bent. The dragon growled and sooty smoke belched out of her nostrils.

Lee turned round, suddenly his usual height again, with a smooth face and soft bright clothes. He nodded to Helen, sheathed his sword and led the others out, by the nearest ground-level arch, without saying a word.

Rona hesitated at the arch. "I could stay with you, Helen," she called back. "I didn't bring any weapons. I'm not threatening anyone."

Helen knew it was harder for Rona to be brave than it was for Lee or the other trained fighters, so it meant even more. "I'll be fine. Please go. I'll see you soon."

Helen turned round. The Great Dragon was shifting her landscape-sized body, swinging her tail like a giant cat, staring at Helen with huge red eyes.

Helen was tempted to run after her friends.

She had no chance of answering the third riddle correctly. How could she, when she wouldn't understand the question? Riddles were hard enough when they were asked in English.

The Great Dragon grunted. A low resonating questioning grunt.

Helen knelt down, partly to show respect for this ancient dragon, partly because her legs were shaking.

The Great Dragon repeated the question impatiently.

And Helen knew that if she gave the wrong answer, she would be this dragon's next meal.

Chapter 22

Helen gave the only answer she could to the Great Dragon's riddle. "I don't know what your question is, Great Dragon, so instead, let me introduce myself. I'm Helen Strang, I'm a bard and a healer, and I'm not here to answer questions. I'm here to ask them. I'm here to save the life of my friend Yann."

The Great Dragon bent down and breathed on her. Helen wrapped her arms around her head and watched sparks bounce off the stone floor, wondering if she was being toasted before being eaten.

The dragon roared so loudly that the ground shook and Helen was deafened. But when her ears cleared, she could hear a voice. "Can you understand me, soft-bodied child?"

She still heard roaring, deep and rumbling, but

she also heard clear words behind the roar. It was like hearing an extra note in the octave or seeing a new colour in the rainbow.

Helen nodded and looked up, to see the dragon move her lips and grunt gently. Again Helen understood, as the dragon said, "Good. The delay and imprecision of translators annoys me. This is a temporary ability, for my convenience, not a permanent gift. Your ears will be deaf to fabled beasts again once you leave my hall.

"But I am intrigued by your response to my riddle. Could you already hear me? Did you understand my question?"

Helen shook her head.

"Interesting. You answered perfectly. I asked the hardest riddle of all: who you truly are. You answered well. You know who and what you are, and you are clear about your purpose here. Such self-knowledge is rare. I hope for the same clarity when you speak to me. You may begin."

Helen spoke in a voice which sounded pathetically small after that huge dragon roar. "I've answered three riddles, Great Dragon, so I believe I have a right to three questions in return."

The dragon nodded. "But only three, child. I shall be counting." She tapped her spear-length claws three times on the floor.

"First I want to ask why dragons have prevented us collecting the tokens which could save the life of our friend the centaur."

The dragon tapped once. "That is one. Now ask the other two."

"I'd rather hear the first answer before I frame the

other questions, Great Dragon." Helen bowed her head politely.

"The wisdom of a bard," snorted the dragon. "I shall answer your first question. Two of my older warriors and a few of my young pupils have indeed prevented you getting the tokens, with sentry duty, ruses, nets and flames, because those tokens are being sought for a darker purpose than saving your friend.

"The Master of the Maze is using you. He needs your naïvety, your innocence and your love for your friend, because the tokens will not reveal themselves to those with evil intent. But once your good intentions have freed the tokens, he will take them from your soft weak hands and use them to build his own strength.

"So we cannot let you have them. I have no enmity towards this son of the centaurs. I do not particularly wish to see him die, but I cannot allow you to have the tokens which would save him."

Helen bit her lip as she tried to think of a way to argue against that rock-solid refusal.

"I see you doubt me, child," said the dragon. "But this is how evil works, turning goodness to its own ends."

Helen needed to find out more, but she wanted to save her second and third questions. She spoke carefully, not raising the tone of her voice at the end of the sentence, so she wasn't asking a question. "The Master wants the tokens to heal his blind eye."

"He wants his eye healed," agreed the dragon, "but he has also been promised that if he uses a healing token at the equinox, the sight in that eye will become greater than ever."

Helen didn't ask. She just waited patiently.

The dragon smiled, which was not reassuring, because her mouth was filled with long cracked teeth. "Wise and patient child! The healing would give him the power to see not just light and dark, but to see the weakness in everyone. Then he could target hidden weaknesses, secret weaknesses, weaknesses not yet known to those who believe themselves strong.

"We cannot risk that. I have watched many conflicts on this land and I do not usually interfere. I let the soft-bodied short-lived beasts fight it out, because the results of your wars are not important to those of us who take the long view. But this creature from the underground maze has a darkness and ambition that is unusual even in his kind. With this ability to see weakness, he would become too powerful. He might even threaten those of us who are usually above all conflict. I do not take sides unless I need to, but I must prevent this healing."

Helen said slowly, "The Master I've met is strong, but he doesn't have magic. He couldn't use the tokens to heal himself."

"He does not need to heal himself. He has the Three to do it for him."

"But the Three are going to heal Yann! How..." Helen stopped herself before that became a question.

The dragon laughed. "The Three do not usually take sides either. They enjoy injuries, suffering and blood. That's why they are healers, to spend time at the bedsides of those in pain. They are especially keen to heal warriors and monsters, those who inflict more wounds for them to heal. The Master is using you to get the token for himself, but the Three are using all of you. They will heal the Master, hoping he will cause more chaos. It is interesting that they are also keen to heal your friend. Perhaps you should question whether the world is a better place with him, or without him."

Helen stood up. "The world is definitely a better place with Yann."

"But it is a much better place without the Master seeing all our weaknesses."

"So you would sacrifice Yann to stop the Master." Again, a statement, not a question.

"Yes. The horse-boy means little to me or my people. He means little to the world. The Master is a real danger. It is necessary to sacrifice one to stop the other."

Helen swallowed her anger. Arguing with this dragon wouldn't help Yann; she had to offer solutions. "If you don't want the Master to see everyone's weaknesses, yours included, then let us heal Yann. Because Yann could stop him."

The dragon snorted. "The child centaur could stop the Master?"

"Yes. That's why the Master injured him. He's afraid of Yann's strength, his bravery, his skills. The Master could have injured any one of us, and the rest of us would have searched for the tokens he wants, to heal our friend."

The dragon nodded. "That is your weakness. I don't need magical vision to see that. Your weakness is that you can't bear to see your friends hurt."

"That's not a weakness," said Helen. "That's a strength."

She kept building her case for saving Yann. "Even though Yann would have been the best one to lead the quests, the Master didn't injure me or Catesby or Lavender or Rona. He injured Yann, because he's afraid Yann could defeat him. He's trying to get rid of a serious opponent and get his healing at the same time. It makes sense, doesn't..." She paused before that became a question.

"So if we heal Yann, he can stop the Master, which will end the problem permanently, unlike your plan. There must be other healing tokens in other places, and other good people the Master can force to collect them. It's not enough to deny him this last Scottish token. We should stop him completely. Send him back to his maze."

"Go on," said the dragon.

"So my second question is this: will you please ask your dragons to stop hindering us in our search for the tokens?"

The Great Dragon clicked her claws once more, and shook her head. "If I call off Jewel, Crag and the others, then the Master will seize the token from you, the moment you have it. That's the flaw in your argument. The Master won't permit you to heal your friend if he is afraid of him. If you collect a token, you are helping the minotaur, not the centaur."

"Not necessarily," said Helen. "Yann is our strength and our bravery, but my other friends have skills and experience too. Lee is his king's champion." The dragon huffed a noise which even Helen's new hearing didn't understand, so she kept talking. "Lavender has great wisdom, Sylvie already leads a pack, Tangaroa is the best rhyme gatherer among the blue men of the Minch, Rona is a true Storm Singer and Catesby is the one who blinded the Master a year ago.

"All my friends have talents. That's why the Master chose us to get these tokens for him. Now that we know what he wants, we won't be easily fooled or overcome. But we can't fight him *and* your dragons. I'm not asking you to help us. I'm just asking you not to hinder us. And if you leave us alone, I promise the Master won't get the token from us."

The Great Dragon stared at her. "You genuinely believe you can better the Master?"

Helen said confidently, "We've done it before."

"But you don't understand what he is capable of. You are too young and naïve to understand the depths of darkness in the world."

"I'd rather be young and naïve, than too old and cynical to remember why good should stand against evil."

The dragon roared so loud that echoes crashed back down from the domed ceiling hundreds of metres above. "You dare speak to me like that?"

Helen looked steadily into the fiery red eyes.

"You do dare! Perhaps that's a good sign. If you can speak to me like that, perhaps you can challenge the Master."

The Great Dragon stretched, her massive scales rattling like a rockfall. Then she nodded. "I want a guarantee from you. If I ask my dragons not to hinder you, I want your personal guarantee that you will destroy the final token rather than let the Master take it. You must not let him have it, even if that means denying it to your friend.

"As with any guarantee, there must be a penalty. A penalty that you must pay if the Master does gain the token, gain his healing and gain his power. Because of an arrangement I've made with your over-confident faery friend, it is not *your* life that will be forfeit. It is the life of one of your friends. The flower fairy, the selkie, the wolf, the blue loon or the phoenix. If you let the Master enhance his sight, I will eat one of those fabled beasts for breakfast tomorrow. Do you understand?"

Helen didn't answer. She couldn't answer.

"Are you prepared to risk their lives on the bet that your centaur is worth saving? On your faith that you have a team which can outwit the Master?"

Helen knew that every one of her friends would risk their life for Yann in the heat of a fight. But could she make a cold-blooded promise of deliberate sacrifice on their behalf?

If she left without persuading the Great Dragon to call off her pupils, Yann would die. She couldn't do that to him, and she didn't think her friends would want her to.

So Helen nodded.

Then, her mind on whether she should tell her friends exactly what she had just agreed, or not quite lie by not quite telling them everything, she said, "May I ask my final question now?"

Helen suddenly realised she'd asked a third question. She hoped the dragon hadn't noticed, then saw the long claw click down.

"Yes. You may. And you just have!" The dragon laughed. "You may ask me another question, but I do not have to answer it, because I have already answered three questions. Foolish child, letting your emotions overcome your caution."

Helen said quickly, "I'll answer another riddle to get another question."

"No, there are only ever three riddles. But do tell me, just out of interest, what else you wanted to ask me. I will listen, but I probably won't answer. Not unless I feel the answer will help, when I take the long view." The Great Dragon smiled.

Helen tried to be polite, though she was angry with herself and with this obstructive, self-satisfied creature. "With your long knowledge of this land, Great Dragon, I wondered if you know where we can find the footprint of a king?"

"What a shame, child. I do know where that footprint is, but I have no obligation to tell you. So, you can try to save your friend and we will not hinder you. But you have only this one afternoon to find the footprint, so I'm confident that the world is safe from the minotaur and that you will have to get used to the loss of your friend. Goodbye."

Helen hesitated. The dragon lifted one massive foot, pointed to the exit, then roared.

Helen couldn't hear any words in the rattling roar. She could no longer understand the dragon's speech. Their conversation was over.

She bowed and walked towards the arch where she had last seen her friends.

She knew the clever red eyes of the Great Dragon were watching her, so she walked with her back straight and her steps steady.

She was leaving with what she'd come for: the dragons wouldn't interfere with the final quest. But she hadn't got the information she needed: she had no idea where to get the final healing token. And she'd promised the life of one of her friends to the Great Dragon if the Master won the token.

After what felt like a very long walk, she stepped into a smaller hall with blurred daylight coming through arches at the other end.

Her friends were there, but so were Jewel and two other young dragons. The white dragon and the green dragons were prodding Sapphire's bandage. Helen didn't have to hear their words to know they were being rude about her short tail.

"What happened?" Lavender asked.

Rona said, "What happened is that Helen's still alive. She can tell us everything else when we're safely away. Sapphire, don't listen to them. They don't know whether tails grow back, they're just tormenting you. Let's get out of here. Up on Sapphire, everyone, then blindfold the person in front of you."

Helen clambered up behind Sylvie. As she tied a blue scarf round the wolf-girl's face, she heard Lee behind her. "Is a red scarf alright for you, Helen? Your cheeks are so pale after your chat with the dragon, I'm not sure bright colours will suit you."

"Don't be daft," she answered. "Any colour will do."

As the faery wrapped the cool silk round her face and pulled it tight, Helen whispered, "Lee, what did you say to the Great Dragon?"

"I told her you were under my protection. I said you were my bard and therefore valuable to me, so if she harmed your fingers or your ears or your ability to play music for my people, then I would hunt her down with all the pent-up power of the faery army."

"Did she believe you?" Helen asked from the darkness of the blindfold.

"She didn't eat you."

"But Lee, can you order the whole faery army to fight for you?"

"Not yet. But perhaps I will eventually. In the Great Dragon's long view, 'eventually' is the blink of an eye. She wouldn't risk me taking revenge even in hundreds of your years' time."

Rona called from the end of the line on dragonback, "We're all blindfolded, Sapphire, you can go."

As Helen felt the dragon lurch upwards, she asked, slightly louder, "So Lee, if it would help Yann, could you threaten the Master in the same way?"

"No, the minotaur is working to a mortal timetable. He wants power now, and I don't yet have the power to oppose him."

Helen nodded. But she still had more questions. "When you spoke to the dragon, did you turn into something else?"

Lee laughed. "My glamour works on different beings in different ways. For you, I glamour a human boy, which is almost the same as my own true form. For a dragon, I glamour something else. Something she can understand. Something she has reason to fear."

"That Great Dragon was afraid of you?"

"Of course," Lee said calmly. And Helen wondered whether she should be grateful for, or wary of, the faery's protection.

Chapter 23

It wasn't possible to talk to everyone on Sapphire's back as they flew away from the Great Hall through cold wet clouds, so Helen stayed quiet during the flight.

When the dragon landed at Cauldhame Moor, they pulled off their blindfolds and leapt down, then all turned to look at Helen.

She took a deep breath. "The good news is that the dragons won't get in our way again. I persuaded the Great Dragon to call off Crag, Jewel and the rest. The bad news is more complicated..."

Helen paused. On the flight, she'd decided not to tell her friends all the bad news. She didn't want to admit that one of them might be eaten for breakfast tomorrow if they let the Master get a token, because she didn't think that knowing the danger they were in would help anyone save Yann.

"The bad news is I know why Yann was injured. The Master injured Yann so that we would search for the tokens. Presumably, if Yann had agreed to work for him, the Master would have asked Yann to find the tokens. But when Yann refused, the Master injured him so we would collect them."

Lavender shook her head. "No, he must have intended to injure Yann all along, because the healing tokens wouldn't give themselves to someone working to help evil."

Lee nodded. "I thought that injury was too perfect. So it was a trap to injure Yann, to force us to do the Master's bidding." He frowned. "I don't like being manipulated."

Sylvie muttered, "You manipulate everyone else..."

Helen broke in before the wolf-girl and the faery, who had a temporary truce rather than a friendship, started to argue. "I also discovered that the Three are playing both sides. They're happy to heal Yann *and* the Master, hoping both of them will cause more injuries and pain. But there's worse news than that. The Master doesn't just want to heal the blind eye and scars you gave him, Catesby. With the Three's help at the equinox, a healing token can give him the power to see everyone's weaknesses."

Her friends looked concerned, even frightened. They understood how dangerous that power could be.

"So we *can't* let him get the token. Agreed?"

She looked round at everyone whose life had been threatened by the Great Dragon. No one disagreed.

Helen sighed, then kept talking to cover her relief. "The other bad news is that I'd planned to ask about the king's footprint, but I made a mess of the last question, so the Great Dragon didn't tell me where it is. However she did confirm it exists." Helen looked up at the sun, already well past noon. "We only have a few hours left. And we still don't know where the king's footprint is..."

"Yes, we do," said Lee. "I've studied places and objects which confer royal power. Long ago the Kings of Dalriada were crowned by standing in a carved stone footprint in Argyll. The new king placed his foot in the carving to connect with the land. Perhaps that connection to the land's power gives the footprint healing force too."

"Where is it?" Helen asked.

"On Dunadd, a hill fort in Kilmartin." Lee grinned.

Helen smiled back. "Excellent! But why didn't you tell us this yesterday?"

"Lavender was right, with no rain it was an unnecessary distraction. But we flew through rain clouds on the way here, so now the footprint might contain genuine rainwater."

"Let's go to Argyll then," said Tangaroa, clambering up Sapphire, his blue skin almost camouflaged against her scales.

"But there's no point getting a fourth token," Rona said, "because the Master's minions will just take it. It's impossible to get a token to Yann if the Master wants it first."

"Of course it's possible," said Helen. "We just need something else to give the Master. It doesn't have to be the true token he takes. What would we put the water in?"

"A small glass vial," said Lavender.

Lee smiled. "I'll see what Mallow has in her kitchen. But I think you want me to get more than one vial, don't you, Helen?"

"Yes. We'll take one empty vial and one filled with fountain water."

So, ten minutes later, with a half-discussed plan, and a full vial of water hidden in Lee's cloak, they flew to Dunadd.

They passed through a band of rain on the way, which Tangaroa confirmed was moving east from Argyll. When they landed on the almost flat summit of Dunadd, it was no longer raining, but the ground was wet and low cloud clung to the hill.

"This weather should keep human tourists away," Helen said, as they all slid down.

"We don't need long," said Sylvie. "Let's get the token and go." She flickered into her wolf form.

"Not so fast," said Tangaroa. "We can't be sure we're here alone."

"And the footprint won't be easy to find." Rona peered through the mist.

Lee said, "I think it's just down the slope to the northeast. But Tangaroa's right, we must be careful."

Helen nodded. "The Three must have told the Master where the tokens are, so his goats might already be here." She was whispering, as they huddled together near Sapphire's head.

Lee drew his sword. "We don't have time for debate. I'm my king's champion and a senior officer in his army. Many of you are skilled hunters, but I'm the only soldier here." He spoke brusquely, as if he was giving orders to troops. "You will all do as I say, so we can get away as fast as possible."

Sylvie growled, but Helen said, "Let Lee suggest his plan, Sylvie, and unless you see any flaws, let's just do it. We don't have time to argue. Yann doesn't have time."

The wolf nodded.

So Lee stood in front of them, back straight, sword in hand, speaking clearly and sharply. "The dragon will remain here, as there is no room down by the footprint. Helen will fill the vial and I will go with her to watch her back."

Sylvie snarled something sarcastic, which no one translated for Helen. Lee raised his eyebrows at the wolf and repeated, "I'll watch her back and you will all cover our exit route. If our enemies are planning an ambush, it will be *after* we have the token. Therefore I will station each of you at a different section of the path from the footprint back to the dragon and you will stand sentry. Once we have the vial, you will cover our exit, follow us back up to the dragon, then we will all leave. Understood?"

Almost everyone nodded.

"But what if the Master attacks the sentries first...?" Tangaora said slowly.

Lee flicked his cloak, which was suddenly a duller green, almost khaki. "Trust me. I'm trained in defensive tactics. Are you all ready?"

This time everyone nodded.

Lee stationed Sapphire at the far edge of the plateau, looking southeast, and Catesby behind her looking northwest. He placed Lavender and Sylvie near the centre of the plateau, and Rona and Tangaroa at the northeast, beside a curved wall of ancient stones.

Then he led Helen down the steep slippy path off the summit. As they walked carefully through the soft grey mist, she said, "The sentries won't be able to see a thing."

"They'll see a minotaur right in front of them, if he's here."

"And what can they do if he is here?"

"Don't worry, Helen. Do your job; let the sentries do theirs. And that looks like your job."

Lee pointed at a flat grey rock with a geometrical pattern scored across it. As Helen got closer she realised the straight lines were natural cracks, framing a deep footprint carved at the front of the rock. A right footprint, pointing off the hill towards the misty expanse of Scotland below.

Lee said, "That must be it. The footprint of Scotland's earliest kings."

Helen knelt down on the slippery wet rock. There wasn't as much rainwater in the footprint as she'd hoped.

As she pulled the empty vial from her pocket, she heard a squawk from Catesby.

She looked towards the summit, hidden in mist, then turned to Lee. "What did he say?"

Lee said sharply, "Just a sentry checking in. All clear. Get the water."

Helen eased the cork out of the vial and lowered the glass vessel into the thin layer of water. She chased the water around the footprint, looking for tiny dips in the stone, catching as much liquid as she could.

She was aware of the cloud getting heavier and darker, of cold silence all around her. Soon she was spilling as much from the vial as she was collecting, so she lifted the vial up and waggled it. It was half full. That would have to do.

As she pushed the cork back, Lee whispered, "I'm going to help you up. When I grab your hand, I'll swap the vials. Don't react, in case we're being watched."

"But then you'll have the true token," she whispered, not looking at him, still fiddling with the vial.

"Yes. Can you trust me with it?"

Helen looked up at him. This Lee wasn't a smiling, colourful, music-loving faery. He was a hard-faced soldier. His clothes looked darker, more severe, more military, and his voice had been harsher since they landed. Helen hardly knew this Lee.

"I trust you to get your job done. I'm just not sure what your job is."

"Today, my job is saving Yann. So do as I ask."

She held her hand out to him. He put his sword in its scabbard, took her hand and pulled her up. She felt the vial in her fingers roll away and another take its place. Then he let her go.

"I heard something," Lee said suddenly. "Look north, check there's no one at the foot of the hill. I'll look south, then we can get back to the dragon."

Helen stepped to the north and looked into the mist, but she couldn't see anything, so she turned back.

Lee hadn't moved south. He was still at the rock, kneeling down, his cloak covering the footprint.

"Lee, what are you doing?"

He frowned at her, then stood up and carefully placed his right foot in the dry footprint. He put his weight on the foot, gazed into the mist, then stepped away.

Helen gasped. "The king's footprint! Lee, is *that* your ambition?"

"Ask me later. Let's get the token to Yann."

So Helen walked with the faery warrior towards the summit of Dunadd. When they were nearly at the top of the path, Helen looked up at the curved wall. The selkie and blue loon weren't there.

Lee put his hand on her elbow. "Keep walking." He pushed her forward.

She shook her head. "Where are they?"

A deep voice called out from the summit. "I have your selkie, human girl. I have all your friends, wrapped up like presents. Unless you want me to skin the wolf or boil off the seal's blubber, come up now."

Helen heard a noise behind her and glanced back to see a line of fauns blocking the path.

"Come up *now!*" boomed the voice.

Lee said quietly, "It's fine. We knew this might happen. We're prepared for this." He said even quieter, "You have the dummy vial. Give it to him, but be reluctant."

Helen shook his hand off her elbow and ran the last few steps up the hill.

The mist was thinning and when she reached the east side of the plateau, she could see the minotaur standing in the middle. Black wiry hair on his bare chest, black leather trousers on his wide legs and a black-handled axe in his hands.

And she could see her friends. Rona and Tangaroa standing still, with swords at their throats and wound all round with glossy brown rope. Sylvie lying on the ground, her back to Helen, covered from muzzle to tail with the same smooth rope. Catesby and Lavender, unbound, sitting on the grass, and Sapphire crouched down with a rope round her snout.

"Helen Strang," rasped the Master, his human voice straining to get past his bull's throat. "Thank you for collecting my token. Though I had hoped for one earlier. Perhaps you aren't as efficient without the horse-boy.

"Your winged friends agreed to stay still and silent to save your other friends from the blades of my minions." He nodded to Frass, the tallest faun, who lifted his sword closer to Tangaroa's neck. The blue loon's face was pale under his swirling tattoos and he was looking straight ahead, not down at the blade under his chin.

"As your friends are being so obliging, human child, I'm sure you will oblige me too. Give me the token."

"No," said Helen. "I won't give you anything."

"Don't you believe I will hurt your friends? Show her the wolf."

A smaller faun rolled Sylvie over with a cloven hoof, and Helen saw blood dripping from the wolf's jaws.

The Master smiled. "You've already collected the token, so I can leave this old fort stained with blood if I have to."

Helen wanted to refuse, to argue, to fight. But there was no point risking their lives for water from a fountain, so she let her shoulders droop. Then she remembered Lee's advice to be reluctant. "How do I know you won't kill us once you have the token?"

"Because I might need you again, my clever little questors. I'd rather leave you alive and in awe of my power than dead and useless. Give me the token, child, and I will give you back your lives. For now."

He stepped towards her.

"But what about Yann? If I give you the token, Yann will die!" She put a note of panic in her voice, even though she knew the real token was safe in Lee's cloak.

The Master laughed. "You can't save the centaur. But you can save the wolf, the seal and the others. Give it to me now."

He stepped closer.

Helen opened her hand and looked at the vial. She held it out to the minotaur and he snatched it.

"Thank you, human girl."

"Now let us go."

"Not yet. I've been tricked by you before, and I will not underestimate you again. Frass?"

"Yes, Master," the tallest faun answered.

"Is your uncle awake, or is he dozing again?"

"Don't be so impertinent, young bullhead," said a frail voice. "I am here, and I am ready to work." A hunched-over faun appeared from behind the curving stones of the old hill fort. He had a lined face, grey goat legs and a leather bag over his shoulder. "Where is that token you want me to test?"

He hobbled up to the minotaur and took the vial.

Helen heard Lee whisper, behind her, in a worried tone, "He brought a magic tester..."

The minotaur nodded to his minions. "Hold them, until we see whether this child has been honest with me."

One faun grabbed Helen's shoulders and pulled her away from Lee, and two uruisks leapt at the faery.

Lee flicked his sword out and up at the face of the nearest uruisk, who brought a mace straight down towards Lee's sword arm, but the faery spun out of the way and knocked the mace out of the goat's claws with one slash.

The faery moved to the middle of the plateau, sword out in front, feet moving, circling round. "No one lays a hand on me!"

"Calm down, faery boy," chuckled the Master. "I don't need to lay a hand on you. Put down the sword, or I will have my goats use their swords, not on you, but on your friends. If this token is all you say it is, you have nothing to fear."

Lee glanced at Helen, and she thought she saw him wink, then he laid his sword on the ground.

They all watched as the elderly faun put his hand in the satchel and pulled something out.

He held it up. A mouse. A small brown mouse, dangling limply from his fingers by its tail.

"Here's one I injured earlier. A field mouse. Unconscious, with a broken leg. It's probably almost suffocated in my bag too, poor wee thing," he said cheerfully. "Let's see if this water heals the mouse."

He pulled the cork out with his teeth, tipped the vial up and let one drop fall onto the mouse's fur.

Nothing happened.

The mouse still swung, nose down, from his hand.

The faun looked at the Master. "This water has no power at all, except the power to fool the unwary. These children have tried to trick you."

Chapter 24

At a growled signal from the Master, the faun gripping Helen flung his arm round her throat, so her chin was forced up and she could hardly breathe.

She strained to look round. Lavender was caught in a faun's hand. Catesby was clutched to an uruisk's chest. Rona and Tangaroa were held by two fauns each, swords at their throats. An uruisk was pointing a sword at Sapphire's eye. Sylvie was struggling against the rope.

The Master said, very softly, "Everyone stay still."

Helen twisted round to look at the minotaur. He was standing to her right, his double-bladed axe held high above her head.

"Everyone stay still and no one will get hurt."

Where was Lee? Helen moved her head slowly. The faery was in the middle of the plateau, both arms held firmly by uruisks. He looked furious, but he was standing very still.

The Master whispered, "You thought you could fool me, Helen Strang. You thought you could give me puddle-water. But I'm not stupid. I'm not naïve and trusting like you. I was prepared for tricks.

"Now I have you under my blade. You will be the first human I control, but not the last. When I have the power to see all weakness, I will use it first to defeat the fabled beasts, but then I will turn my new eye to your people. The modern human world seems so strong, but it must have weaknesses. I will find those weaknesses and use them to rip your world apart, girl.

"So I need that token. I know you have it; my fauns watched you get it. So give me it now, or I will let this fall..." He let the axe drop a centimetre.

Helen stared up at the shining metal arc. "No. I will not give it to you. Not if you plan to rip the world apart with it."

She wished she still had the vial, so she could pour it out, or drink it, or stomp it into the ground.

But Lee had the vial. And he wouldn't give it to the Master either.

So she said again, "I won't give you anything, you selfish, greedy..." The faun behind her shifted his arm up and put his hand over her mouth.

The minotaur laughed. "Silly little girl. If you refuse and I swing this axe, then once you're dead, I'll search your pockets and I'll find the token. That would be a pointless way to die, wouldn't it? So give me the token!"

"She doesn't have it," said a calm voice.

Helen looked round.

Lee repeated, "She doesn't have it. I do. There's no need to threaten her, because it is not her decision. It's mine."

"Then give it to me," growled the Master.

"Why would I do that?"

"Why would you indeed? I'm not inclined to trust the word of a faery. I'm surprised these fabled beasts do. But you can trust my word. If you give me the token and it proves to be true magic, then I will let all of you go, unharmed. All of you, including this human child whose music you value so much." The Minotaur grinned. "I know the weakness of your kind already." He let the axe slip closer to Helen's scalp.

"Don't damage her!" Lee yelled.

Helen was panicking. If Lee gave the Master the token, not only would Yann die, but she would lose another friend to the old jaws of the Great Dragon.

Helen tried to pull away from the faun behind her, but he was holding her too tightly. So she bit his sweaty fingers and he let go long enough for her to scream, "*No!* Lee! This isn't just about..." then the faun gagged her again.

Lee looked at her. "I know it's not just about Yann. It's about other lives too."

She nodded frantically, hoping he would see the desperation in her eyes, hoping he would see how important it was not to give the vial to the Master.

But Lee just stared at her, his face cold and still. "Don't struggle, Helen. Don't fight it. I can't let this monster kill what I'm planning to steal, can I?" He turned to the minotaur. "Get these animals off me."

The Master nodded and the uruisks let the faery go.

Lee smoothed his shirt and tidied his hair. Then he put his hand inside his cloak and, with a flourish, pulled out the vial.

Helen felt tears at the back of her eyes. Yann's heart would fail. Rona or Lavender or Sylvie or Catesby or Tangaroa would be eaten. Then the Master would take over the world. All because that stupid faery liked the way she played the fiddle.

She watched as the faery and the minotaur walked towards each other.

She watched as the faery's pale hand dropped the vial into the Master's hairy hand.

She watched as the old faun limped forward and took the vial.

She watched as he let a glistening drop fall onto the mouse's fur.

And she watched as the mouse wriggled, fell to the grass and scurried away.

She couldn't even feel happy for the mouse.

She could barely stay on her feet. When the faun let go, she fell to her hands and knees.

She heard the Master say, "Thank you, dear children, for fetching this healing token for me. Now go home and watch your friend die. I will summon you next time I need you. And you will do my bidding again or I will kill another of you."

Helen crouched on the damp grass, as hooves and feet thundered away, wondering who would be left alive for the Master to threaten once the Great Dragon had finished with them.

Then she realised she had to untie her friends, but when she sat up she saw the ropes slithering off the selkie, the blue loon, the wolf and the dragon. The ropes had become snakes, which were sliding swiftly into the long grass.

Helen hoped the mouse had kept running, then said, "Is that how they trapped you all so fast and quietly?"

Tangaroa nodded and said hoarsely, "So much for your defensive tactics, soldier!"

"No," Lee said. "Not here, not now." He pointed to a sharp cut end of brown rope, still visible at the edge of the plateau. "I'm not sure if those are snakes turned into ropes, or ropes turned into snakes, but I don't want them listening to us and telling tales to their Master. The footprint is empty, there's no reason to stay. We have to get off this hill."

"Yes." Helen stood up. "We have to chase them, get the token back."

"Don't talk here," Lee said again. "Get on the dragon."

He picked up his sword.

"He's right," said Rona. "He's a useless tricky unreliable faery, but he's right. We can't stay here. Sylvie's bleeding and we have to get away from the Master's spies."

They climbed onto Sapphire in shocked silence and flew away from Dunadd.

Sapphire landed five minutes later on a higher hilltop. Helen slid off, grabbing Sapphire's leathery wing to help her down, because her legs were still wobbly.

Once they were all on the ground, Lee backed away a few steps, followed by the others in an angry group: Tangaroa throwing his spear from one hand to the other; Sylvie snarling, blood staining her fur and teeth.

Lee straightened his bright green cloak and flicked his sword-point from side to side. "I just saved your lives. Why do you look so annoyed?" He grinned.

Lavender spoke for all of them. "Because you've killed Yann! And you've given the Master the power to take over the world."

Helen said soothingly, "Lee has some explaining to do and so do I, but let's not fight. Please. Sylvie is bleeding."

"I'm not fighting," said Tangaroa, banging the butt of his spear on the ground. "Not yet. I'm just asking questions. Before we ask why you caved in to the Master so fast, you need to explain your tactics, faery. You lined us up for him to attack."

As Helen knelt by Sylvie to find the source of the blood, Tangaroa's soft Hebridean voice rose. "Didn't you even consider there might be a trap?"

"Of course I did," Lee said calmly. "I knew there would be a trap. My job was to arrange you far enough apart that he could take you all out easily, with as few injuries as possible."

"You *knew* there would be a trap? You *expected* it?"

"Yes. The Master knew where we were going, so of course he was waiting for us. We had to give him the dummy vial at some point. I thought it was wiser to give him it at Dunadd than have him chase us back to Cauldhame Moor."

"You set us up?" Rona said quietly.

Lee smiled. "I was surprised you all agreed so readily, but yes, I set you up. I assumed that he would immobilise you all, block our way back to the dragon and demand the token in exchange for your lives. And it worked. Exactly as I intended."

"No, it didn't," said Helen, "not if you were aiming for as few injuries as possible. Look at Sylvie."

Sylvie growled, blood flecks spitting out of her mouth.

"Sorry about that, dear wolf, but I suspect you resisted when it was already too late, didn't you?"

"She bit the rope and it bit her back," explained Rona.

As Catesby began to squawk angrily at Lee, Helen examined the wolf's muzzle. Her lips and nose weren't cut. Where was the blood coming from?

Lee was saying, "Yes, of course I heard you on the hill, my feathered friend. I knew it was a warning, but I had to let Helen fill the vial, so..."

Catesby screamed at the faery, but Helen interrupted, "When Catesby called out at Dunadd, was that a warning? You said it was fine. You lied to me!"

Lee nodded. "Yes. Because we needed to collect the token first."

Helen shook her head in exasperation, then turned back to the wolf. "Did the rope turn into a snake when you bit it?"

Sylvie nodded.

"Did it bite you *inside* your mouth?"

Sylvie nodded again.

"Open up, then." Helen wasn't keen to put her fingers in the wolf's mouth, past the long teeth and the saliva, but she could see blood welling from Sylvie's tongue. "You have puncture wounds in your tongue. Was the snake poisonous?"

As Catesby screeched at Lee, Helen looked up at Lavender. "Were the snakes poisonous, do you think?"

Lavender shook her head. "I don't think so. One of them bit a faun when he put his sword too close to the rope round Rona's throat, and the faun just laughed. She'll be fine if you can stop the bleeding."

Helen opened her rucksack to get wipes and swabs, and explained quietly to Sylvie that she didn't need to sew the wounds in her tongue, just slow the bleeding. As she cleaned Sylvie's fur and checked for any other wounds, she could hear Sapphire snarling at Lee and Catesby squawking at him. It was frustrating that she couldn't follow what was going on. She tried to hear the extra note in the octave she'd heard in the Great Dragon's roars, but she couldn't concentrate, not with the blood on her fingers, the anger in the air.

She glanced up. Lee was standing, his back to a rock, his sword at waist-height, not aiming at anyone, just creating a space in front of him. Everyone was yelling at him.

Helen said, "Could you all stop shouting! I need to calm Sylvie down. My mum once treated an Alsatian with an injured tongue, and she slowed the blood flow to the wound by calming and cooling the patient. So if we could all stop yelling and if someone could fetch me cold water..."

"You need water?" Lee said. "What about this?"

He opened his left hand. He was holding a small glass vial.

A vial, half-filled with water.

Everyone was silent, staring at the faery.

Then Helen said slowly, "But you gave the vial to the Master."

"I gave him the vial *you* filled. This is the vial *I* filled, under the cover of my cloak, when you had your back to me. This is also filled with healing water. This will also save Yann's life. Or cool the wolf's sharp tongue!"

Sylvie growled, but Helen noticed the blood flow was lessening already.

"So you brought another vial with you from Cauldhame?" asked Helen.

"Yes. I got three from Mallow's kitchen rather than two."

"You set us up for an ambush, because you expected the Master to be there before us. And you took an extra vial, because you expected him to bring a magic tester?"

"I hoped he wouldn't. But I did prepare for all eventualities. I brought a spare, so that even if the Master got one vial, we could still save Yann." Lee grinned. "Sometimes a tricky unreliable faery, trained in glamour and deception, can be quite useful. So, can we all stop shouting now and go back to the Borders to save Yann?"

Helen sat with her back against Sylvie, feeling the wolf's warmth on her spine. "But Lee, now the Master will have the power to see everyone's weaknesses."

"I know. It's not ideal. But we'll have Yann. What would you rather have: a dead centaur and a scarred minotaur; or a living, breathing, kicking Yann and a powerful Master?"

"It's not that simple. There's another cost to the Master having the token..."

Helen was going to have to tell them.

"Sorry everyone. I'm about to make this situation worse. Because the Great Dragon made a deal with me. She promised to call her dragons off, but only if I promised we would *not* give the token to the Master, under *any* circumstances. And there's a penalty: if the Master gets this powerful vision, then the Great Dragon will ... em ..."

“What?” Lavender prompted her.

“The Great Dragon will eat one of us for breakfast. Tomorrow.”

There was silence. A deep cold silence.

Helen felt Sylvie turn into a girl behind her. Helen looked round warily.

Sylvie wiped blood from her lips. “Eat one of us. Which one?”

“Em ... she’ll choose when the time comes.”

“And who is on the menu, human girl?” Sylvie was lisping, but her words were clear and angry.

Sylvie pushed Helen away and stood up. “Not her pupil Sapphire, I suppose, but am I on the menu? What about Rona? Or Catesby? Who else is insignificant enough?”

Helen whispered, “She mentioned you, Catesby, Tangaroa, Rona and Lavender. I’m sorry. I’m so sorry, but if I’d refused, Crag and Jewel would have been breathing fire on us and evaporating the water before we filled even one vial. And I would offer myself, but ... she didn’t want...”

“Yes,” snarled Sylvie, “Lee pulled rank, and extended his faery protection over you. We all heard him. He’s given you a charmed life, human girl, but you have sold our lives for Yann’s.”

“I didn’t think it would happen,” Helen protested weakly, “because we all agreed we wouldn’t give the token to the Master.”

Lee stepped forward. “We didn’t all agree that, because we didn’t know what was at stake! Why didn’t you tell us?”

Helen stood up to face him. “You’re a fine one to talk,

Lee! You set up that whole performance on Dunadd without telling anyone. If you'd told me your plan, I could have explained why it wasn't going to work!"

"If I'd told you my plan, Helen, then you wouldn't have been so wonderfully appalled when I gave him the second vial. The only reason he didn't suspect we might have more than one false vial, and search us all, was because your anger at me convinced him he had Yann's last heartbeat in his hands."

"So it was ok for you to trick us, in order to trick him? How dare you do that?" Helen's anger at herself was spilling over into anger at Lee.

"You, my dear human, have offered one of your friends as a snack to a dragon. How dare *you* do *that*? Because you thought it was the best thing to do in difficult circumstances. That was my calculation too."

"But I didn't think it would ever happen! I thought we'd agreed not to let him take the token. I didn't think anyone would do anything so daft."

"Not even to save you?"

"*No, not even to save me*, you self-centred ambitious faery!" she yelled at him, then she took a deep breath and spoke more calmly. "If I had told you what I'd promised, what we risked, would you have set up that ambush, and given him the vial?"

"Of course not. I would have come up with another plan. You could have trusted me with their lives too."

Helen realised that no one else had spoken for ages. She looked round. Everyone was silent, staring at the ground. Rona was stroking Lavender's soft feathery wings.

"Sorry. I'm really sorry. Don't give up yet..." Helen didn't know what else to say.

Lavender fluttered into the air. “We’ve all been far too clever for our own good. Now we must concentrate on the simple things. We must heal Yann. Then we must stop the Master.”

Lee nodded. “Wise words, flower fairy. But I thought we’d have more time.”

Tangaroa looked up. “You always planned to stop him?”

“Of course. You didn’t think I’d hand the Master the token, then let him trot off and conquer the world, did you? I hoped we’d have a few weeks to gather our forces and plan our attack. But this just gives us a more pressing deadline. Now we must stop the Master before that dragon has her breakfast tomorrow.”

Chapter 25

They were all quiet and sombre as Sapphire flew back to Cauldhame Moor. When the dragon landed and Helen leapt off, she saw that the sun was nearly resting on the horizon. It was almost halfway through the spring equinox.

Epona galloped up, ignored Helen and spoke to Catesby, who was hovering above Helen's head. "The Three are here, fire-bird. Time is running out!"

Lee pushed the vial into Helen's fingers. "You hand it over. That will make it harder for her to hate humans."

Helen said, "But you got it. I didn't."

"We all got it, it was a team effort."

Epona was questioning Catesby, but gabbling so much the phoenix couldn't get a squawk in. "Petros and Mallow have nothing to offer the Three, nothing to heal Yann with! Did you find the token? Have you brought it?"

Helen walked up to Epona. The dappled centaur took a step back, then stamped a hoof. "Keep away from me, human, unless you want my hoofprints on your ribs!"

Helen held up the vial.

Epona snatched for it, but Helen pulled her hand back. "Are you sure you want it, Epona? Do you want to touch something that's been in a human's hand?"

Epona said, "Give me the token, so I can take it up there in time to save Yann."

Tangaroa said, "The sun is still free in the sky. It isn't quite sunset yet. We have time to take it ourselves."

All the friends rushed past Epona. They sprinted along the lawn, past the fountain, up the steps and through the columns. Helen heard Sapphire flap overhead, swooping over the green-tiled roof to land at the back.

As Helen got to the front entrance, she grabbed Lee's cloak to slow him down. They walked in together, behind the rest of the friends, who were skidding on the smooth floor as they ran towards the room in the back corner.

Helen asked, "Lee, that bit of panto with the king's footprint, was that just to cover you filling the extra vial, or is being Faery King really your ambition?"

He answered quietly, "It would be my ambition, Helen, if you'd promise to play at my coronation."

He smiled at her, waiting for a reply. Helen sighed. "Ask me later. Much later. Let's concentrate on Yann right now." She hurried off towards Yann's room.

When she stepped into the warm space, she saw the Three, red cloaks glowing in the firelight.

She saw Petros and Mallow, arms round each other, looking down at Yann, who was lying still under a striped blanket.

And through the window to the west, she saw the sun just touching the horizon, as Sapphire stuck her head through the window to the north.

Helen held out the vial to Yann's parents.

Petros gasped. "A token! You got it! I never really believed you could … Thank you so much, all of you." He bowed his head slightly to Helen and her friends. "But don't give it to me. Give it to them."

Helen turned to the Three, who were standing in front of the fireplace, warming their hands.

"What do you bring us ... human girl?"

"Water from the footprint of a king," Helen whispered.

"And did you meet ... the Master of the Maze there?"

"Yes," Helen admitted.

"Did he get ... a token too?"

"Yes."

The Three laughed. "That should be fun ... But first..."

They each reached for the vial. Helen could see a red-nailed hand, a plump hand and a wrinkled hand. She didn't know which to put it in. So she just held out the vial and watched as all three hands moved forward, then a blur of fingers grabbed it.

Helen stepped back, and stood beside Rona and Sylvie.

The Three approached the still silent shape of Yann on the low bed.

First they dragged the blanket off him.

Then they ripped the dressing off his chest.

The centaur shuddered, but his eyes didn't open.

The youngest of the Three reached out her slim hand to his chest and jabbed her red-tipped fingers into the wound. Blood started to flow again.

Yann moaned, as new pain dragged him out of his warm slide into death.

The Three moaned back, "*Aaaah!*" But their moan was of happiness, not pain.

The youngest held the open vial to the slow flow of blood, and the blood slid slowly in. Then she replaced the cork and handed it to the oldest of the Three, who shook it up and down to mix the water and blood.

Helen tried not to gasp when she saw the youngest of the Three put her bloodied fingers to her mouth and suck them.

The middle woman pulled the cork out and threw it behind her into the fire.

Then three hands clutched the vial and held it up to the setting sun. The light shone through the red liquid and they poured the liquid out.

It fell, like a long red thread, from the vial to the wound, where it sizzled and smoked.

Then the blood stopped flowing from the wound, as it closed up. It closed like a flower closes at night, or a hand closes into a fist.

It stopped bleeding, it closed up and it healed. In just a few seconds, there was no scar, just blood-matted hair and a mess of blood and ripped dressing on the floor.

Yann's eyes opened.

He looked at the Three, leaning over him.

"How do you *feel*?" they chorused. "Is it still painful?"

"No," he said, and smiled, then shut his eyes again.

The Three sighed and moved away, gliding over to Petros and Mallow.

Helen slipped behind their trailing cloaks and knelt beside Yann.

She heard the Three say, "It was a joy to meet your son ... We fully expect ... to see him again soon."

Helen placed her ear on Yann's ribcage. She heard the strong, thumping beat of his horse heart.

She sat up and grinned at her friends, as the Three said, "His heart is beating again ... He will wake ... when the sun has set ... but the healing will not hold for certain ... until dawn ... so he should rest until then."

Helen looked at Yann's face. His eyes were closed, his mouth still, but his cheeks were no longer white and his breathing was stronger. He was asleep, not unconscious.

She looked up to see the Three gliding towards the door. "We cannot stay to watch ... we have another appointment ... once it is full dark."

Petros and Mallow trotted over to Yann. Mallow bent down to clear up the bloody dressing and Petros laid the blanket over his son.

Helen walked back to her friends and whispered, "Yann is healed. Now let's stop the Master."

But Mallow spoke too. "We cannot ever fully repay you for saving our son, but we can start by feeding you. Please join us in the hall, and we'll let Yann sleep off the healing in peace."

Rona started to say, "But we still have to..."

Helen spoke over her. "That's very kind, Mallow. We would love to eat with you. But first we have to debrief after our quests, so we'll go outside where we won't disturb Yann." She pulled Rona out of the room, and the rest followed.

"But why can't we ask them for help?" Rona muttered, as they walked past the columns.

Once they had settled by the fountain, Helen said firmly, "We can't ask them, because we don't have time for long crisis meetings and full-blown military assaults on the Master. Do we, Tangaroa? When will it be full dark?"

Tangaroa answered quickly, "At this time of year, twilight lasts less than two hours."

Helen nodded. "So we have to go now and deal with my mistake. Or I have to go, because this is my fault. You don't need to come with me."

"But if we involved the elders, they could protect us from the Great Dragon, hide us, keep us safe," Rona insisted.

"I'm no keener than you to be eaten," said Lavender, "but hiding from the dragon won't help; it might even provoke a war between fabled beast families."

"Helen's right," said Lee. "This needs to be dealt with fast and simply, not with lots of hooves and noise. And those who caused the problem should solve it, so it's only right that Helen and I deal with this on our own. You enjoy the centaurs' hospitality, while we find the Master and destroy the token."

Sylvie growled, "I won't trust my life to anyone else. Not to tricksy faeries or truth-slicing humans. I'm coming too."

Tangaroa nodded. "I've discovered that most of you, fairies and phoenixes as well as humans and selkies, are capable of cheating and lying, so I must come too, as the only person I can trust."

A familiar voice cut through the evening air. "Tricks and truth-slicing and cheating and lying? That doesn't sound very friendly. What *have* you all been up to?"

Yann pushed Lee and Helen aside, and sat down in the circle.

Everyone stared at him.

"I gather I have to thank you all for saving me. So I thought I'd find you celebrating my return to life. Instead I find you whispering in dark tones and accusing each other of trickery and treachery. Have you had a difficult couple of days?" He grinned at them.

Everyone spoke at once: Helen admitting to stupid promises, Tangaroa asking why Yann had helped Rona cheat, Sylvie complaining about being used as a bargaining chip, Sapphire waving her stumpy tail.

They all spoke over each other, until Lavender yelled, "Do you want me to use the silence spell again?" Everyone quietened down.

"We all have confessions and complaints, but Yann doesn't need to hear them now," the flower fairy said firmly. "Yann needs to go back to bed and rest."

Helen reached up and grabbed the centaur's wrist. His pulse was strong, but she agreed with Lavender. "You rest, and let us sort this out."

He pulled his wrist away. "Sort what out? You found a token, and the Three healed me. What do you need to sort out?"

They all looked round. No one wanted to admit it into the silence.

"I'm not going to rest easy with a mystery in my garden. Tell me."

Catesby perched on Yann's shoulder and began to tell him a story.

As Catesby squawked, Yann looked first at Sapphire, "I'm sorry about your tail, but if Helen says it will grow back, then I'm sure it will." Catesby chattered again, and the centaur shook his head at Rona. "You couldn't keep quiet, could you?" He turned to Tangaroa. "You have a valid complaint against me, my blue friend, but now is not the time to settle it." Tangaroa nodded. Then Catesby added more, and paused. Yann looked down at Helen. "I appreciate your loyalty, human girl, but my life was not worth theirs. You should never have made that promise."

Catesby flew down to Helen and perched on her hand. He rubbed his head against her shoulder and nodded at her. She smiled back. Maybe the phoenix was the only one here who thought she'd done the right thing. The only one who genuinely didn't mind sacrificing himself to save Yann.

Sylvie said, "Now you know the highlights of our bad decisions and foolish mistakes in the last two days, you can go back to bed and let us sort this out."

"Oh no." Yann stood up and stretched. "I'm coming with you. You risked your lives to save me. Now I must risk mine to save you."

"Don't be daft," said Helen. "You were dying an hour ago. You can't fight the Master tonight."

"Why not? I feel fine. I feel fantastic. I have the healing force of Scotland running through my veins. I've never felt better."

"The Three said the healing wouldn't be fixed until dawn."

"The Three, my dear girl, do not always follow the path of truth. They're probably hoping I'll stay out of their way while they heal the Master. I'm willing to take the risk."

Helen shook her head. "You can't. We've all risked so much to save you."

"You didn't go to all that trouble to save a centaur who sits out a fight while his friends go into danger, though, did you?"

"But too much effort now could kill you."

Yann shrugged. "If I have to risk my life to stop the Master and save my friends, then I'm risking a life which was very nearly lost anyway. I do appreciate all you have done for me. But the Great Dragon may be right. Perhaps my death was a price worth paying to stop the Master. If I really am worth saving, maybe I can stop him. And if I die stopping him, then at least I'll achieve something with my death."

Everyone stared at him silently. He grinned. "Cheer up! I'm back. And I'm looking for a fight. So where are we going?"

"He's the Master of the Maze," said Lavender. "His healing will be strongest at the heart of a maze. We should go back to Traquair."

Tangaroa looked at the western horizon. "The sun is down, the equinox is in the dark half of its cycle. We don't have much time."

Yann said, "We're not aiming to outwit the Master. We're going to fight him. So gather your weapons and your courage."

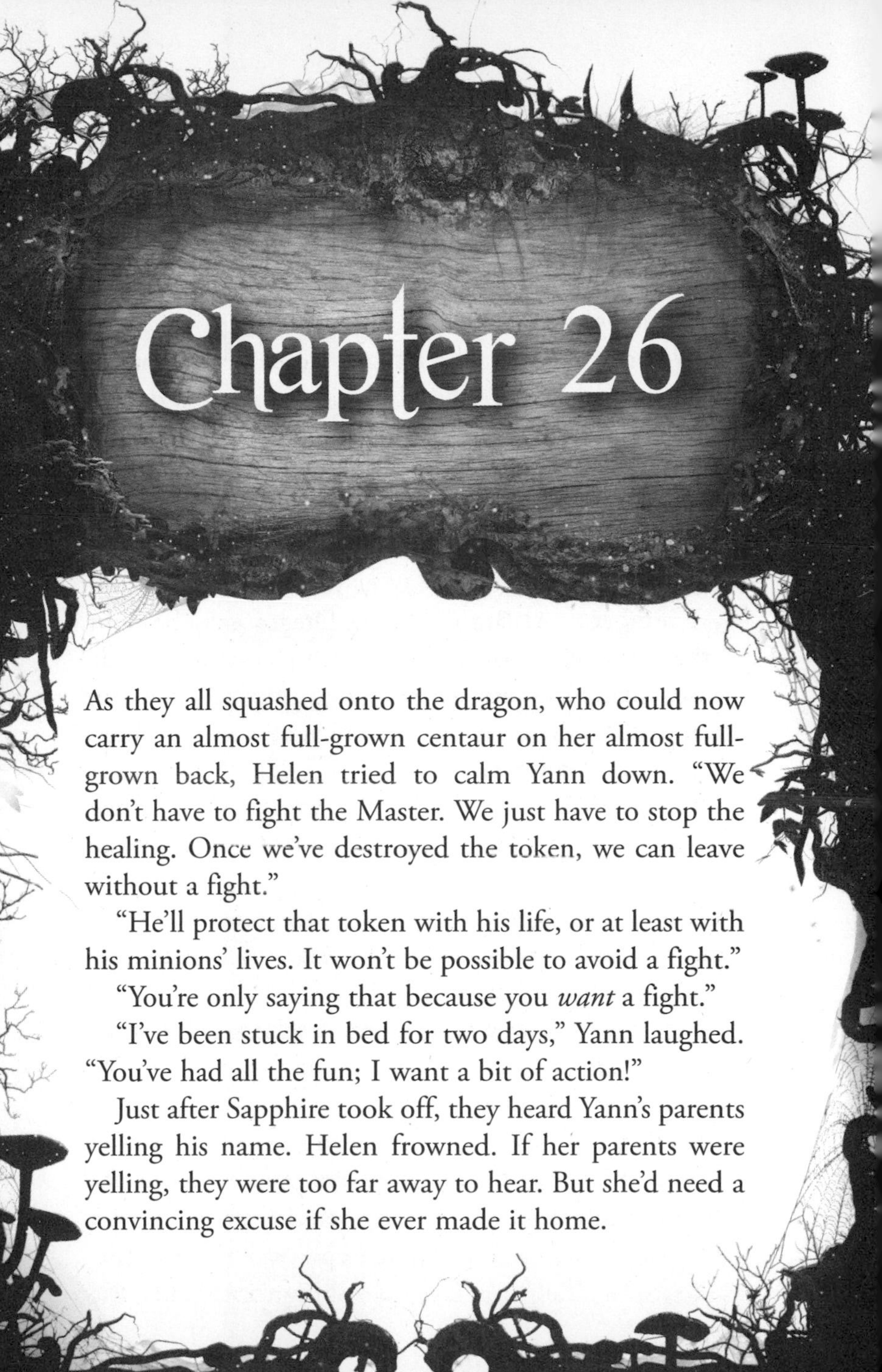

Chapter 26

As they all squashed onto the dragon, who could now carry an almost full-grown centaur on her almost full-grown back, Helen tried to calm Yann down. "We don't have to fight the Master. We just have to stop the healing. Once we've destroyed the token, we can leave without a fight."

"He'll protect that token with his life, or at least with his minions' lives. It won't be possible to avoid a fight."

"You're only saying that because you *want* a fight."

"I've been stuck in bed for two days," Yann laughed. "You've had all the fun; I want a bit of action!"

Just after Sapphire took off, they heard Yann's parents yelling his name. Helen frowned. If her parents were yelling, they were too far away to hear. But she'd need a convincing excuse if she ever made it home.

On the flight to Traquair, Yann and Lee spoke quietly on the dragon's back, and when they landed in front of Traquair House, the two of them announced their joint plan.

Yann spoke first. "The Master will be in the middle. I know the layout of that maze pretty well by now, but I don't want to get into scuffles with fauns on the way through. It's a waste of time, energy and arrows. We have one priority: the token. So we're going straight to the heart of the maze."

"How?" asked Helen.

Lee said, "We'll fly there. Sapphire can drop the two of us in the middle, we'll destroy the token, then get out."

"How will you get out?"

"We'll have to fight our way out."

"But you don't know the layout, Lee."

"He can follow me, covering my back," said Yann confidently.

"That's a stupid plan," said Sylvie. "There are nine of us, and your selfish plan only uses three of you. Why don't we *all* leap off Sapphire into the maze? One team can concentrate on the token, the other team can clear the way out."

"I like the wolf's plan," said Lee. "Is everyone up for a full-on fight?"

Helen looked round. She was the only one not nodding, and the only one without a weapon.

Sylvie would have teeth when she changed, Lavender had her wand, Sapphire had fire, and Catesby had his beak and talons. Rona had remembered to bring her golden spear, Tangaroa had his fishing trident, Lee was bristling with swords, and Yann had his bow and a full quiver of arrows.

Helen was about to say she didn't have anything to fight with, when Lee handed her a sword. "You've fought with this one before. Please be careful."

"Of the sword?"

"No, of your fingers."

She laughed. "You don't want me to punch any goats then!"

He smiled. "Just be careful. You don't have to save everyone on your own, they can fight for themselves."

She nodded, and they all climbed back on the dragon, as Yann split them into two teams.

Sapphire flew low over the maze, to its very heart, where they all leapt, screaming, yelling, howling...

Onto a bare wooden altar.

The middle of the maze was empty.

There was a stepped arrangement of smooth tree trunks, the tallest trunk charred by the interrupted unicorn sacrifice, but there was nothing else there. No goats. No minotaurs. No red-cloaked women. No healing tokens.

"Have we dropped into another trap?" asked Helen. "Are they hiding in the maze?" She looked up. "Sapphire, can you check?"

The dragon breathed a flare of flame and spun round, keeping the fire safely above the hedges, but lighting up every corner. She growled a negative answer.

Yann led his friends out of the maze and Sapphire landed beside them on the grass.

They stood in puzzled silence for a moment, then Rona asked, "What do we do now?"

Helen looked to the west. There was still a glow in the sky.

"We have more than an hour of dusk left," Tangaroa said. "But we don't know where they are!"

"We should have followed the Three," sighed Lavender. "I should have thought of that."

"They wouldn't have been easy to follow," Lee pointed out. "And if they caught a spy they would enjoy taking painful revenge."

"They weren't easy to follow," said a new voice, "but they didn't catch me."

Epona trotted out of the splintered trees.

"I followed the Three to their destination and when I came back home to tell you, I saw you all fly off. So I followed you too. I can gallop," the dappled centaur said proudly, "almost as fast as a dragon can fly!"

Sapphire rumbled and Yann laughed. "A fully laden dragon, to be fair to her, Epona. But why did you follow the Three?"

"Because the herd did nothing to heal you except keep you warm. Your friends showed us what we should have done." She glanced at Helen. "They worked together, they risked their lives for you. I wanted to help too. I've never trusted the Three, so I followed them. And I have smaller hooves than you, Yann, so I kept silent behind them all the way. They went to an old house called Whitestane Tower, in the hills towards the border."

"Thank you so much, Epona." Yann patted her shoulder.

"I could show you the way," Epona offered.

Yann shook his head. "I know the way to Whitestane. And you must be exhausted after your gallop. Anyway, we're a team, we know each other, and we work together."

As Yann gave Sapphire directions and everyone else clambered onto the dragon, Helen looked at Epona, left on her own at the corner of the maze.

Helen walked over. "Thank you. Your quick thinking and bravery might mean my stupidity doesn't cost my friends their lives. Next time, I hope you can come with us."

Epona frowned. "Perhaps." She walked off, limping a little.

Back on Sapphire, Helen was crushed between Sylvie and Lee. She could hear the faery behind her and the centaur behind him chatting. They decided to see how the Master's forces were arranged around Whitestane Tower before they came up with a detailed plan, then Yann asked quietly, "At the hill fort, did you actually set them all up in a line, like skittles, for the Master? And they fell for it?"

Lee said, "Every single one of them," and laughed softly.

"How did you manage that? Did you glamour them?"

"Just a little, but they haven't realised."

"Well done. Thanks. But don't ever do that to me..."

"I won't. You wouldn't fall for it, my strong-minded friend." Then Lee leant forward and whispered in Helen's ear. "No one ever thinks they can be glamoured. That's why everyone can!"

It was a short flight in the darkening sky to the hills around the tower, where Sapphire circled high above the old house.

Whitestane Tower wasn't tall, thin and pointy, like a fairy-tale Rapunzel tower. It was a large house that was higher than it was wide, with small windows and one big wooden door. There were no lights shining inside, but a circle of dark figures outside suggested they had come to the right place.

Sapphire landed round the side of the low hill to the west of the house.

"I don't understand why the Master isn't in a maze," muttered Lavender once they were on the ground. "Why isn't he being healed where his power is greatest?"

"He knows his enemies expect to find him in a maze," said Yann. "Perhaps he's avoiding mazes until he's healed?"

"Or perhaps there's a maze under the house?" suggested Helen.

"There isn't," said Yann. "I played hide and seek in there when I was young. It's just a big old house. The roof is half-collapsed, the stairs are falling down, most of the rooms are filled with ancient human furniture. It doesn't even have a cellar, let alone a maze. It's just a hideout. If we get in, we can find him. But first we have to get past those sentries. Are they fauns or uruisks?"

Lee scrambled up the side of the hill, peered over, then came back. "Uruisks. I saw long horns and heard one of them bleat."

"That makes sense," said Yann. "His hired help outside, his closest followers inside. How many are there?"

Sylvie said, "I counted ten sentries as we flew round, four at the front and two each at the back and sides."

Yann laughed softly. "Ten means one each, except for the lucky warrior who gets two."

Sylvie and Lee raised their hands, but Yann said, "Come on, guys, I missed the giants, the lizards and the rope snakes. Can I have the double act? Please?"

Yann was enjoying himself, but Helen was getting nervous. Did he really expect her to walk up to the house and attack an uruisk? In the dark? On her own?

Though as she watched Yann draw a rough sketch on the ground, marking out the sentries' locations, she could see the sense in it. The sentries were all the way round the tower. A concerted attack in any one place would leave sentries on the other sides of the tower free to raise the alarm. They had to silence every sentry at the same time.

Yann announced that he would take both sentries at the back, Catesby and Sapphire would attack from above on the east side, Lee and Lavender would deal with the west side. Which left Helen, Rona, Sylvie and Tangaroa with the sentries at the front.

"I don't want a feud with the uruisk tribe, so try not to kill your sentry. Just disarm, disable or knock them out when you see Sapphire's signal," said Yann. "Then we'll meet at the front door. Once we're inside, Sapphire will gather the unconscious wild goats into a heap and guard them. Alright?"

Everyone nodded. Even Helen, who couldn't suggest anything better. Then the friends moved away carefully.

Helen muttered to Rona, as they crawled through the black heather, "Are you happy about this? Sneaking up to fight a monster on your own?"

"Not really, but I seem to be spending the whole weekend proving to Tangaroa that I'm not a complete wimp."

"Because he found out you cheated?"

"Yes," Rona whispered. "He didn't take it very well."

"So why did you tell him?"

"He sort of guessed. Then I admitted it. Telling lies beside the seven waterfalls didn't seem like a good idea."

"This doesn't seem like a good idea either," Helen murmured, then stopped talking as they got nearer the tower.

She was responsible for the sentry to the west of the door. She crouched in a shallow dip, close enough to smell the hot meaty stink of her uruisk.

He was chatting to the sentry on his left, the one Tangaroa was going to tackle. Helen tried again to open her ears to the meaning she knew was there, but all she could hear were grunts and bleats.

She grasped the sword hilt tightly, then realised she couldn't attack the uruisk with it. She didn't want to kill him, and she wasn't sure how to inflict a minor wound with a sword, so she put it down.

She felt around the ground and found a rock which might make a decent weapon. But the uruisk was taller than her. To hit him on the head, she'd have to stand right beside him and stretch upwards. That would leave her vulnerable to the axe he was swinging around.

So she opened her rucksack quietly, pulled out several packets of bandages and pushed the stone deep inside. She slowly zipped it closed and gripped the straps.

Surely everyone must be in place by now? She was getting even more nervous waiting.

Suddenly a silent fountain of flame blazed above the tower.

Then Helen heard thumps and groans from all around. Her uruisk stepped forward, raising his axe.

Helen jumped up in front of him.

He looked surprised. He took a step back. And Helen

swung the rucksack as hard as she could, right into his long-nosed hairy face.

There was a crack and a squelch, which she hoped was first aid equipment breaking, not his bones, and the uruisk fell backwards against the wall of the tower.

"Sorry," she muttered, and she almost meant it.

Then she picked up Lee's spare sword and ran to the front door. Within moments, the friends were all there, breathing hard but smiling.

As Sapphire dragged the floppy uruisks into a heap, Yann said, "How long do we have until full dark, blue loon?"

Tangaroa looked at the pale line on the horizon. "Fifteen minutes, maybe twenty."

Yann grinned. "Plenty of time if they're easy to find; not much time if we have to play hide and seek. So let's get inside."

Yann reared up and kicked the door of the tower to splinters.

Chapter 27

They shoved the shattered door open and walked into the entrance hall.

It was narrow and low ceilinged, not high and wide like halls in other old houses Helen had visited. It was built of stone and brick, with furniture and pictures, but nothing was where she expected.

The walls were made of rubble, with broken legs of furniture and backs of framed pictures mixed in with the stones and bricks. The ceiling was lengths of floorboards with carpet and lino hanging down, balanced on top of the patchwork walls just above Yann's head. And the corridor split into two narrower tunnels ahead.

"The Master has built his own maze," Lavender whispered. "He's ripped the rooms apart and built his own maze with the debris."

"So let's find the middle," said Yann. "That's where he'll be."

"How?" asked Helen. "This isn't a maze we know, and Catesby and Lavender can't fly above and guide us."

Rona pointed to the choice of ways ahead of them. "Should we split up or stay together?"

"Split up," said Yann.

"Stay together," said Lee.

They looked at each other.

"Stay together," insisted Lee. "We don't want to find the Master and lose each other."

Yann nodded. "I'll go at the front. You go at the back, Lee. Tangaroa, stay beside Rona. Sylvie and Helen walk together. Lavender and Catesby, can you be scouts?"

"We need a plan, so we don't get lost," said Lavender. "Let's turn right at the first five junctions, then see where we are. That way we can get back here by taking five left turns. If we stick to that theory, we won't get lost, and it might even help us find the middle."

So they followed the flower fairy, quietly and carefully, through the dusty lanes of the dark maze.

Lavender's lightballs brightened their way, but she kept the bobbing lights close, while Catesby peered round corners to check they were clear.

Helen walked beside Sylvie, who'd turned back into a girl, whispering that wolves weren't keen on small indoor spaces.

They turned right at every junction, but that didn't take them in a square spiral, because there were lots of corners, left and right, which gave them no choice at all. As they crept deeper into the labyrinth, Helen soon had no idea which way she was facing.

Every time they had a choice, they turned right, and after five rights, they found themselves in a wider space: the wreck of a bedroom. A rusty iron bed had been jammed into the wall. Opposite was a door, upside down. Helen pushed at the door gently. It didn't budge, so she pulled, and it creaked open. Behind it was a solid wall of more rubble, including a chamber pot at head-height, and a single leather boot above that.

Helen shut the door and turned round. She caught sight of movement to her left and slashed out with the sword.

Lee laughed. "Good reaction time, bard, but you just attacked yourself!" He pointed at the wall and Helen realised she had seen her reflection in a tall mirror, stuck lengthways at waist-height in the wall.

The friends looked at the two exits from the ruined bedroom.

"Do we keep going right, or head back to the door and try left this time?" Yann asked Lavender.

"Stand still. Listen," Lavender instructed.

They all listened.

But there was nothing. No voices, no footsteps, no hoofbeats. Just silence.

Lavender sighed. "Let's keep going to the right and see if we can get nearer the middle."

So her friends followed her through the maze.

They passed a bath standing on its end. A whole wall of fenceposts covered in moss. A bookcase with no books. A baby's cradle filled with bricks.

When they had chosen right four more times, Lavender held up her wand.

Everyone listened carefully, standing by a wall of velvet striped wallpaper slashed by claw marks.

They heard faint voices.

Helen whispered, "We don't have much time. Can we follow the voices?"

Lavender shook her head. "Following sound in a maze can be confusing. We must stick to the theory."

"We could kick our way through," whispered Yann.

"Not if we want any element of surprise," said Tangaroa.

So they walked through tunnels of angled wooden steps and banisters, and a space hung with velvet curtains, the voices getting louder, then quieter and then louder again.

After another two junctions, as they crept along a corridor lined with broken roof slates, the voices became overwhelming. Three chanting voices.

The friends bunched together and peered round the next corner. They saw a large open space. A square room with black and white floor tiles, lit by candles high on the crumbling walls.

The heart of the maze.

Helen could see the Three chanting and the Master kneeling at their feet. And she could see the vial held high in the hands of the Three.

The youngest of the Three was forcing the minotaur's eyelids open with her red-nailed fingers.

There was no one else there, no fauns, no uruisks, no ropey snakes. The Master was keeping this healing private.

The friends pulled back into the slate-lined corridor.

"What do we do?" Yann whispered. "I could have taken the vial from the Master, but I can't steal it from the women who saved my life."

"We don't have to steal the vial," said Lavender. "Could we make them spill it?"

"Or offer them something else?" suggested Rona.

The chanting reached a higher pitch and Sylvie said, "Don't be daft. This is about our lives, not about being nice to old ladies." She flickered into a wolf and sprinted past Yann.

Her friends ran after her, just in time to see the wolf leap up at the Three.

Before she reached them, the women tilted the vial and poured the water into the Master's eye.

Then the Three turned as one and flicked their cloak, which was suddenly as solid as a shield. Sylvie bounced off and fell to the floor.

"If it's too late to stop the healing," said Yann, "then I can't let him live." He lifted his bow, an arrow on the string, and aimed it at the Master.

But the Three had the stunned wolf wrapped in their red-hooded cloak. "No boy ... We will only free the wolf ... if you put the bow down."

Yann sighed and lowered the bow.

Suddenly the walls opened. A tabletop swivelled on one wall. A Turkish rug lifted on another. A picture of a deer pivoted right over on the third wall.

A long line of fauns entered through each hole. More fauns than Helen had ever seen.

She noticed Lee, Rona and Tangaroa raise their weapons. She remembered she had a sword and lifted it too. But the fauns didn't attack.

They gathered at the other side of the space and lined up between the Turkish rug and a faded green tartan couch, chattering softly in a foreign language and watching as the Master stood up. He had tears streaming from his left eye, but a fierce grin on his face.

The scar tissue on the minotaur's head smoothed and sprouted soft black hair, his left eye opened fully and started to glitter.

Then he turned to Frass. "How touching, you have summoned your whole family to watch my triumph!"

Frass, standing in the middle of the fauns, smiled but said nothing.

The minotaur pointed at the faun. "I can see your weakness, Frass. I can see your lack of faith and your doubts swirling round you. But let me put your mind at rest. My plan has worked. Look! I am healed and I can see everyone's weaknesses." He whirled round. "Everyone's!"

Frass folded his arms. "Your plan has worked, Master, because the Three have healed you. But it hasn't worked entirely as you promised, because the centaur is still alive, still challenging you, and at this moment of your triumph the centaur is standing in the heart of your own secret maze."

The minotaur stamped a bare foot. "A minor detail, easily solved. We have numbers on our side, so grab those insolent children and show them who is the Master!"

The friends pressed together, aiming their weapons.

Before the fauns could move, the Three said, "Oh no ... that's not what we want..."

They glided over to the green couch in the corner. As they moved, Sylvie fell out of their cloak, scrambled to her paws and slunk over to her friends.

The Three settled themselves, patting cushions and

pulling cloak edges out from under each other, then spoke again, "We do like a nice big battle ... but today we'd rather watch ... a duel."

The Master shook his head. "With respect, ladies, why would I bother to duel with any of these children when I already have them at my mercy?"

"Because your healings ... are linked," the Three said, sharing the sentences. "We were given two tokens tonight ... but they were from the same rainfall ... from the same footprint ... so each contained only part of the healing force ... You're both healed *now* ... but come the sunrise ... the healing force ... will settle in only one of you.

"So you must fight a duel to decide ... who keeps their healing ... The winner stays healed ... the loser returns ... to how they were this afternoon ... On the verge of death," they nodded to Yann, "or blinded and scarred," they nodded to the Master.

Helen glanced at Lee. The faery's face was white. "I'm sorry my friend," he said to Yann. "I didn't realise my trickery meant you only got half a healing token."

Yann smiled. "It was enough to get me here, for which I thank you all. But now I must earn the rest of my healing myself."

The Master frowned. "But I'd be mad to agree to a duel when I already have them trapped in the heart of my power, surrounded by my loyal soldiers. If you want to see a victor, then I will force this colt to bow to me. That will show who is the winner here."

He turned to Yann. "Horse-boy, bow down to me and I will let your friends go."

"I will not bow to you."

The Master said, "Frass. Grab his friends."

Frass said calmly, "Are you sure, Master? It would be an unfortunate start to the story of your triumph if you let others win your fight for you. The world will only get a true sense of your power if you defeat this young challenger on your own. I think the Three are right. I think you have to win this duel for yourself." The faun leant back against the wall and smiled at the Master.

The Master stared at the faun. "I will not forget this, goat." Then he glanced at the Three, who pulled their hoods round their faces. "So, you want a duel. To the death, or surrender?"

"That sounds lovely, dear ... either would be nice," they said.

"And the winner stays healed and the loser, if the loser is still alive, loses his healing?" asked Yann.

"Quite right, dear ... so get on with it."

The Master turned to Yann. "You can't fight with bow and arrows. It's a long-range weapon, it wouldn't be fair."

"No weapons at all," said the Three. "We healed your bodies ... so you must fight with your bodies ... with hooves, horns, hands ... Come on, we're waiting."

Yann laid his bow and arrows down in a corner, then looked round the space, as if he was measuring how many paces he could take.

Helen looked round too. To her left was the wall with the upside-down painting of the deer. Opposite them, the wall with the Turkish rug, where the fauns were standing. The next wall had a large wardrobe, which hadn't swivelled, and the long tabletop, which had.

The only furniture on the floor was the saggy couch the Three were sitting on.

The Master stared at Yann. "You are so young, so arrogant, and you have so many weaknesses."

He turned to the group of fabled beasts, then, before any of them could react, he plucked Lavender out of the air.

Yann shouted, "Let her go!"

"No, boy. I'm just testing my new sight. The duel hasn't started yet, so keep your distance or I will squash this little one."

He stared at the fairy for a minute, then kept hold of her as he examined the rest of them. "If I describe all your weaknesses, you might learn to overcome them. Perhaps I will keep my new knowledge to myself."

He looked hard at Lee and nodded. "I know that feeling." He just shook his head when he looked in Rona's face.

Then he looked at Helen, standing behind Lee and Tangaroa. "A human. I see your weaknesses just as clearly as I see those of my fabled neighbours." He grinned. "This sight will allow me to conquer every world!"

He opened his fist, let Lavender go and strode back to the middle of the space. "Ready, boy?"

Yann said, "Almost," then stepped closer to his friends and whispered, "Get out of here if it looks like I'm losing. Lavender will lead you out. You've saved my life once today, don't risk yourselves for me again."

The Master looked at all the friends gathered beside Yann. Then he frowned, and turned towards the Three.

They pulled their hoods tighter. "Don't look straight at us, minotaur ... we would prefer you did not see..."

"Of course, ladies, my apologies." He spoke to the air above their heads. "But the sight you gave me is fading already. I can't see the children's weaknesses from here. Does it only work close up?"

The Three laughed. "It works from any distance ... but you are now seeing them as a team ... Perhaps as a team ... they have no weaknesses at all?"

Yann smiled at his friends. "I wonder if that's true?"

"Even if it is," said Lavender, "you have to fight this duel on your own."

So Yann stepped into the middle of the maze, to meet the Master.

Chapter 28

As Yann and the Master circled each other, Helen tried to work out who was bigger and heavier. There seemed to be more of Yann, because of his long horse body, his two arms and his four legs. But the centaur was slim and elegant, not heavy and muscular like the minotaur, who had a huge chest and shoulders holding up his massive head. The Master had longer, stronger arms too. If he managed to grab Yann, he could probably crush him.

Though Yann had laid down his bow and the Master's axe was leaning against the tartan couch, they both had weapons. Yann had four heavy hooves and the Master had two long horns.

The Three watched the centaur and the minotaur walking round the space, but they were also busy with their hands. The oldest was knitting a mitten, the middle one was darning a sock, and the youngest was braiding a friendship bracelet.

Suddenly the Master lowered his head and charged at Yann, his horns aimed at the centaur's human chest.

The centaur stepped out of the way and let the minotaur run past him. The Master skidded to a stop, so he didn't run into the deer painting on the wall.

Yann said, "Do you want to try that again, bull? I think you missed."

The Master roared and charged again. Yann leapt away, his fast hooves keeping him safe.

Helen relaxed a little, wondering if Yann's speed meant he could survive this duel.

But escaping injury wouldn't win a fight. And Yann had to win, to keep his own healing and to deny the Master the power for which the Great Dragon would punish her friends.

Yann couldn't spend the whole duel dancing on his hooves, he had to attack.

She needn't have worried. The next time the minotaur rushed at him, Yann stepped sideways, then reared up and crashed both front hooves onto the Master's back.

The Master grunted with pain and stumbled forward.

Yann reared up again to attack a second time. But the Master spun round, seized Yann's front legs and threw the centaur to the ground.

Before the Master could lower his horns to gore him, Yann rolled and leapt up again.

The two of them stood still, staring at each other, reassessing each other's strength and skill after those first attacks.

The Master smiled. "But your long delicate legs aren't your real weakness, are they, colt?" He circled round, dipping his horns occasionally, slashing the sharpened tips towards Yann, laughing when the centaur jumped out of the way.

"I know what your soft centre is, centaur!" The minotaur strode over to Yann's friends. "It's them, isn't it? I could throw you down, stamp on you, stab you, and you'd bounce back up again, because you're young and arrogant and don't mind a bit of pain.

"But if I hurt *them*..." He grabbed for Lavender again, but she'd already dived behind Helen.

The minotaur stared at them with his glittering left eye. "I see their weaknesses. The fairy's fear of being ripped apart. The selkie's fear of teeth." He opened his bull mouth and bellowed, showing his huge crushing molars.

He turned back to Yann. "I won't hurt them *now*. I'll hurt them once I've killed you. I'll pull the fairy apart, feather by feather. I'll give the selkie to some long-fanged friends of mine, so they can chew her to bits."

Helen heard Rona gasp behind her and felt Lavender nestling deep into her hair.

The Master boomed, "I'll hurt them once I've killed you. Unless you surrender right now. Unless you *bow down to me!*"

He jabbed his horns at Yann, who backed off and kicked out, almost losing his balance as he tried to watch the Master and look over to his friends at the same time.

"It's not honourable to threaten the audience at a duel," gasped Yann. "This is between us."

"Don't be ridiculous, boy. I don't care about honour. I care about *victory!* So surrender. Put down those hooves, or I will tell your friends what else their weaknesses suggest to me."

Yann kicked out at the bull's left eye. The Master twisted away just in time.

"Don't you care about them? The faery boy, I could scar his face so badly with barbed wire that he would never glamour anyone again; the blue boy, I could tie him down in a desert and let him dry out until his tattoos flake off."

He charged at Yann again. The centaur leapt to the side and cantered over to his friends. "You have to get away! Please..."

"No," said Lee. "We will stay here and we will watch you win. That big bully's threats don't scare us."

But that wasn't true. Lavender was shivering in Helen's hair. Rona was sobbing behind her. Tangaroa was barely breathing in front of her. She'd even heard an unfamiliar shake in Lee's voice.

The Master knew how to get to the heart of each of their fears.

Helen could hear him now, threatening to pull out all Sylvie's teeth or lock Catesby in a freezer.

Helen wondered what he would suggest for her, what weaknesses he had seen in her face. But the Master had stopped talking, to concentrate on avoiding Yann's angry flurry of kicks.

Then Helen wondered what weakness the Master would see in himself. What he would see if he looked at his own face in a mirror? Would he see his own fears, his own nightmares, his own hidden weaknesses? Would that make him shake the way her friends were shaking?

She watched Yann, less sure on his hooves now he was worried about his friends.

She watched the minotaur, striding about the heart of his own maze.

She watched the Three, busy on the couch.

And she wondered if she could force the Master to look in a mirror.

She had seen that bedroom mirror out in the maze, but she wondered if there was anything in the heart of the maze which would show his reflection.

She stared at the walls, past the fast-moving bull's head and horse's legs.

Yann landed a kick on the Master's chest, but while the centaur was close enough, the minotaur swung his horns and cut open Yann's left arm.

Now Helen was distracted by blood on the floor, as well as her friends' fear. She tried to concentrate on the walls again. Picture, rug, couch, table, wardrobe...

She remembered the antique wardrobe in her gran's old house. It had a wire tie-rack, a shelf marked 'hats' and an oval mirror on the inside of the door.

Would there be a mirror in that old wardrobe? Could she ask Yann to open the door, without alerting the Master to her plan?

She whispered, "Lavender, can you get a message to Yann?"

"Not if I have to go near the Master's hands!"

"He's not going to hurt you now," Helen murmured. "He's just using your fears to hurt Yann. He's only going to hurt you if Yann loses, and I have a way to stop Yann losing. Fly over there and ask him to kick the wardrobe door open. But don't let the Master hear you. Pretend to be saying something else."

"What else?"

Lee turned round and whispered, "Pretend to be begging Yann to surrender. The Master will believe that, even if Yann won't."

Lavender wriggled out of Helen's hair and hovered in front of her. "The wardrobe? Kick it open?"

Helen nodded.

So Lavender fluttered round the walls to the corner nearest Yann and called out, "Yann, please. I can't bear the Master knowing my weaknesses and threatening me with them."

She flew closer to Yann and landed on his shoulder, as the Master backed off, listening intently. The tiny fairy said loudly, "I beg you to surrender, to put our lives above your own."

Yann frowned at her and she moved closer to his ear, as the Master strode over to his fauns, yelling, "You see, Frass, knowing his weakness is the way to defeat any warrior! However many hooves he has!"

Helen saw Yann nod. Lavender had delivered the message, now the flower fairy had to escape the battle ground. So Helen shouted, "Lavender, how dare you! Get back here and stop undermining Yann. We don't all feel like she does, Yann. The rest of us think you should keep fighting. Her wishes don't reflect ours. They don't *reflect* ours at all."

Yann frowned again and Lavender, sobbing noisily, flew back from the centaur to Rona's arms.

Yann looked at Helen. At Lavender. At the Master. And at the wardrobe.

Then he edged round the walls, ducking fresh horn attacks, flicking fast hooves back in return. When he reached the wardrobe, he kicked out with his left front hoof at the top corner of the door.

The door flew open with a crash and shards of glass clattered onto the floor.

Yann's kick had opened the door, but he'd also broken the mirror.

Chapter 29

Helen watched Yann limp round the room, blood dripping from his front leg. She sighed. Her stupid idea, asking a centaur to *kick* a mirror, had weakened Yann rather than the Master.

The Master was taunting Yann. "You missed that time, boy! But please, blunt your hooves on my maze as often as you like!"

Helen sighed again, but with relief this time. The minotaur hadn't understood what Yann was trying to do. So they could try again. But with what?

Lee leant back and whispered, "What was that about?"

Helen replied, "I wondered what the Master would see in his own reflection. What weaknesses he'd see, what that would do to him."

The faery smiled. "Clever. Sneaky. So we need

another mirror. You attacked a mirror halfway through the maze. We could go and get that."

The Master was rubbing his toes in the blood on the floor. "Your poor weak hearts are working hard to pump this blood out. Can they take the strain?"

As they circled each other, Helen saw that Yann was still managing to use his speed to keep out of reach of those sharp horns and huge hands.

She said to Lee, "But if we brought a weapon in for Yann, wouldn't it be cheating?"

Tangaroa whispered, "Don't worry about cheating. The Master is using us and our weaknesses as weapons against Yann, so we can take part in this fight. Do you want me to get the mirror?"

Lee nodded. "Tangaroa and I will go back for it."

Helen said, "No, you're both as obvious as peacocks, with your bright blue skin and bright green cloak. If you go, you'll be missed. I'll go. Rona, will you help me carry the mirror?"

Rona nodded.

Lavender said, "Where will we put it?"

Catesby chattered, the rest of the friends nodded and Lavender translated quickly, "That deer painting is about the same size. Catesby says we could put the mirror on the back of the painting and flip it round. Look, it's not swung back flush to the wall, it's hanging squint."

Helen said, "Great idea. Lavender, you fly to the picture, nip through the gap at the corner and mark where it is on the other side of the wall, so we can find it once we've got the mirror."

"Are you sure you won't get lost?" said Lavender.

"Six left turns," said Helen, "then six right turns on

the way back. But how will we find you and the picture?"

The flower fairy smiled. "I'll think of something."

Helen took one more look at Yann, bleeding from his arm and his leg, and at the Master, with purple bruising on his ribs, then saw Lavender flutter casually over to the deer picture and slip behind it.

Sylvie flickered into a girl beside Helen. "I'll move around behind the boys and try to look like three girls at once. But please hurry, Yann doesn't look as strong as he did when he woke."

Helen and Rona stepped back into the corridors of the maze.

Helen whispered to Rona, "Choose left every time and count to six." The girls held hands, and ran through the maze.

As they sprinted round the tight corners, Rona asked, "Why do we have to fix the mirror to the picture? Why don't we just take it in and hold it up?"

"Because if the mirror is part of the maze, the Three might not think it's a weapon and might not think it's cheating."

They ran past slates and baths and curtains, running full pelt along corridors they had crept through earlier. As they ran the maze, using her bright torch beam to light the way and not slowing to check round corners, Helen hoped all the fauns were watching the duel.

They skidded round the final corner, into the wider space of the old bedroom, and Helen dashed to the mirror on the wall. Only it wasn't really on the wall: it was part of the wall. Helen tried to pull it off, but it was tightly wedged in.

"How do we get it out?" Rona ran her fingers round the bumpy golden frame.

Helen stood back. "That's what's holding it in." She pointed to a chair leg, overlapping the corner of the mirror. "That and the weight of the whole maze over it."

She opened her rucksack and took out the rock.

"You're carrying rocks now!" said Rona. "What does that cure?"

Helen smiled. "This gives uruisks headaches, rather than curing them!"

She bashed the chair leg until it splintered, then she shoved Lee's sword behind the frame. Rona forced her spear in as well, and they tried to lever the mirror out of the wall. Rona's spear broke after two tries, and Helen bent the sword, but eventually they levered the mirror out.

It was heavier than they'd imagined and chunks of wall crumbled into dust as they pulled it out, but when they stepped back, the mirror awkward in their arms, the wall was still standing.

"Six right turns back," said Helen. "And watch out for Lavender on the way."

They left the broken weapons on the floor and ran back through the maze. They weren't as fast now, because it wasn't easy manoeuvring a long mirror round tight corners.

They could hear hoofbeats and grunts from the middle, fading in and out as they ran round the maze.

When they got to the third junction, Helen saw something to their left. "Wait! Did you see a glow down that corridor?"

Rona shook her head.

Helen said, "I thought I saw a faint light. It might be one of Lavender's lightballs."

"If we turn left, we'll get lost."

"No, we won't." Helen put her end of the mirror down, rummaged in her untidy rucksack and pulled out a scalpel.

She scraped an arrow on the wall at eye-height, pointing right, and led Rona to the left. Then she switched off the torch. In the sudden darkness, she saw a pale glimmer. A lightball, hiding behind the next corner. Helen moved fast to follow it, running round two more corners and taking left at another junction.

"The mark!" Rona called behind her. "You didn't mark this corner!"

Helen turned round, marked their way back on the wall, then ran after the lightball. She found it floating in the middle of the corridor, and followed it round one more corner to...

Lavender, perched on the string on the back of the painting. "At last," she murmured.

"How's the duel going?" Helen scratched an arrow on the wall, then stood the mirror up to measure it against the picture.

"They're both tiring, but no one has landed the winning blow."

The mirror was slightly narrower than the picture but a similar length.

Rona whispered, "How do we fix it on? Lavender, could you stick it on with magic?"

Lavender shook her head. "Not firmly enough to hold it in place while it swings right over. Do you have glue in there?" She pointed to Helen's green rucksack.

"Only enough for fixing mermaids' tails, not enough to hold a mirror. We need nails."

They searched the rubble and found rusty nails in the base of a wooden desk. Then Helen, listening nervously to the laughter of the Master on the other side of the wall, wrecked a pair of scissors prising nine nails out.

Rona, who'd been holding the mirror in place, held her hand out for the nails.

Lavender whispered, "What do we hammer them in with?"

"Helen has a good rock," said Rona.

"What, the rock I left in the bedroom?"

"Oh. What else do we have?"

Helen was starting to wish that she carried a tool kit rather than a first aid kit. Lavender peeked round the picture. "Hurry up. Yann has two wounds on his flanks now and the Master is still looking confident."

Helen wondered if her torch was heavy enough to use as a hammer, then she saw a frying pan in the wall near Rona's knees, and tugged it out by its greasy metal handle.

"Lavender, let me know when Yann's hoofbeats will cover a hammering noise."

The fairy smiled. "Just start hammering now. I'm getting pretty good at silence spells."

Rona held the mirror and picture together so they didn't swing round, Lavender muted the noise, and Helen whacked at the nails with a frying pan.

When all nine nails were in, Rona let go, Helen stood back, Lavender fluttered away, and the mirror stayed where it was. They stared at it for a minute and it still stayed where it was. So they all nodded and turned in different directions.

Lavender sighed, "I'm lost, how do we get back?"

Helen pointed to the arrow she'd scratched into the wall. "That's how to master a maze."

They sprinted back to the last corner she'd marked, then counted right for another three and almost ran into the back of Lee's shining cloak.

"What took you so long?" said Sylvie.

Helen replied, "We didn't bring enough tools." She realised she was still gripping the frying pan, so she put it down.

"Yann has been holding his own," said Lee, "but the Master hasn't been bedridden for days, so he's got more energy."

Helen looked between Lee and Tangaroa's shoulders. Yann was now bleeding from an arm, two legs, his horse's flank and his human chest.

The Master wasn't bleeding at all, but was bruised all over.

The Three were still watching, chattering quietly and smiling.

The fauns were watching too, arms folded, heads to the side.

And the picture was still hanging slightly squint. No nails poking through, no mirror visible. Just a nervous deer, with unwieldy antlers, hanging upside down.

"Now Yann has to turn the mirror and force the Master to look at it." She frowned. "How do we tell Yann without telling the Master?"

Lavender said, "I could fly over again."

"That would look suspicious."

Catesby chattered an offer.

But Helen said, "Let me try from here." She pushed between Lee and Tangaroa, and called out, "Yann, dear, why don't you try something new? All you're doing is dancing around, dear. What about trying something else? Dear!"

Yann frowned at her. "If you'd like to give it a go, *dear*, I'd be happy to take a break. It's not easy out here."

Helen said, "It's not been easy in the corridors either, *dear*. So I suggest looking round, dear, and trying something new. More gently this time, dear."

"Stop calling me ... oh!"

Yann looked at all the walls in turn, then grinned at Helen. "Thanks, dear." He trotted across the open space towards the picture of the deer.

As Yann stepped away, looking at the wall rather than his opponent, the minotaur ran at him and punched the centaur in the chest with both huge fists.

Punched him in both chests.

Two punches, landing hard on his human heart and his horse heart.

One heart which had been overworked for the last two days, the other heart which had been injured and only healed two hours ago.

As the two hammer-blow punches landed, Yann gasped and fell to the ground.

The Master laughed. "That was your real weakness, horse-boy. Not your legs, not your friends, but your weak and ailing hearts. Thank you for finally letting me near enough to attack them."

Yann lay on the floor, legs limp, looking up at the deer picture. Unable to reach it.

Chapter 30

The minotaur stood over the centaur, prodding him with dirty toes.

Yann's breath was coming in shallow irregular bursts. Helen wondered if either of his hearts had stopped when they were punched. But he was still conscious. His head turned towards the Master, then towards his friends.

The Master put a foot on his flank. "Surrender, horse-boy."

"Not yet," Yann whispered. "Both my hearts are still beating and I'm not giving in."

The Master lowered his horned head, aiming one point at Yann's human torso and the other at his horse chest. "I wonder if I could pierce both your hearts at the same time?"

Yann's breath was coming easier and he tried to roll over. But he was pinned down by the Master's foot.

Helen muttered, "This is my fault, I distracted him." She took a step forward, wondering if she could reach the picture to turn it over herself.

But Lee held her back. "Wait. Have faith in him."

Yann looked up at the Master and spoke clearly, "At least I have hearts to pierce. At least I have friends who would miss me. At least I don't have to pay uruisks to protect me, and I don't have followers who are waiting eagerly for me to fail..."

The Master glanced at the fauns. And the moment the minotaur's attention shifted, the centaur rolled to the right, got his long strong legs under him and pushed up, knocking the Master off balance.

Yann leapt to his hooves.

He took one step over to the deer painting and very gently, with his human hand, pushed the top corner of the frame.

The picture swivelled, the deer swung out of view and the mirror swung into the heart of the maze. Before the picture frame stopped moving, Yann cantered behind the minotaur and grabbed him.

They struggled and scrabbled on the black and white tiles, Yann's pale arms round the minotaur's wide chest, the Master bellowing and jabbing back with his elbows.

The centaur shouted, "I can't hold him!"

Lavender yelled, "Yes you can. You have the healing power of Scotland in your veins!"

"So does he!" gasped Yann.

"But you were healed at sunset on the spring equinox. You have the strongest power, Yann. He only has a shadow of it. You *can* do it."

As they watched the two wrestle in the middle of the maze, Helen muttered, "Is that true?"

Lavender whispered back, "If it gives Yann confidence and weakens the Master, it becomes true."

The centaur's hooves smashed tiles as they fought, and the minotaur's bare feet bled on the sharp corners. Yann's arms held tight, the minotaur's breathing faltered and Yann slowly forced the minotaur round to face the mirror.

The Master shut his eyes and whimpered, "No! Don't make me look!"

Yann adjusted his grip and shifted one hand up to the bull's face.

Helen looked at the mirror. The weight of the glass was pulling it forwards. "Hurry up, Yann!"

Yann yelled, "Which eye?"

Helen called back, "His left!"

Yann used his fingers to push the Master's left eyelid up, then Yann held the Master's squirming head still and forced him to look at the mirror.

The Master stared at his reflection. He stopped struggling and just stared. Then he laughed. "I never knew that!"

Helen could see the mirror tipping very slowly, the nails slipping out of the picture frame.

The Master stopped laughing and tried to back away. Yann dug his hooves in. The Master said, "I never ... That's not..."

Then he moaned, "That can't be true!"

He started struggling again, trying to close his eye, trying to get away from the mirror, trying to get away from Yann. The minotaur was whining, "No, that's not me," and clawing at Yann's hands, clawing at his own eye.

But Yann held firm.

The Master screamed. "NO! That can't be me..."

The mirror fell, and shattered on the ground.

Yann let go of the Master.

And the Master fell onto spikes of glass and tile.

Suddenly, there was complete silence in the maze.

The minotaur lay unconscious in the middle of the floor. Yann stood, both hands pressing against his human chest.

The Three tucked the wool, needles and thread away in their cloaks.

The fauns moved forward.

Helen saw Lee lift his sword and Sylvie flicker into a wolf.

But Frass knelt on his hairy knees beside the Master. Then he nodded to four younger, beardless fauns, who grabbed the Master's arms and dragged him across the floor, through the broken glass.

Frass looked up at Yann. "He failed the Maze. He is no longer the Master. Those of us who run the Maze will elect a new Master and train him better, so he doesn't put his faith in such complex plans and doesn't underestimate his opponents."

Lavender called out, "How long does it take to elect and train a new Master?"

Frass smiled. "About ten years."

Helen felt the group around her sigh with relief.

The fauns pushed the scarred tabletop aside and jumped through the hole, bumping the unconscious minotaur along with them. Once the last of the fauns had leapt through and the table had swung shut, the Three stood up.

"Well done, dear boy." They laughed. "Dear boy! ... What an amusing end ... to a fascinating duel ... Congratulations, son of Petros ... Your healing will hold ... and your hearts will be strong."

They smiled at Yann, then at his friends, from the depths of their hoods. "It was a pleasure ... to work with you all ... We will see you again ... to heal your wounds, or even better ... the wounds you inflict on others." They pulled their cloaks around them and left by the Turkish rug.

Helen crunched over bloody glass to Yann.

"Thank you," he said quietly. "That was a very good idea. Though you could just have said, open the wardrobe door, rather than kick it open. And you could just have said, look at the back of the picture."

She shrugged. "I didn't want the Master to know what we were doing."

"I didn't know what we were doing either, which made it a little difficult." He winced and held his hands to his chest again.

Sylvie howled and Lee said, "I agree. Let's get out of here. The wolf isn't the only one who'd be happier in the fresh air."

Yann nodded. "We've left Sapphire out there with all the uruisks, so let's go and give her a hand."

They wound their way out of the maze, turning left and left and left again, until they found the splintered front door.

Helen followed her friends into the clean dark Borders night, and they saw Sapphire, sitting in the moonlight all on her own. She roared. Yann laughed, then turned to Helen. "She built a bonfire of the uruisks' weapons, so when they woke up with no shields or axes, and saw her crouching over them blowing little flames, they ran off!"

Then he coughed and bent over in pain.

"What's wrong?" Helen asked. "Is it those cuts?"

"The cuts look bad and they feel bad too, but I think several of my ribs are broken and they feel much worse. I need some of your first aid, Helen."

She dropped her rucksack on the grass. "I have nothing left. I dumped or used or broke everything to get us into the maze and through the maze, and to fix that mirror to the picture. Anyway, you don't need first aid. You need proper medical treatment. And not from the Three this time. So let's head back to Clovenshaws, and get an expert to look at you."

Yann said, "Back to Clovenshaws? Are you inviting me to your *house*?"

"Yes, I am. If you can trust me, you can trust my family. Come on everyone, let's go and have supper at mine."

The centaur said, "But we could go to Cauldhame Moor, to my herd's healers."

"We could," said Helen, "but I'd like to stop lying to my family, and I think showing is probably easier than telling with fabled beasts, don't you?"

Yann laughed. "But isn't that a bit ... risky?"

"We've been taking risks all weekend. Let's take one more."

So they all clambered onto the dragon, Sylvie growling unhappily even in her human form, but everyone else murmuring in surprised excitement.

As they flew, Helen could hear Rona and Tangaroa

in front of her, chatting about swimming to St Kilda together on a hunting trip.

Then Lee leant forward and whispered in Helen's ear, "Now that Yann is healed..."

"He isn't healed," Helen interrupted, "he's just collected lots of new injuries."

"But those injuries aren't magical, so we don't have to hunt for more scabbards or footprints. Now that our quests are over, will you consider playing for my people?"

Helen shivered. "I'm not ready."

"Yes, you are. You're the greatest fiddler I've ever heard."

"But I haven't learnt everything I can. I want to go to music school, to study with the best teachers, to learn everything this world can teach me."

Lee sighed. "How long will that take?"

"Ten years. Maybe more. By then I hope I'll be able to prove that music is so valued in this world that I don't need to come to your world for my music to be worthwhile."

"Do you really hope that, Helen?"

Helen smiled into the dark. "Neither of us needs truth to open a door right now, so you'll have to wait to find out."

The dragon landed in her usual spot and everyone peered through the trees at the bright windows of Helen's house.

Sylvie snapped, "This is stupid."

"No, it's not," said Rona, as they all slid down the dragon. "I've met her parents plenty of times in my human form and they're very nice."

Lavender added, "And her little sister is really sweet."

"How do *you* know?" Helen asked.

Lavender giggled. "I chat to Nicola sometimes when I'm waiting for you to get home from school. She's just as good at keeping secrets as you are."

"So it seems!"

Lavender smiled. "And she's far more interested in building little rooms and making tiny hats."

Helen led everyone down the hill, then over the wooden fence. Yann jumped, stumbling as he landed.

"Are you sure this is a good idea?" he said, gasping with pain.

"Yes. It's what we should have done months ago. My mum might be a scientist who doesn't believe in magic and myths, but you're all real, and she won't deny the evidence of her own eyes."

She led Yann to the back door and knocked.

Her mum flung the door open. "Helen! I've been so worried!"

"Sorry I'm late, Mum. But I need your help, because my friend is injured."

Helen moved out of the way to let her mum see Yann, standing on the doorstep with blood on his chest, clutching his ribcage.

The light from the kitchen also lit Tangaroa's blue skin, Lee's polished swords, Sylvie's suspicious face, Rona's sealskin bag, Catesby's orange feathers, and, landing on Helen's hand, Lavender's purple feathers.

And nosing between them all, Sapphire's scaly snout.

Helen's mum looked at them, then rubbed her eyes and looked again.

She stepped forward and examined Yann more closely. "An interesting combination of injuries, to go with your interesting combination of limbs." She glanced at Helen. "This explains a lot. I was starting to doubt the birdwatching excuses. You can give me the details later, but first we need to treat these injuries."

She spoke to Yann. "So, young man. What happened to you?"

"I fought a duel with a minotaur, and your daughter's quick thinking saved my life. But I think I have some broken ribs, in both ribcages. Helen thought you were the best person to help."

Helen's mum nodded. "Let's get you inside and see."

Yann took a step towards the house.

"Oh no. You'll all be welcome in the kitchen later, but this much blood needs to go into the surgery." She pointed to her left and they all walked towards the large animal surgery, where Helen had first treated Yann.

They crowded in, though Sapphire could only get her head and neck through the door. They watched Helen's mum clean the wounds and feel gently along Yann's ribs.

Helen watched her two worlds fit together at last. She felt her shoulders relax and her breathing slow.

Then she heard Catesby squawk above her. She heard the phoenix say, "Hey, Yann, do you think you can count the one where the mirror cut you as a battle scar? Or is that more of a girly hairdressing injury?"

Helen started to smile. Then Sapphire roared gently beside her.

Her mum turned round. "Helen, did the dragon say something?"

Helen grinned as she translated, "Yes. She's very impressed with how you're treating Yann, so she wonders if you could look at her tail. Because she thinks I made a mess of it."

Yann shook his head, as Helen's mum strapped up his ribs. "Even if you did make a mess of it, Helen, I'm sure it'll grow back perfectly, because everything else you've made a mess of this weekend has turned out fine..."

Catesby agreed. "Even asking a centaur to kick open a door with his hoof, which was pretty daft."

Sapphire growled, "Even promising to feed our friends to my granny, which was very awkward for me."

Helen laughed. "This should make it easier to discuss our next quest!"

She leant back against the dragon's neck and heard her rumble, "Hello, my soft-bodied little friend. Nice to meet you properly, Helen."

"And you, Sapphire. It's nice to meet you too."

Enter a world of magic, adventure and destiny! If you've enjoyed the Fabled Beast Chronicles, you'll love

ROCKING HORSE WAR

The triplets were stolen on a sunny Monday morning.

Pearl ran upstairs to call them for breakfast. She'd heard her sisters and brother singing one of their made-up nonsense songs just a few minutes before, but now the schoolroom was empty.

Surely they were too old to be playing hide and seek with her? She glanced between the school desks, behind the piano and under the kilts in the dressing-up chest.

"Emerald! Ruby! Jasper! Come out! I'm not in the mood for games. I don't want to spend all day chasing after you."

There were no toes poking out under the red velvet curtains, but Pearl stomped over to the windows to punch at them anyway, and saw that the middle window was wide open.

She sighed. The triplets weren't trying to fly again, were they? She was tired of building steps out of chests of drawers, or bumping long ladders through narrow corridors, to fetch the triplets down from impossible places before anyone noticed.

She glanced up at the sky first to check it was empty. Just a couple of swans, no truant triplets. Pearl shook her head. She didn't really expect to see her brother and sisters flying. There must be a rational explanation for their habit of appearing on top of unclimbable trees and locked buildings.

Then she looked down at the ground. The triplets weren't there either. The lawn, three floors below, led to the rockery and the garden wall, then to the woods, moors and mountains beyond. But the smooth grass was torn, clods of dark earth clustered around a pattern of round holes and deep gashes. Had the triplets jumped down, hitting the ground so hard they'd ripped into the grass when they landed?

The trail of damage continued across the lawn, not towards the northern mountains which Pearl had climbed with Father, but towards the southern ones which Mother had forbidden anyone to approach.

Pearl considered jumping straight out of the window to follow the triplets. But even if they had stayed on their feet after such a long leap, she would probably break her legs, so she decided to run down the stairs instead.

As she swung round, her big toe banged against a hard object. She bent down to rub the pain away, and suddenly noticed six long pieces of wood lying flat on the floor round the open window. Each one was shaped in a smooth curve like the cavalry sabre on Father's study wall. The wood was dark and varnished, but towards the ends of each curve were scars: round patches of wood, paler, unvarnished, splintered. Scars where something had been torn off.

Then Pearl recognised the wooden shapes. They were the rockers from the triplets' rocking horses. Their beautiful wooden rocking horses, with jewelled bridles, leather saddles and real horsehair manes and tails. Emmie always said they looked like warriors' horses, chargers from the age of chivalry, with their flared nostrils, bared teeth and sharp hooves.

The horses had been a gift on the triplets' fourth birthday. No one knew who'd sent them, though Mother had ransacked the house for the missing gift tags.

Even at the age of ten, far too old to play with their other wooden toys, the triplets still rode their rocking horses every morning. They galloped off on imaginary quests Pearl couldn't join, because her tatty brown horse was too short for her twelve-year-old legs. But as the triplets' legs grew, their horses seemed to grow with them. Pearl had mentioned this to Father once, and he had chuckled, "Everything seems to change size as you grow up, dear girl. Wooden horses don't really grow."

She touched the splinters on the nearest curve of wood. The horses' legs had been wrenched free of the rockers, and the horses had vanished too.

Pearl stood up and looked out of the window at the hacked holes slashing away across the grass.

Hoofprints.

The triplets and the rocking horses had disappeared together.

But had the triplets taken the horses? Or had the horses taken the triplets?

Pearl frowned. Whatever daft or dangerous nonsense the triplets were up to this time, she had to find them before Mother realised they'd gone. So she jumped over the rockers and sprinted out of the schoolroom.

As she hurtled down the main stairs into the entrance hall, she passed the new Chayne family portrait, finished just last month. She stuck her tongue out at it. The artist had been so enthusiastic about painting the triplets. "Classically perfect," he'd called them, with their golden curls, green eyes, clear skin and sincere smiles on demand.

The artist was told of their angelic voices, so he'd put sheet music in their hands. But the triplets never bothered to read music, they just sang new tunes suddenly in harmony with each other, while Pearl struggled with her scales on the piano.

No one could suggest an artistic accomplishment for Pearl, so when she stood in front of his easel, the painter asked her to clutch a new illustrated geology textbook. Then he sketched her at the back of the picture, brown plaits and scowling face in the shadows of the triplets' brilliance. She would have preferred not to be in the painting at all.

Her running slowed as she reached the bottom of the stairs. Why was she bothering to chase the triplets? If they wanted to get into trouble, perhaps she should let them. She glanced back up at the portrait. Ruby and Jasper simpered at her; Emerald twinkled.

She slithered to a stop on the hall tiles. The triplets were probably off having an adventure together. But if she didn't follow them, she'd have to listen to Mother worry about them all the way through breakfast.

"Weren't you fetching the triplets for me, Pearl?" Her mother's quiet voice startled her. Pearl spun round to face the pale figure in the dining room doorway.

"They're up already, Mother, and … em … we're going out for a picnic breakfast. Emmie's idea. She packed the baskets last night."

"Going *out?* Not going far, I hope."

Mother's fingers were already twitching. She hated

not knowing where the triplets were. She got nervous when they left the house and frantic if they were out of sight of the windows. She never seemed bothered about where Pearl went, which was usually very convenient.

"You will stay with them, won't you? Look after them? Bring them home?"

"Of course. I'm following them right now. We'll be back when we run out of food."

Pearl turned and stepped out of the front door.

Behind her, she heard Mother wrench open the nearest cupboard. Mother always tidied when she was worried about the triplets. She would dust and sweep as if she could find her missing children on the mantelpiece, behind old photos of her eldest son in uniform, or in the shoe cupboard, reflected in the polished toes and heels of the family's boots.

If Pearl took too long to find the triplets, Mother would empty drawers and bookcases, rearrange pictures, and move furniture from room to room. It would be the cleanest, neatest house in Scotland, but no one would be able to find anything for weeks.

Pearl dashed to the stables, hoping the groom had already brought her bay pony in from the field. She saw Conker's dark tail flick at the entrance to his loose box, so she saddled him as fast as she could, then leapt on his back.

Pearl trotted her pony round to the south lawn, feeling his strong warm muscles stretch as he enjoyed the morning air. Much better than riding on a cold wooden horse.

But when Conker reached the churned-up grass

below the schoolroom window, he stopped so abruptly that Pearl crashed forward onto his neck.

"Walk on," Pearl ordered. But he backed away, shying at the hoofprints, shaking his dark brown mane.

"Come on, let's have an adventure, searching for those precious triplets and their mighty steeds. Walk on, boy." She clicked her tongue and urged him on with her hands and legs, but the pony refused to follow the trail.

Pearl grunted in frustration. She considered getting off and leading him, or using the crop and forcing him. But Conker was even more stubborn than she was, and she was in a hurry, so she loosened the reins and let him gallop the short distance back to the stables. She put him in his box, and took off his saddle and bridle.

"If you won't take me, I'll just have to go on my own two feet," she murmured, looking around for a treat to distract him from his fright.

She stuck a hand in the biggest pocket of the old-fashioned navy pinafore hanging up on a nail. Pearl wore it for expeditions and experiments, so its deep pockets were filled with string and pencils and other useful things. There was usually leftover food too. She found a slightly chewed carrot and offered it to Conker.

Then she tugged the old pinafore over her grey dress. Today already felt like an expedition.

Pearl sprinted from the stables to the damaged lawn. She looked up at the open window, the red velvet hanging limp on the sill. Then she turned her back on the house and followed the rocking horse hoofprints.

TIME TRAVEL TROUBLE

from Scottish Children's Book Award winner Janis Mackay

Time travel is a tricky business. From getting a lost girl back to *when* she came from, to finding lost title deeds when the world is on the verge of war, Saul and Agnes's time-twisting adventures could lead to a whole host of problems…

discoverkelpies.co.uk

Lewis and Greg might have *accidentally* summoned Loki, the Norse god of mischief. Not to mention his hammer-wielding big brother Thor, who's trapped in the boys' garage… But it wasn't their fault!

With a gang of valkyries chasing them from St Andrews to Asgard, can the troublesome twosome outwit Loki and save the day?

Mischievous fairies? Smelly troll? Werewolf snatching your sheep? Email the Really Weird Removals company!

Luca and Valentina's Uncle Alistair runs a pest control business. But he's not getting rid of rats. The Really Weird Removals Company catches supernatural creatures! When the children join Alistair's team they befriend a lonely ghost, rescue a stranded sea serpent, and trap a cat-eating troll.